"In this delightful tale of Kat... characters revolving around ... Rhodes has given us a story o... lives shared and burdens carr... one of those novels that helps you ... laughter in the darkness, reminding you that the sun really will rise tomorrow."

Sheridan Voysey, BBC Radio 2 presenter and author of *Reflect with Sheridan*

"Written in Pam's characteristic gentle and humorous manner, *Summer's Out at Hope Hall* appears to be just a light-hearted book, but it powerfully demonstrates the strength of community and the importance of faith."

Debbie Duncan, author of *Brave: Showing Courage in All Seasons of Life*

Summer's out at Hope Hall

PAM RHODES

LION FICTION

Published by
Lion Hudson Limited
Wilkinson House, Jordan Hill Business Park
Banbury Road, Oxford OX2 8DR, England
www.lionhudson.com

ISBN 978 1 78264 287 9

e-ISBN 978 1 78264 288 6

First edition 2021

A catalogue record for this book is available from the British Library

Printed and bound in the United Kingdom, January 2021, LH26

Editor's note

The Hope Hall series was commissioned before Covid-19 reared its ugly head, and fortunately Kath Sutton's community and its environs have been fortunate enough to escape any trace of the virus. You won't find any masks, vaccines or hand sanitizer between these pages, but you will enjoy the warmth, humour and human touch so many of us have missed since the pandemic began.

Chapter 1

The house martins were back!

There was no mistaking those glossy blue-black wings, forked tail and the flash of white rump when the bird swooped over Kath's head as she stood on the pavement edge waiting for a chance to cross the road to Hope Hall. With aerobatic precision, the bird headed straight for the tip of the gable of the hall's roof and disappeared from sight.

Once the road was clear, Kath broke into a run, a broad grin spreading across her face as she reached the front door of the hall and looked up. The telltale signs of muddy drips down the stonework drew her eye up to the dark brown ball of mud and grass that the martins were carefully crafting into a home for their new family. There didn't seem to be any sign of chicks yet, but just the thought of those small, noisy, elegant lodgers returning to the hall for yet another year was enough to lift her spirits. Summer was here at last!

April had brought a mixed bag of weather, from flurries of snow and chill winds to glorious blue skies that promised warmth in the bright sunshine, but mostly didn't deliver. Now, as May arrived, with scarlet red tulips in flower beds, bluebells carpeting local woods, and lilac and cherry blossom hanging in swathes of pink and purple along pavements and garden paths, it was tempting to throw off coats and cardigans and turn her face to the sun. At that thought, Kath smiled to herself again as she remembered how her mum warned her every spring about the old saying "Cast ne'er a clout till May be out". Kath was never sure if that meant the month of May or the May blossom that now graced every hedgerow, but did it really matter? The house martins were back!

"Morning, Kath!" called Liz, wiping her hands on her white apron as she crossed the foyer towards the kitchen door. "Maggie's not here yet, in case you wanted her. She's going to take a look round that new wholesalers first thing today, to see what sort of deals are on offer. Want a coffee?"

"Thanks, Liz, but I know you're busy and I've got Muriel Baker coming in at eleven. I'll take her up to the balcony for coffee and biscuits then."

Liz frowned. "Muriel Baker – I know that name…"

"She's the unit leader for the Sea Cadets."

"Oh yes, of course! My nephew Callum went to Sea Cadets for quite a while when he was a teenager. He loved it. Gosh, that was ages ago. Is Muriel *still* running it?"

"'Formidable' and 'unstoppable' are words I've heard to describe her."

Liz giggled. "Oh, I've heard her described in a few more colourful words than that. I remember Callum saying that whenever she talked to them about the sailing manoeuvres that won sea battles in Nelson's time, the lads were convinced that she was old enough to have been there!"

"I hope I don't bump into her," called Kevin, the work experience kitchen assistant who was sorting out the display cabinet at the other end of the serving hatch. "I only went to Sea Cadets for a fortnight when I was about thirteen, but she was terrifying. I don't think I'd be able to stop myself jumping to attention and saluting even now."

"Why is she coming, anyway?" asked Liz. "We're a long way from the sea here."

"Apparently, after all these years, they've discovered asbestos

8

in their hut roof. They've got to find somewhere else to base themselves for about three months. We can let them have a room in the old school building to store their kit, and their meetings are held on Wednesday nights when our main hall happens to be free."

"They do most of their training outdoors, if I remember rightly," said Liz. "And don't some Sea Cadets have a band too?"

"They've not asked about that. It would be nice if they did. I hope we can come to an arrangement to help them out. It will be interesting to have them based at Hope Hall for a while."

"And they all look very smart in their uniforms," sighed Liz. "I'm a sucker for a brass band. The moment they strike up 'Hearts of Oak', it's all I can do to stop myself marching along with them. That's what happens when you have generations of military men in your family."

"See you later then!" laughed Kath as she opened the glass-panelled door at the end of the foyer and walked through the main hall towards a side door at the far end. That door opened on to the small corridor that linked the main building at a right angle to the old school which had stood immediately adjacent to Hope Hall for decades. Once inside the school, the first room on the left was Kath's office. In spite of the modern technology and office furniture, the room still bore a trace of the look – and, Kath often thought, the smell – created by a succession of headteachers who had been its previous occupants down the years. On the other side of the corridor were cloakrooms and a flight of stairs leading up to three classrooms on the floor above. Straight ahead were double doors leading into the assembly hall, and those doors suddenly burst open to reveal thirty under-five-year-olds squealing with excitement as they sat in ball ponds, dug up sand pits, fitted together jigsaws and scribbled with crayons, all at the top of their voices.

It was Management Assistant Shirley Wells who came storming through those double doors and into Kath's office.

"Had a parking problem with a particularly inconsiderate mum delivering her little darling off in their 4x4 this morning. She couldn't think of a single reason why she shouldn't park right in front of the main gate and leave her car here while she nipped out to get her nails done in town."

Kath smothered a smile, knowing that no parent, 4x4 owner or not, would ever win an argument with Shirley. She was a force to be reckoned with, a big-hearted woman with the voice of a foghorn and a strict sense of how people should behave, especially in a community facility like Hope Hall.

"Where is she now?"

Shirley shrugged. "Don't know. Don't care. I made it clear that she had to move her precious car, and eventually she did, but not before she came back inside to give the playgroup staff a piece of her mind."

"How did they react?"

"They rang me straight away, and after we'd had another word or two, the woman left, taking her daughter with her."

"Oh dear," frowned Kath. "Is she likely to come and bash my ear too? Should I have a word with her?"

"Nope," smiled Shirley. "The playgroup staff said she's always been a pain in the neck, making demands that disrupt the experience for everyone else. Apparently, she told them she intends to remove her daughter from our playgroup and enlist her at Tiny Tots on the High Street instead. Tiny Tots has got no parking spaces at all, so that should go well!"

Now, *that* was why the recent decision to create the new role of Management Assistant for Shirley had been such a good idea, thought Kath. Shirley had been taken on at Hope Hall at the start of the year to help caretaker Ray after his wife Sara was diagnosed with terminal cancer. Shirley attacked the role like a whirling dervish, busying away with her mop, duster, paintbrush and sewing machine until Hope Hall was gleaming from top to bottom. But it had soon become clear that her efficiency at hall maintenance was just a small part of her talents. That loud authoritative voice of hers had a way of cutting through confusion and chaos so that calm and order could quickly be restored – and that was in stark contrast to a much softer, compassionate side of Shirley that was revealed in her care for Ray and Sara, which went beyond anything that was expected of her. Her worth was truly recognized when she masterminded several imaginative and entertaining ideas to involve all age groups in the Easter Monday Fayre, which was the first event to mark this centenary year of Hope Hall. And so, when Ray announced that he was keen to resume his caretaking duties, which he felt was an important step towards dealing with bereavement after the loss of his beloved wife, the management team recognized that Shirley was too good an asset to lose – and her new part-time role was created.

Shirley's distinctive voice jolted Kath out of her thoughts.

"I want to organize a school reunion in the main hall on the first Saturday in June. I've checked the diary. It's free, and we'll pay the usual fee. All right with you?"

"Of course," said Kath, opening the bookings file on her computer. "Which school is this?"

"We all went to Walsworth Road Comprehensive, which was demolished a few years back now. A group of us realized that our year left in 1992, which is nearly thirty years ago, and we've never had a reunion in all that time. So, we thought we'd organize a get-together!"

"Great idea. How many do you think might come?"

"We plan to open the invitation up to any pupils who went to the school during the eighties and nineties, so it could be quite a lot. Some people are still living locally, but I reckon the majority have moved away now, so it will depend how successful we are at spreading the word. I hope we'll get at least a hundred. I'll organize a buffet and a disco of all the music we danced to then. It should be a good night."

"I remember going to our reunion a while back," mused Kath, "when we hadn't seen each other for more than twenty years. I hardly recognized anyone. We all had a copy of the guest list, so we knew who was there, but it was so difficult to put names we could remember to faces that were so much older. The boys were the worst. So many grey-haired and bald-headed old fellas with paunches and prescription glasses, I didn't recognize any of them!"

"Did they recognize you?"

"Some did, so I can't have changed all that much, thank goodness. But the big change I recognized after that reunion was that schools in my day had a very different attitude to discipline compared with schools today. Mike, the man who came up with the idea for the event, got in touch with the secretary of our old school to book everything, and she said that on the night, all the guests could come in through the main entrance of the school, past the headmaster's office and straight into the hall. Mike immediately said that they wouldn't want to do that, because they'd never been *allowed* to go in through that entrance, past the headmaster's office. The secretary laughed, and said that for the last twenty odd years pupils *had* been allowed to come in that way. So, later that night, when Mike was telling his son about the conversation, his son asked him what would have happened if they'd disobeyed orders and gone through that main entrance when they were at school. Mike said that he didn't know, because they'd never dared to try it!"

Shirley nodded in agreement. "You're right; it can be a bit of a free-for-all where discipline's concerned in schools these days. Who'd want to be a teacher?"

"You, I reckon," smiled Kath. "You're great with the kids who come in here – and the grown-up kids too! You certainly don't let any of our cheekier pensioners take liberties, but then you're so full of great ideas to keep them happily occupied, they love you for it."

"Me, a teacher? Never!" huffed Shirley, getting to her feet, but not before Kath saw a flush of pleasure bring colour to her cheeks. 'I'm going to see if Ray needs a hand up in that middle classroom. The lights have been playing up."

And she was gone.

Sometime later, on her way to greet Muriel Baker, who was due at eleven, Kath walked through the foyer where the weekday café was comfortably busy, with groups of people sipping coffee and tucking into a variety of cakes around tables covered in bright flowery tablecloths. Thinking it would be good to spot Muriel as soon as her car arrived, Kath made for the main entrance door, but then had to stand back to allow someone else to come inside. The young woman was probably in her late teens or early twenties, with long pale blonde hair, and an expression that made it clear she was uncertain where to go.

"Can I help?" smiled Kath.

"I come for English class," was the girl's careful reply as she fumbled in her pocket for a piece of folded paper, which she held out towards Kath. "Hope Hall. This Hope Hall?"

"It certainly is," nodded Kath, realizing that the girl's English was very limited. "Let me show you."

Gratefully, the girl followed Kath back out of the entrance door, then fell into step beside her as they turned right across the playground towards the main door of the school.

"Where are you from?" asked Kath as they walked.

"Czech Republic, near Prague."

"And is this your first visit to this country?"

"Yes, but I learn English at school, and watch TV. American movies."

Kath smiled. "Well, that will certainly help!"

"I am Mili Novakova."

"And I'm Kath. Pleased to meet you, Mili!"

Opening the school door for them both, Kath led the way up the stairs and pointed to the first classroom along the corridor, where there were already several students waiting for their English as a Foreign Language lesson to begin. Mili was plainly nervous as she stepped inside, so Kath kept watch until she saw a couple of the group smiling a welcome as they beckoned the newcomer to join them.

Back in the playground, Kath was just in time to see an estate car turning into the parking area at exactly eleven o'clock. There was no mistaking Muriel. She was short and round, with an air of solid authority that came from her no-nonsense haircut, dark-rimmed glasses, and the Sea Cadet uniform that seemed to be her constant form of dress. Her smile was formal as she offered a firm handshake.

"How nice to meet you, Miss Sutton."

"Everyone calls me Kath. Welcome to Hope Hall!"

Turning to look across the playground, Muriel surveyed her surroundings with interest, paying particular attention to one area after another.

"This would all be available to us?"

"Absolutely – and the main hall inside is also free on Wednesday evenings at present. I gather that some of your activities are held indoors?"

"Our cadets are each studying for particular modules to

14

achieve skill goals and qualifications. Some of that is practical and often physical, and would be best suited to this outdoor area – but inclement weather conditions, or quieter study, would make the main hall a better environment at times during our meetings. Can I take a look at the facilities inside?"

"Of course," agreed Kath, matching Muriel's businesslike tone.

Ten minutes later, after a comprehensive inspection of all the areas on offer, including the storage room on the outside of the school building which could be made available for the exclusive use of the cadets, Kath waited to hear Muriel's verdict on whether Hope Hall might prove suitable.

"We are required to maintain a high level of parade skills, which means we need to practise marching and drill techniques on a regular basis. This can sometimes prove quite noisy as orders are shouted out and responded to. How are your neighbours? Can you see any problems from them as far as that is concerned?"

"Well," replied Kath, "as you can see, we have no near neighbours. There's waste ground on one side of us, and a road junction on the other, so apart from St Mark's Church across the way, who are likely to be making as much noise as us on some occasions, we have no worries on that score."

"Well, Miss Sutton – er, Kath," Muriel announced, "I think this could well suit our purpose. I'd like to make certain of the health and safety arrangements and, of course, the necessary insurance cover. Most important of all, I need to run the proposal past our trustees, but I feel this could be an excellent temporary base for our work."

"When would you like to start?" asked Kath.

"Perhaps we could arrange to move our equipment across to our storage facility during our usual meeting time this Wednesday evening? Then our activities can start in earnest on the same evening a week later."

"That's good news," smiled Kath. "Let me organize a coffee for you in the balcony lounge and I'll bring over all the relevant paperwork for you to inspect and have available to show your trustees."

In response, Muriel clicked her heels and stiffened to attention before turning abruptly and marching off in the direction of the main building.

The Call-in Café was in full swing at midday when Catering Manager Maggie staggered into the kitchen carrying a big cardboard box, with bulging supermarket carrier bags on each arm. Liz rushed to grab the box from her as Maggie laid out the bags on the work surface.

"You liked the new wholesaler then?" grinned Liz. "Is there more to come in?"

"A couple of big boxes in the back of the car," puffed Maggie, "but just give me a moment to get my breath back."

Liz grinned before turning towards Kevin, who was leaning against the work surface taking large gulps from a can of coke.

"Be a love, Kev, and bring the rest of those boxes in for us, would you?"

Always keen to help, Kev immediately headed for the door.

Maggie sighed. "It's my own fault. I need to go on a diet. I keep saying I should go to a gym or Zumba, or something else that's just as awful, as long as it gets me exercising – then I never get round to doing anything about it. But I have to. I'm a stone heavier than I was this time last year."

"This time last year, you had just celebrated your silver wedding anniversary surrounded by loving family and the husband you thought was yours for ever. Then that slimeball ran off with a glamour girl half his age and told you he was about to become a father again when he's already a grandfather, totally humiliating you in the process. No wonder you've put on a bit of weight! Besides, you make the most wonderful cakes. We all love eating them, so is it any surprise that you do too?"

Maggie grimaced in agreement. "Isn't there a saying about people who work in a chocolate factory ending up being really sick of chocolate? Why doesn't that happen to me with my cakes? Why can't I resist a chocolate éclair or a jammy doughnut or lemon sponge with custard? Why haven't I got any willpower?"

"Because you've been very unhappy, and extremely busy now your home is having to be packed up and sold to pay for Dave's new family. You've got a lot on your plate, Maggie."

"Yes. Mostly cakes."

"And the upheaval of moving! But just think, in a couple of weeks' time you'll be getting your completion date on that gorgeous new flat of yours. How amazing that you've found such a lovely place in a house you used to visit and love when you were a schoolgirl!"

A slow grin spread across Maggie's face. "It is rather gorgeous, isn't it? Honestly, in the end I know I'm going to like being there—"

"...but it's all a bit daunting right now, packing up the memories from quarter of a century of family life."

"Oh, for heaven's sake, a quarter of a century? I feel old now as well as fat!"

"That's enough sympathy for one day. Come on, you! Let's make some room for all this lot in the store cupboard. That's where we'll be if you need us, Jan."

At the hatch, Jan gave a wave of agreement before turning her attention back to the lemon meringue pie that needed an extra dollop of thick fresh cream at the request of the customer she was serving.

"They've got a great fruit section at that wholesalers," said

Maggie as she and Liz made their way towards the walk-in storage cupboard and cold room at the back of the kitchen. "And a wet fish area too, which was very well stocked. Their meat is good as well – some interesting cuts that are sometimes hard to find, and a proper butcher who was happy to discuss exactly what I needed."

"My dad was a butcher – did I ever tell you that?"

"Really? Where – here in the town?"

"No, we lived up in Stockport then. His family had a butcher's shop for years, so my dad was working there as a 'butcher's boy' when he was still in short trousers. It sounds like his father had no qualms about cutting a few corners, though. I remember Dad telling me about a lady who came in just as the shop was about to close asking for a six-pound chicken. His father only had one chicken left, which weighed four pounds, and when she saw it, she said that wouldn't be big enough. So he told her he'd see if he could find another bigger chicken out the back. He took the chicken outside, pulled it about a bit and puffed up the flesh, then brought it in with a great big smile, saying he'd managed to find a six-pounder, just what she wanted."

"And did she fall for that?"

"Oh, she was delighted. So delighted, in fact, that she said she'd take them *both*!"

Every Monday afternoon between two thirty and five o'clock, volunteers from Churches Together in the town set up an emergency Food Bank in the foyer, so that local people struggling to keep food on the table for their families, or who were living hand-to-mouth on very little money and few resources, could get a range of rations, basic goods and clothing to help keep them going throughout the week ahead. In the three years since it was started on a trestle table at Hope Hall with barely any groceries or supplies on offer, the Food Bank had grown into a large and complex operation which reflected the rapid and shocking growth in the number of those in need within their own community.

The organizers had soon recognized the importance of allowing each volunteer to work to their strengths. Some were good at collecting, transporting and lugging in big boxes of supplies, often direct from local supermarkets. Others were good at organizing emergency bags of goods, some for families, some for single people, some specifically with older folk in mind. And then there were the more experienced volunteers, who became known for their insight, empathy and ability to read between the lines of what they were told by those coming for help. Their embarrassment, their reticence to be drawn into conversation, so often concealed deep despair, fear and emotional turmoil, often as a result of domestic situations that were oppressive, inadequate or simply inescapable.

Throughout her working life, Sheelagh Hallam had been a social worker, not just with the local council for many years, but also with several charitable organizations that supported the most vulnerable people in society. Always a regular churchgoer and now a grandmother, retirement made little difference to her energy and determination to support anyone who needed a helping hand. She volunteered for several sessions each week in the local Citizens' Advice Bureau, and on Mondays she was always at Hope Hall helping out at the Food Bank. Whereas others were busy unpacking supplies and giving out bags of essentials, Sheelagh preferred to be near the kettle, always ready with a cup of tea and one of the delicious cakes or savouries left over from Hope Hall's daily Call-in Café. Years of experience combined with a natural intuition meant Sheelagh was astute at sensing when it wasn't only food that was needed, but a listening ear, an arm around the shoulder, and practical support to help with the desperate situations in which people often found themselves.

As one young mum who was a regular visitor to the Food Bank came in through the main door, Sheelagh caught sight of a dishevelled-looking man standing close to one of the trees lining the pavement at the front of the hall. He was trying to peer inside without making his presence too obvious, flattening himself behind the trunk of the tree for fear of being noticed. Picking up a couple of cardboard cups, Sheelagh poured out two teas, one with a large spoonful of sugar, then stuffed a couple of packets of biscuits in her pocket before stepping outside the door just in time to see the man pull back from the nearest tree to one that was several yards further along the pavement. Moving slowly and casually in his direction, Sheelagh walked up until she was nearly level with him, then sat down on the small wall that divided the old school playground from the road.

"I wondered if you might like a cup of tea. I've got biscuits too."

At first there was no reply, but then, after a while, he leant out a little to take a closer look at her.

"Shall we drink them while they're hot? This one's got sugar, the other hasn't. Which would you like?"

Placing the tea with sugar on the wall quite near to the tree that was shielding him, she busied herself with the biscuits, opening one packet, then the other.

"Bourbons and ginger nuts. Do you fancy either of these?"

There was no reply, and Sheelagh pretended not to notice when he moved out enough to pick up the cup.

They drank together for several minutes before Sheelagh lifted her arm towards him to offer the pack of ginger nuts. Seconds passed before he stretched out to grab them from her, shoving them quickly into his coat pocket. Sheelagh noticed immediately that the coat was torn and filthy, and the one boot she could see that wasn't hidden behind the tree was scuffed and gaping, with a hole at the front where the sole had become detached. Even from a few feet away she was catching the musty smell of stale body odour.

"I'm Sheelagh," she said at last. "It's nice to meet you."

Silence.

"I've not seen you here before."

Nothing.

"I wonder if you need anything – food perhaps, or some basic essentials. Could I make up a bag for you? Is there anything in particular that would be useful right now?"

Still hesitating, the man was gradually revealing more of himself from behind the tree.

"Shall I just bring you a selection?"

He nodded.

"You wouldn't like to come in with me to see what we have available? You could make your own choices then."

He shook his head in definite refusal.

"Will you stay here and wait for me?"

He nodded again.

"Right, I'll be back in a minute then. Oh, I didn't get your name…"

"Michael," came a reply that was so gruff and muffled that she could barely hear it.

"Help yourself to those other biscuits then, Michael. I'll be as quick as I can."

And although she walked away at a steady pace, she knew she had to be quick to make sure he didn't disappear before she returned. Having an urgent word with Brian, the overall organizer of the Food Bank, she picked up a ready-prepared box, which contained long-life milk, fruit drinks, tinned food, boxes of cereal, bread, crackers and cake, as well as washing-up liquid, soap, toothpaste and a brush, deodorant and toilet rolls. Another quiet word in the ear of the lady in charge of the freshly washed donated clothes meant that minutes later she was on her way back out to Michael, clutching not just the box of supplies, but also some trousers, a thick jumper, two T-shirts, pants and a couple of pairs of socks.

His expression didn't change as he saw what she'd brought him, but she noticed that he peered at the clothes with particular interest. Then he nodded towards the box.

"Get that lot from the supermarket, did you?"

"They're very generous. We collect from them every week."

"*Very* generous, when they're the ones that cause the problem."

Sheelagh said nothing, hoping that Michael would fill the silence, which eventually he did.

"They're good at throwing stuff out. Two hundred and fifty thousand tonnes of food that could be eaten every year."

"Really? That's shocking."

"Around two million tonnes of food wasted by the food industry in this country. That's a lot of meals no one ever had."

"Well, you certainly know your statistics. Is this something that's always interested you?"

"It does now," he retorted, looking down at the box of supplies. "I didn't care much when I had enough to eat."

Sheelagh took a moment before she spoke again.

"What happened to you, Michael?"

In an instant, he picked up the clothes and grabbed the box awkwardly, nearly tipping out the contents as he turned to scuttle across the road.

"See you next Monday!" she called after him. "I'll be ready with your cup of tea."

But he was gone.

Chapter 2

Kath was fumbling to get her key in the apartment door when her phone rang. By the time she'd pushed the door open, grabbed her bags, pulled her phone out of her pocket and got it to her ear, it was just about to go to voicemail. Seeing that it was Jack who was ringing, it was a relief when she managed to answer the call before he rang off.

"Hi, Kath, you all right?"

"I'm just back from work. It was quite an interesting day really, because you remember I mentioned—"

"Sorry, love, I'll have to stop you, because I'm due down in theatre in five minutes."

"Oh, of course. I'm sorry."

"So, very quickly, I just wondered if you'd like to come up to Southampton on Saturday week? The hospital is organizing a Family Fun Day with lots of stalls and displays. Do you fancy coming along?"

"That would be nice. Haven't you been roped in to help on some stall or other?"

"Apparently they've put me down to go in the stocks so people can throw water balloons at me."

"Nice!" chuckled Kath. "You're really popular there then!"

She could hear the smile in his voice as he replied, "I think if I were a tyrant they'd never dare put me in the stocks. I'm not looking forward to it, but I don't think the team would rate me very highly if I didn't enter into the spirit of the occasion."

"So you need me to come and mop your dripping brow, do you?"

"That would be nice, but we also need someone to oversee all the prizes and awards that need to be given out at the end of the afternoon – you know, whoever's guessed the Name the Doll competition, or the right number of sweets in a jar, or won the tug-of-war or the pie-eating competition."

"Pie eating? Does that comply with NHS dietary advice guidelines?"

"Definitely not," he laughed, "and you've guessed straight away that I have absolutely no idea what competitions and awards there are. I just know that it needs someone who can gather all the relevant information, sort out the prizes and arrange the award ceremony at the end of the afternoon. And suddenly, you popped into my mind."

"Oh, I did, did I?"

She could hear the affection in his voice as he replied, "Well, who else do I know who's been a senior administrator at a major London hospital, and kept even the most difficult doctors toeing the line? My darling Kath, this will be a piece of cake for you!"

"What's wrong with your own hospital administrator stepping up for that job? Or is she lined up for a dunking in the stocks along with you?"

"*He* has wangled a day off for himself. Says he's got a family event to go to."

"Now, he sounds to me like an excellent organizer. I could learn a thing or two from him!"

"So, will you come? You organize events like this all the time at that place where you work. This is right up your street."

"Do you remember that story about the army officer who lined up all the squaddies to ask them to volunteer for something or other – and all of them in the know took a step backwards, so just one chap was left at the front who seemed to be volunteering? Well, I am that soldier—"

"Thanks, Kath. I knew you'd help. Look, I've got to go. I'll ring you before Saturday, okay? Loads of love."

"Love you too," replied Kath – but Jack never heard her because he had already rung off.

Looking at the blank screen, she sighed, then kicked off her shoes and threw the phone down on the sofa before collapsing into the cushions herself. She knew she shouldn't feel so deflated that all their phone calls seemed to be like that these days, with Jack usually in a rush, or exhausted, or called away suddenly, so that their conversations never lasted more than a minute or two. A man who apparently couldn't even remember the name of the place where she worked. But then he had said "loads of love" before he ended the call. That was something, wasn't it?

On the other hand, had she ever really understood what Jack meant when he said he loved her? They had been colleagues in that London hospital for several years, while he worked his way up the ranks as a consultant paediatric surgeon and she had a senior role in the running and administration of the whole hospital facility. His timetable had always been unpredictable, so she'd learned to expect him to let her down at the last minute whenever she'd booked tickets for the theatre or dinner with friends. After all, he was a doctor, devoted to the care of his patients, always ready to go the extra mile or allow a bit more precious time knowing the difference it could make to the outcome of his patients' treatment.

Being part of the same circle of friends, they had drifted into a romantic relationship that was undemanding and comfortable – at least, that's how he probably would have described it. For Kath, there had been a growing realization that she was losing her heart to this compassionate, talented, dedicated man whose skill saved lives every day. There was no doubting the way they complemented one another, supporting, encouraging and totally understanding the demands of each other's work. Everyone thought they were a great couple – and they were, but did Jack actually realize that? She wondered if he had ever realized how good they were together. Had he ever thought about putting a ring on her finger? At that time they had both been in their mid-forties, too late in life to be thinking about a family, but they had so many interests in common. Wouldn't marriage have been the obvious next step?

If life had gone smoothly, she would probably never have had to put that question to the test. However, when her mother was suddenly taken very ill and unable to live alone, Kath had known what she should do. Her sister Jane was happily married and living in Australia, so Kath had been the only one able to help her beloved mum. The only thing that would have stopped her leaving London to come back and look after Mum was a marriage proposal from Jack. Her mother would certainly have approved of that, because there was nothing she wanted more than to see her much-loved daughter happily settled.

That proposal never came, and Jack hadn't made the slightest attempt to stop Kath leaving. He simply showed his usual understanding of the difficulty of her situation and the inevitability of her decision to leave. With a heavy heart, she had packed her bags and turned her back on the job she loved. Jack had hugged her and wished her well, and as he walked away Kath knew he would not be keeping in touch.

And, as expected, there had been no contact for the four years she'd been here until just a few months ago when she'd reluctantly accepted an invitation to a gathering of former work colleagues at the hospital. One of those colleagues was Jack, who had recently accepted the post of Senior Consultant Paediatric Surgeon at the major hospital in Southampton, a city that was less than an hour's drive from her home town.

That evening, when they found themselves slipping back into the familiar ease of each other's company, they agreed to carry on seeing each other, even though the demands of their jobs and the geography of where they now lived would be a challenge. Neither of them had given this rekindling of their relationship a name. Were they a couple? Were they just old friends enjoying the comfort of many years of knowing each other well? And what about love? Was that part of what they now shared? Was she still in love with him?

Kath was aware that, because she couldn't answer that last question with any certainty, she was keeping Jack slightly at arm's length. That wasn't difficult when they lived an hour's drive apart. Occasionally they had met up in a restaurant halfway between them, which meant Jack always had his eye on the clock, because his call time the following morning was extremely early. On one occasion he came to look round Hope Hall to see what her job now entailed, but he had seemed preoccupied and restless. He had also invited her to spend an afternoon with him in Southampton, starting with a tour of the hospital, but he was plainly exhausted, his phone never stopped ringing and finally he had to cut her visit short because he was urgently needed for emergency surgery.

And now this. He did ring, but only every four or five days, and then often, in the way of this last call, leaving an impression that ringing her was not something that ranked very highly on his list of priorities.

She closed her eyes to help clear her mind a little. This thing with Jack was just whatever it was, with no conditions or expectations. She needed to understand and remember that. She would go along to the Family Fun Day at the hospital and do her best to make a success of it. She would enjoy his company, based on the long and loving friendship they shared, but she didn't fool herself that he was in love with her. And, with surprise and even a little relief, she realized that, although she loved him dearly, she was no longer in love with him either.

From the moment Mili had walked into the English for foreign students class, her life looked up. Until then, the three weeks she'd spent in England had been thoroughly miserable.

The whole idea had been suggested by her priest in the local Catholic church back in the Czech Republic, to which every member of her family went each week without fail. To do otherwise would be unthinkable. In their small town on the outskirts of Prague, being Catholic was simply a way of life. All occasions, great or small, were celebrated and marked in church along with the neighbours – weddings, funerals, first communions and a dizzying calendar of saints' days that had shaped her life for as long as she could remember.

But Mili had wanted a change. Not from the Catholic faith, because that was as much a part of her as her character or intelligence, but a change about where she practised it. The life she had always known was choking her. She watched documentaries on television, she read magazines, she listened to the news, and she longed to break the chains of her smothering family and their small-town existence. She wanted to travel, see the world, experience life in all its adventure, challenge and beauty.

Mind you, trying to tell her father how she felt had resulted in a row during which he told her in no uncertain terms what a stupid and ungrateful idea her moving away was. Her mother had said much the same thing but in kinder tones, reminding Mili how lucky she was to have a good, solid job at the local food-processing factory, and how much Pavel, the next-door neighbour who liked to think of himself as her boyfriend, loved her – and how he had told his parents he planned to ask Mili

28

to marry him as soon as he'd saved up enough money for a ring. She was left feeling deflated and full of frustration, but her determination to leave had been stronger than ever.

With her twentieth birthday looming, and no proper idea about how to make her dream a reality, she had found an ally in the most unexpected place. One evening when she was leaving the church after taking her turn to refresh the flower arrangements, she bumped into Father Peter, who had come to see if the church was now empty so that he could lock up.

Father Peter was new to the church, in his early thirties, with an enthusiasm for faith and evangelism that didn't sit all that comfortably with the more conservative members of the Catholic hierarchy in the town. But his sermons rang bells in Mili's heart whenever she heard him, as he spoke of the two years he'd spent with the monks in the monastic community in Taizé, near Cluny in France, where young people in their thousands flocked every day to be part of their fellowship. He had studied for a while in Canada and travelled across the States, and he had trained in a seminary in Rome in the shadow of Vatican City. He connected with young people, but also seemed to have the general approval of their parents, who mostly warmed to his enthusiasm and obvious devotion.

"Hello, Mili. You're here late. Are you finished now?"

"Yes, I'll just drop this bag of rubbish in the bins on the way out before heading home."

"If you wait a minute or two, I'll walk with you. I have to call in to see a neighbour of yours this evening. You know Eva? She's recovering physically now, but I hear she is still feeling very low and in need of encouragement."

"She'd like that," agreed Mili. "Losing her baby so late in the pregnancy was a terrible blow. They have been longing for a family for so long."

That fifteen-minute walk back from the church changed everything. She couldn't quite remember what led her to start telling Father Peter how trapped she felt, but once she realized he was listening with genuine interest and not just dismissing her thoughts as rebellious and outrageous, she found herself pouring out her heart to him. More than that, he responded by telling her how he'd felt exactly the same way at her age, but had finally found the courage to leave home in spite of his parents' protestations.

"How do your parents feel about you now?" Mili had asked.

Father Peter grinned. "They are a devoted Catholic family, and they now have a son who has chosen to become a priest. God has answered their desperate prayers, and I am redeemed!"

"Did you ever imagine becoming a priest when you were living at home?"

"Never in a million years! That was the last thing I ever thought would happen. I hated the church. I hated the routine of having to go every week. I hated confession, and usually lied my way through it just so no one would know what I had really been up to. I hated the way in which my life seemed to be planned out for me, so that I had no choice in my future. So, I ran."

"They didn't know you were going?"

"I left a letter on the table when I left one morning before the sun was up. I caught the milk train to Prague and found a bed in a youth hostel until I met a few other boys who were sharing a very cramped apartment and invited me to join them. They helped me get myself a job working nights in a factory, and I grabbed every hour of overtime I could until I'd saved up enough money to start my journey."

"How did you travel?"

"Sometimes by bus, if I had the fare. Often I hitched. God was good. I always found a way to move on."

"Where did you go?"

"Across Europe. It took me about a year, because I didn't really know where I was heading, but God did. He brought a couple of young Christians into my life who had just spent several months at Taizé. I only spent one day in their company, but I knew from what they told me that Taizé was where I had to be."

"What was it like?"

"It was the body of Christ. It was the gathering of Christians from all countries, traditions and backgrounds. It didn't matter what denomination of church they came from, or if they'd never been inside a church at all. Christ called them there. He called me. I found true, lasting faith there in a God who is present and real."

"So did you decide to become a priest while you were at Taizé?"

"No, not at all. I knew that my life was God's and that he would show me where he wanted me to be, but it took a long time for me to realize that he had always had a plan in mind for me."

"And now you're here."

"I'm here, just fifty miles from the town I grew up in, and a priest in the Catholic church that nurtured me. This is my home, but God understood that until he took me away from what I'd always known, I couldn't recognize that this was exactly where I belonged and where I had most to give."

Mili was silent as she wondered how his experience could possibly be reflected in her own.

"Do it, Mili. Follow your heart. Trust God to show you the way."

She gave a rueful smile. "I might need more practical plans than that. Where would I go? How would I live if I weren't with my parents?"

"Step out in faith. Ask for help. I will help you."

"You will?" Her eyes were huge as she turned to him in hopeful astonishment.

"Have you thought about becoming an au pair? Many young girls go to other countries around the world to learn the language, and earn their keep by helping out with the care of children in families there."

"I love children! I have two brothers and a sister who are younger than me, and four nieces and nephews. I'm always babysitting."

"Then you have the perfect qualifications and experience for the job."

"Where would I go?"

"Where would you like to go?"

Mili thought for a while before answering.

"To England, I think. It is not as far as America, and I already speak a bit of English."

"Then we'll find a family who would like you to join them."

"How?"

"There's sure to be somebody in the church who knows someone who knows someone who lives in England. Let me put a few feelers out, not mentioning your name at this stage, of course."

Mili's face shone with excitement. "What about my parents? Should I tell them about this conversation?"

"Why don't you wait until we have something really positive to report to them? If your ideas are vague and indefinite, of course they will worry about letting the daughter they love head off to heaven knows where."

"So, I'll wait to hear from you."

"And I promise I will start my research on your behalf as soon as I can."

Mili felt as if her feet were inches off the ground, she was so elated.

"Thank you," she said at last.

"Wherever you go, dear Mili, I know you will go with God. I will come back to you the moment I have some real news."

And that is exactly what he had done. Just a week later, he introduced her to a lady she only knew by sight in the congregation. The lady explained that her daughter had married an Englishman and now lived in London, but her husband worked with a colleague whose wife was looking for an au pair to join their family at their home in a town not far from the south coast of England. There were two children, one of them at school and another who was younger, but their current au pair, also from the Czech Republic, had announced unexpectedly that she was leaving within the week, and they were desperate for help. Bubbling with excitement at this news, Mili listened as she was told that she should send by email a resumé of her experience, along with a reference as to her character and honesty. If that looked promising, the English mother would like to have a conversation with her online. All being well, a flight would be organized immediately so that she could join them within the week.

Seeing that Mili's head was reeling, Father Peter quietly took her arm and suggested that he should come with her to tell her parents about this exciting opportunity, so that their permission could be sought for Mili to take it further. Her parents were filled with curiosity and a sense of foreboding when Father Peter invited them to join him for a quiet talk in the vestry, and they listened in stunned silence as he explained the offer that was being made. Her father's immediate reaction was complete refusal, but it was a priest who was asking, so he held his temper in check as Father Peter quietly explained that this family were recommended through members of their own congregation. It was Mili's mother, once she'd got over her surprise, who quietly asked questions that she sensed would provide answers her husband could not dispute. In the end, although he was plainly put out and felt his authority had been undermined, he had no choice but to recognize that his own priest would not recommend an arrangement unless it was safe and proper.

After that, things moved quickly. Father Peter had helped her to write a resumé that sounded a lot more impressive than Mili thought she actually was, but by the end of that day, a message had come back from the English family saying they'd like to speak to her over the internet the following morning. That interview took place in Father Peter's office, with Mili's mother and father watching from the corner of the room. They all saw a woman on the screen who looked to be in her mid-thirties, smartly dressed with a fashionable hairstyle and immaculate make-up. She spoke rapidly in English so that Mili struggled to follow her, but then a young girl, the present au pair, was introduced on the screen so that she could translate into Czech. She didn't smile much, perhaps because she was concentrating on getting the translation right, but she explained that Mili's duties would be to look after the house and the children, do the shopping, cook the meals and generally be in charge while the mother, a lawyer, was at work. She explained that Mili would have a nice room of her own and access to a car during her working day, and that she would be paid £60 a week. To Mili, that sounded like a very respectable sum of money, and she looked across anxiously to gauge her father's reaction. He didn't smile. He didn't ask any questions. He looked straight into the eyes of his wife for several seconds, and when she gave the smallest of nods, he turned to Father Peter and also nodded his agreement.

By that evening, a flight had been booked for Mili to travel to London, a new suitcase had been bought for the journey, her wardrobe had been updated, she had been given a new pair of boots – and she was off! Father Peter came to bless her before she left the house, and her brothers, sisters, cousins, nephews and nieces lined up alongside her father's car as she climbed into the back next to her mother.

And suddenly, she was here – and she cried herself to sleep each night thinking of all she'd left behind. She hated living in a household where everyone spoke at breakneck speed in a language she barely understood. She found the children difficult – Savannah, a precocious seven-year-old who was rude, dismissive and pretended she couldn't understand anything Mili said to her, and Brandon, a whining three-year-old who hated going to his pre-school class on three mornings each week, and thumped her in the face whenever she tried to comfort him. The parents, Alan and Samantha, were hardly ever there. He commuted to London every day, where he worked somewhere in the City, and she was something called a barrister, which Mili didn't really understand except that it meant she was some sort of lawyer. The previous au pair had left for home the day before Mili arrived, and Samantha found it difficult to fit in any time to explain to Mili what her duties would be. She was given a list of tasks: several pieces of paperwork covered in tick boxes which she had to fill in throughout the day to ensure that the children read enough, had sufficient exercise, ate healthily and had plenty of sleep. Mili also had to ensure they didn't watch too much television, were limited in their use of electronic gadgets, and that they attended a range of out-of-school activities that included horse-riding, ballet, French lessons and piano for Savannah, and Music for Toddlers, Tumble Tots and Tiny Talk Sign Language for the under-fives for Brandon.

Mili was up at six thirty each morning, and literally didn't stop working until she fell into bed, totally worn out, before nine each night. Once she'd bathed both children, got them into their pyjamas, heard Savannah do her homework reading, and read a bedtime story to Brandon, she had to make sure they were both settled and ready for the parents to sweep in and kiss their offspring goodnight as soon as they got home, which was never before half past seven and often later. And while Samantha and Alan checked their emails and drank gin and tonics while they swapped stories of their day, Mili would be preparing their supper in the kitchen, then filling the dishwasher so that she could leave the couple to enjoy a nice meal and a restful evening in peace.

At the end of the first week, during which she'd worked every day, neither of the parents made any mention of paying her. When she finally plucked up enough courage to ask for some payment, the little she understood from Samantha's answer was that she wouldn't be paid for the first week, but that money would be kept to give her when she left the family, whenever that might be. She got the message that this arrangement was usual in the UK, but she couldn't for the life of her understand why. All she knew was that there was no money, and that was that.

It wasn't until the third week that she saw a poster about the activities at Hope Hall, and realized that there were daily classes there teaching English to foreign students. She only had a two-hour window to go to the class between the time she dropped Brandon off at playgroup and the time she'd have to leave to collect him again, but that was just enough for her to pop in for that very first visit.

And walking through that door made everything different. She met Terezka, a Czech girl who was nearly four years older than her, and who'd already been in England for eighteen months. Whereas Mili was small, blonde and petite, Terezka was more like a rugby player, strong-limbed and solid, with a loud voice and very definite opinions on everything. By the end of that first lesson, Mili had learned that the average weekly wage for au pairs in the area was £85–95, not the £60 for which she was working, and that there was no such thing nowadays as the family keeping the first week of wages "in hand", as she discovered it was called. More than that, apparently the rules governing the employment of au pairs dictated that they should work no more than thirty-five hours a week, with at least two clear days off.

"I think I should come and talk to your employer," announced Terezka. "She's treating you like a slave. This is not allowed."

Mili's stomach knotted with panic at the thought of Terezka facing up to Samantha.

"Okay," retorted Terezka, "then we must speak to Mrs Morgan, the teacher here. She knows the rules. She has been working with foreign students for years. She can talk to your Samantha. This situation must stop."

Sure enough, at the end of the lesson, while Mili was glancing anxiously at the clock to make sure she was on time for Brandon, Terezka marched up to Mrs Morgan and explained Mili's circumstances. After that, things moved quickly. Mrs Morgan wrote a short letter to Samantha, explaining that she was Mili Novakova's English tutor, and she hoped Samantha could spare time for a conversation about Mili's employment and progress.

With her heart in her mouth, Mili left the letter on the kitchen work surface for Samantha to read during supper. Minutes later, her employer stormed into Mili's room without knocking. Struggling to understand the furious tirade, Mili got the gist of what Samantha was saying – that she couldn't imagine why there was any need whatsoever for her to be approached out of the blue by an English tutor she didn't even know, especially when she wasn't even aware that Mili was wasting hours during the working day on English lessons! She went on to say that she was disappointed that Mili should act in such an underhand way, especially when all her other au pairs had been more than capable of learning all the English they needed just by being in their family situation. She finished by asking if Mili had any idea how fortunate she was to be allowed to live in their lovely home, and that if there was any more nonsense, she would be packed off on the first flight back to the Czech Republic.

Mili said nothing, and spent the next day and a half quietly going about her duties, terrified that at any moment Samantha would send her packing. While teaching her class at Hope Hall the following day, Mrs Morgan was deeply concerned for Mili's welfare and set about writing a formal letter listing the points that needed to be addressed, and enclosing a form which clearly explained the conditions under which au pairs were allowed to work in England. In the meantime, Terezka's mind went into overdrive trying to work out what she could do to help. After all, Mili came from a town quite near to her own in the Czech Republic, and it was such a pleasure to have another girl around with whom she could gossip in her own language.

By the following week, Terezka had decided that the room she rented was far too big for one person, and that Mili should move in with her. When Mili protested that she had no money for rent, Terezka grandly announced that The Bistro in the High Street at which she had been a waitress for nearly a year was looking for an extra pair of hands. Hours later, after a hurriedly arranged five-minute interview with the owner, Martin, who was plainly desperate for help, Mili had got herself a job. Mrs Morgan rang Samantha during that day, saying that because she'd had no response to her previous correspondence, and conditions for Mili had clearly not improved, she would be calling in the next morning, which happened to be a Saturday. She would collect Mili and her belongings, and the money the au pair was owed after three weeks of work should be paid in full. That evening, Samantha once against barged into Mili's room shouting that there would be no wages, because Mili owed her a huge amount for her plane ticket to England, and the sooner she left, the better!

And so it was that by lunchtime the following day, Mili had left that house for the last time, without a backward glance. Terezka's room really wasn't huge, but it did have its own tiny bathroom and a kitchen area that was concealed behind a curtain in the corner. And as she put her few possessions in the wardrobe and placed a picture of her family beside the bed, Mili listened to the comforting sound of Terezka's chatter, and decided she was going to be happy here – very, very happy.

Ida was in full flow, regaling her three lady companions at the Grown-ups' Lunch Club held every Tuesday in the foyer at Hope Hall, her raised voice reaching far beyond her own table.

"These youngsters can't even count without one of those flashy phones they've got glued to their hands morning and night. Whatever do they teach them at school these days? Plainly nothing sensible like mental arithmetic."

"That's what my Bert always says," agreed Doris. "He won a cup for doing sums in his head when he was at junior school. We've still got it on our sideboard, although heaven knows why! I'd much rather put flowers there than all those dusty old medals and certificates, but he won't hear of me moving them."

Ida gave Doris a withering look, plainly offended by the interruption. "I was saying," she continued with dogged emphasis, "that they have no common sense. Yesterday I was in the Pound Shop. I bought two items – fragranced disinfectant and a pack of loo rolls—"

"Were they fragranced too?" interrupted Percy from a nearby table. "I can't bear toilet paper that smells pongy, but I like it nice and thick and quilted. Don't you, lads?"

His lunch companions, Robert and John, nodded their heads in enthusiastic agreement.

Ida's eyes narrowed as she stared at Percy with icy fury. "I see, Percy Wilson, that your hearing aid seems to be working properly this morning and without the high-pitched squeal it usually emits. Unfortunately, that means you can very rudely eavesdrop on other people's conversations and interrupt when you are not welcome!"

"Oh, my dear Ida," retorted Percy, his face a picture of innocent concern. "I'm not wearing my hearing aid today. I don't need to when your voice is bellowing across the restaurant for all to hear. So, pray, do continue! What happened to your disinfected loo rolls? Were they going cheap?"

Ida snorted her disdain and turned back to direct her story towards Betty, Flora and Doris, who were keeping a tactful silence.

"To continue," Ida announced huffily. "The total bill for my two items was four pounds twenty pence, so I gave the sales assistant a five pound note along with a twenty pence piece. But the dope of a girl told me that I'd given her too much money, so I had to explain to her that this way she could just give me back a one pound coin."

"I do that," agreed Flora. "I always do that."

"Me too," added Betty.

"That is because both you ladies have brains in your head," pronounced Ida, "but brains were sadly lacking in that young woman. She just gave a great big sigh – very impolitely, I thought – then called over the manager, who was only a spotty teenager himself. He asked me to repeat my request, which of course I did, but he just looked at me and said, 'We don't do that sort of thing here,' and gave me back my twenty pence piece! Then he instructed the sales girl to open the till and take out eighty pence in small change, which she promptly handed over to me."

"Oh, I hate that," said Doris. "All those small coins cluttering up my purse."

"I can't read the values on them these days," mused Flora. "I think those little coins are very confusing. Why can't they make the numbers on them bigger?"

"I never go shopping," replied Robert. "My daughter Joyce won't let me. She just gives me the money I need when I come here to the lunch club, or when I go to bowling, but she sorts out everything else."

"I find that too much change in my pocket really spoils the line of my trousers. Don't you, lads?" guffawed Percy.

"My point," insisted Ida, "is that basic arithmetic is no longer on the school curriculum, and nobody seems to care."

"I remember when Marion and I," started John, "before she passed, you know... I remember that we needed to have our garage door repaired. The man came to look at it and said that our problem was that we didn't have a large enough motor on the opening mechanism. Well, Marion remembered that when we bought that garage door, the man at the shop said that we were buying the largest motor available, a half horsepower, and she told the engineer that. He shook his head and told her that we needed a quarter horsepower. So I pointed out to him that a half was larger than a quarter, and he said, 'Nooo, it's not. Four is bigger than two.'"

"Did you get your garage door repaired?" asked Flora.

"Not by them," replied John.

"I wouldn't have bothered with those new-fangled electric doors," said Percy. "They're very temperamental. My cousin got locked in his own garage by one of them a few years back."

"Oh goodness, whatever happened?" cried Betty. "How long was he in there?"

"Until his missus came out to get some of that Neopolitan ice cream she loved."

"But hadn't she noticed he was missing?"

"Apparently not. He'd gone out after breakfast with his golf clubs, and wasn't expected home until tea time."

"So he was stuck in there all day!"

"Oh, he didn't mind. He rather liked the peace and quiet. His wife was not one to be argued with, shall we say? So he just switched on the car radio to the sports programme that she wouldn't normally let him listen to indoors, and nodded off at his leisure. He said it was the best day he'd had for years!"

Chapter 3

"What do you mean, you're moving back home?" Shirley's voice echoed around the main hall as she held her phone to her ear. Whatever the answer to her question, she wasn't having any of it. "Tyler, your dad and I made it quite clear that if you were old enough to move out and live with Jasmine, then you were old enough to pay your own bills."

There was another silence while she listened to Tyler's reply.

"Then you need to get a job, Tyler. That's what Jasmine's been trying to tell you for months, and who can blame her? And it's what we're telling you too. If you want to eat, drink and have an iPhone, you've got to earn money, just like the rest of us do."

Tyler's next reply was plainly cut short.

"Well, if she's thrown you out, good on her, and don't come whining to us. Grow up and sort yourself out, Tyler. And don't ring me again when I'm here. I'm working to earn money to pay my own bills. You get a job and pay yours!"

And with that she switched off the phone with a flourish and shoved it unceremoniously into her overall pocket.

"Trouble?" asked Kath, who happened to be passing.

"That boy is twenty years old and hasn't an ounce of responsibility in him," sighed Shirley. "Mick and I told him he couldn't afford to live in a flat, even with Jasmine paying most of the rent. She's far too good for him, that girl. I'll miss her, but honestly I hope she's got the sense to kick him out of her life and find someone worthy of her."

"Will you let Tyler come home?"

43

"Well, *I* wouldn't…"

"But Mick might?"

"In the end, probably."

"Where would he go if he couldn't come home?"

"Well, that's the problem. Some of his friends are a bad lot, into all sorts of things we'd rather not know about. He's a follower, our Tyler. If he's not under our roof, we'll be worrying about who he is keeping company with."

"Is he at your house now?"

"Apparently. He's raiding the fridge and making himself comfortable, knowing that if he can get round Mick before I'm there, he's home and dry."

"What a worry for you, Shirley."

"I'm off to scrub a few sinks. I'll take my frustration out on those with a Brillo pad!"

Once Shirley had stomped off and out of the side door towards the school building, Kath continued her way through the main hall, looking down at the notes in her hand as she walked. It was Thursday morning, and she had been working on the Annual General Report of the Good Neighbours scheme which she managed as part of her role at the hall. The scheme connected willing volunteers in the community with those who needed a helping hand. That might be transport to the weekly activities and facilities on offer at Hope Hall, or it could be collecting shopping, help with work in the house or garden, facilitating hospital visits, or organizing shopping trips out of town for a group of pensioners who all fancied a day out courtesy of a kind driver. It had become a wide-ranging and complex operation over the four years she'd been running it, and it took quite a bit of her time to keep those in real need catered for, awkward pensioners behaving, volunteers feeling loved and cherished for their work and goodwill – and the money coming in to pay for it all.

"Oops!" She had been so preoccupied that, as she arrived at the foyer door, her papers were suddenly flying through the air and she barged headlong into someone coming the other way. She looked up into the blue-grey eyes of a man who was observing her with a mixture of amusement and concern.

"Oh, I am so sorry," she exclaimed. "Are you okay?"

"I'm in much better shape than your paperwork, I fear," he grinned, bending down to join her as she scrambled to gather up her notes, which had gone skidding across the floor in all directions.

"Please don't worry. I can manage!" Kath was uncharacteristically flustered.

"Of course you can, but it would be ungentlemanly of me not to offer help to a lady I've practically knocked off her feet!"

Bending down to pick up the last of the papers, Kath wasn't sure if she was grateful or just surprised by the way he took her hand to help draw her upright again. "No harm done," she reassured him, hoping she sounded suitably efficient after her initial display of clumsiness. "I'm Kath Sutton, by the way, the administrator here."

"Ah, then you are just the person I need to see. Is this the area the Sea Cadets are now using for their meetings?"

"Our main hall, yes, for indoor activities during their Wednesday night sessions, but they also make very good use of the old school playground outside. Would you like to see that?"

"No need. I assumed that's what happens, so took a look on my way in. I gather they also have a storage facility here?"

"We've made a room available which can be accessed from the outside of the school building. They moved all their equipment in the first evening they arrived."

"Under the direction of the Mighty Muriel." His eyes were glinting with amusement.

"Yes," she agreed, hoping her expression was serious enough

to hide the fact that laughter was bubbling up inside her. "Muriel is a very forthright woman."

"She is indeed," he said, as the two of them grinned at each other.

"Richard!" The Hope Hall accountant, Trevor Barrett, was striding towards them, a sheaf of papers tucked under his arm. "Good to see you. You're bang on time!"

"I was early, in fact. I haven't been inside Hope Hall before, so I thought I'd take a look at the facilities first. This charming lady has been showing me round."

"Well, you couldn't be in better hands," replied Trevor, beaming in Kath's direction. "Is your other half with you?"

"Celia's coming under her own steam. She'll be here shortly."

"Let's get started then, shall we? I didn't book a private room for our meeting, Kath, because we'd prefer to make ourselves comfortable in that far corner up in the balcony lounge, if that's all right? It's quiet and secluded there."

"Of course. How many of you will there be? I'll organize coffee."

"Five of us in all, I believe. Sheelagh Hallam is already upstairs with William Fenton."

William Fenton, thought Kath, the organizer of the Money Advice Service that had recently started holding weekly sessions on Friday mornings in one of the schoolrooms. Of course, this was the meeting of the trustees of that group, and Trevor was Secretary for those trustees.

"Ah, here's Celia now!"

The woman making her way through the foyer towards them was the picture of elegance. She was probably in her mid-forties, but looked much younger, with a stylish haircut, subtle make-up, and a dress and jacket that Kath recognized straight away as coming from a high-class designer label. Richard immediately moved towards her, kissing her warmly on the cheek, his arm protectively round her shoulder as they shared a few private words before walking over to join Trevor and Kath.

After Trevor had greeted Celia in a more formal way, he indicated towards the stairs up to the balcony, explaining that they could have coffee up there. Celia looked back over her shoulder to glance briefly in Kath's direction.

"Decaf, one sweetener and almond milk, please!"

Kath watched the couple as they walked away arm in arm, Richard smart but casual in a light brown jacket and chinos, alongside his "other half", who looked as if she'd just stepped out of the pages of a fashion magazine. Glancing down at her serviceable trouser suit that worked well for all the different jobs she was likely to find herself involved with during any average day at Hope Hall, Kath sighed before making her way to the kitchen to organize coffee and a selection of Maggie's cakes for them all.

Mili loved working at The Bistro. From the age of fifteen, she had taken on various waitressing jobs in her home town, and had always enjoyed not just the challenge of helping customers choose from the menu, often encouraging them to order just a little bit more than they'd intended when they first walked in, but also making sure that the service they received was efficient and friendly. Very occasionally when she'd been serving tables in the Czech Republic a customer might have given her a small tip, but here the tips were something else altogether! Most customers left a gratuity that was at least ten per cent of the price of their meal, which to Mili's mind was a huge sum. Better still, Martin, the owner of The Bistro, was not one of those employers who simply pocketed the tips for himself. He insisted that they were shared out at the end of every night between all the staff on duty, from Mili or Terezka waitressing out front to the chef and his assistants working in the kitchen.

Terezka was turning out to be the most wonderful friend, knowledgeable and hard-working, with an infectious sense of humour and a very wide social circle. Having worked at The Bistro for more than a year, she had got to know many of the regular customers, greeting them with affection, remembering what dishes and drinks were their "usual", and accepting with nothing more than an acknowledging smile the occasional five pound note that would be quietly slipped into her hand by a grateful regular customer whispering, "Here's a little extra *just* for you."

The Bistro was open throughout the day, starting with breakfast when they served freshly baked croissants and pastries, along with the typical "full English" – bacon and all the trimmings like black pudding and old-fashioned fried bread, which some of their customers thought was really quite trendy. At lunch, there was a tempting range of baguettes and open sandwiches, herby home-made soups, hearty hot meals and creamy desserts. In the evenings, the staff worked hard until the last customers left, ensuring they were delighted with their meals, which were likely to have matched in taste and style the delicacies on offer in the most popular bistros of Paris.

Knowing that Mili had to earn enough to pay her rent and keep herself fed throughout the week, Martin offered her as many hours as he could, avoiding the three mornings she went to her language classes at Hope Hall. Mili was finding it easier and easier to speak English. Her better grasp of vocabulary meant that she could converse more comfortably with customers. It also meant she could watch British television and get the gist of what was happening in the story. She could even walk around the town without worrying about notices, commands or greetings that previously she really couldn't understand.

One regular customer at The Bistro soon caught her eye. He came in every morning around eleven, and sat at the same table in the far corner, where he'd get out his laptop and a lined writing pad on which he would make notes as he drank his espresso coffee with a dash of milk. The young man looked to be in his mid-twenties, with straight brown hair that fell across his forehead as he wrote. His expression was always one of concentration and deep thought, except when Mili came towards his table. Then his face would light up with a smile as he requested the same coffee every time.

That routine continued for several days before eventually he asked, "I've been trying to recognize your accent. Where are you from?"

So Mili told him about her home town in the Czech Republic, and then also found herself telling him about her opportunity to come to England, and about this job, which had been offered just when she needed it. The conversation stretched over the several visits she made to his table bringing him coffee, then coming back later to check whether he needed anything else. By the end of the morning, Mili had discovered that his name was Andy and he was a musician, a piano and keyboard teacher, a music therapist and a songwriter.

"You write songs here?" asked Mili, glancing at the pad on which she could now see musical chords and lines of words.

"I'm trying to," he replied, conscious that her English vocabulary was limited as he tried to explain. "I have many tunes in my head. I like to come here to think about words for those tunes."

"Does anyone sing your tunes?"

"Sometimes. I've already sold some of them to a record company. Perhaps one day a big star will choose my song and it will be a hit. You'll hear it on the radio and TV."

"Perhaps *you* will sing your song and be famous!"

"Oh, I can sing okay, but that's not what I want to do. I like to be at the back, playing the keyboard and making sure the music is right."

"You're in a band?"

"Two or three bands over the years, but for a long time now I've played in a band called Friction."

"So, I can hear you?"

"You can. Sometimes we play at Hope Hall. You could come and see us."

"I know Hope Hall!" she exclaimed. "My English lessons are there."

"Well, on the third Friday of each month, they have a Dance Night and different bands are invited to play."

"What sort of music?"

"A bit of everything really. We have to play the favourites that everyone likes – you know, all those popular songs that people can sing to as they dance. Sometimes we play something new, but mostly we choose songs that we know people will really enjoy."

"Friction? I don't know that word."

Andy's brow creased with concentration as he thought about how to explain, eventually holding his hands up, then clapping them together like cymbals.

"Friction is when one thing hits another thing and goes bang – *whoosh*!"

"Oh! And that happens in the band?" Mili held her hands up and clapped them together. "One person goes *whoosh* with another person?"

Andy smiled. "Well, yes. That's not why the band is called Friction, but there *is* quite often friction between our singer and all the rest of us. Actually, you may know him? Carlos? He's Spanish and I think his girlfriend goes to your English class. Do you know Mariana?"

"Mariana Lopez? Yes, she's an au pair. Very nice, beautiful."

He nodded. "She is. She's far too good for Carlos, I think."

"He's not nice?"

Andy chose his words carefully. "Carlos can be difficult. When he first started singing with us, his English wasn't good. But he knew the really popular songs well enough to sing them so no one noticed that often he was getting the words wrong. And he has a really good voice. Audiences like him, but—"

"But you don't?"

"He's a bit of a prima donna, if you know what that means."

Mili shook her head a little.

"He wants to be the only star of the show. He doesn't care about the other players in the band. He's not good at being part of a team."

"A prima donna," Mili repeated slowly. She had plainly got the picture.

"The band has a lot of equipment to get ready before we play – amplifiers, control panels, the drum kit, the electrics and lights. But Carlos thinks he's too important to help us set everything up. We have many big boxes and electric cables, so we all help to load up our van, and travel together to wherever we're playing. Then we each know which jobs have to be done to make sure we have everything ready on stage. It's a lot of work and it can take us a long time to set up our equipment so that the sound is just right. But Carlos expects to walk in and find we've done it all. Later, he'll go off to have a drink at the bar immediately at the end of the gig, leaving us to clear everything up!"

"*Whoosh!* Friction!" repeated Mili, clapping her hands together dramatically.

"Friction," agreed Andy. "Anyway, why don't you come along when we next have a dance? It's in two weeks' time on Friday evening. Bring your other friend who works here, if you can both get the night off."

"Yes. I'd like that."

"Mili!" Martin caught her attention from where he was standing behind the bar, making it clear that he thought she was paying too much attention to this one customer who never bought more than a couple of cups of coffee.

She smiled as she turned back to Andy. "I see Mariana at class tomorrow. If she goes that Friday, then maybe I come with her."

And with a wave of her hand, she pulled out her sales pad and moved across to a new group of customers who were ready to order.

The sun was low in the sky on Saturday evening as Kath drove away from Southampton. The glare was so bright that it almost made her squint. At least, she thought that was what must be causing the moistness in her eyes. She was tired, she knew that. It had been a long day.

She'd arrived at Jack's hospital by nine o'clock sharp that morning, where the setting up for the hospital Family Fun Day was already in full swing. About a dozen men were struggling to erect a large marquee alongside a display arena, which another team were marking out with pegs and ropes. A pile of trestle tables had been delivered, and various stallholders were taking theirs away to transform it into an eye-catching display – different stalls selling crafts, sweets, home bakes or greetings cards, as well as others that were covered in bric-a-brac, tombola prizes or running competitions of various kinds. There was a barbecue area around which a chattering group of helpers were setting out an array of chairs and tables – and nearby a tea and coffee stand was being put together not far from a children's play area, which also seemed to have a petting compound that later in the day would house some cuddly rabbits, guinea pigs and a litter of puppies.

So much to see, Kath had thought, but no sign of Jack, who had said he would be waiting at the gate to greet her. Two phone calls and ten minutes later, he came hurrying over, a familiar companion at his side. Kath had been introduced to Monica Freeman on her previous visit. The two doctors worked in the same team, and Kath had been struck by the comfortable companionship between them straight away.

Jack had greeted Kath with a hug, but hadn't wasted time on chit-chat because he wanted to introduce her to Joan Cusack, who was the chief organizer of the whole event. Wearing sensible jeans and a smart denim jacket, Joan was a nursing sister who allowed no nonsense on her ward and certainly wasn't putting up with any nonsense in the arrangements for this Family Fun Day. She shook hands with Kath saying how delighted she was to have her help, and led her off to see the list of competitions taking place and what she had in mind for the Awards Ceremony at the end of the afternoon.

"Thanks, Kath," Jack called out as she followed in Joan's wake. "Monica and I have to go and sort out the sound tent and a platform for the microphone. See you later."

But, in fact, Kath saw practically nothing of Jack later – or for most of the day, for that matter. To be fair, she was kept busy making herself known to the Grand Raffle team, and all the stallholders who were organizing individual competitions of various kinds. In the marquee there would be a Cookery Fayre, with prizes on offer for the best cakes, tray bakes, jams and pickles. It didn't take her long to realize there was cut-throat competition for these coveted prizes, and there were even whispers that some entrants wouldn't be above sabotage in a bid to take the Star Baker cup!

Then there were the family races that were being held in the middle of the afternoon, for which she'd set up an easy system of recording the entrants for each race, many of whom might not choose to commit themselves until the last minute. She managed to find a stopwatch for the hospital porter who allowed himself to be roped in as timekeeper on the finish line – and made sure there was an easy way for his girlfriend from the Accounts Department to keep a record of the winners of the first, second and third prize in each race. Back in her office at Hope Hall, she'd already designed and printed out some winners' certificates, which she'd brought with her. As soon as she'd got her bearings at the site, she'd arranged for a desk to be placed next to the sound tent where she could base herself so that all the results could be delivered to her there, and certificates filled in immediately.

Jack and Monica had passed by with a wave on several occasions as they busied themselves with their own part in the preparations, and Kath saw them standing together alongside the microphone platform when the local MP arrived to open the whole event. Noting in the programme the time Jack was due to be pelted by water balloons, Kath made a point of going over to wish him luck, but by the time she arrived he was already installed in the stocks, and Monica was first in the queue with an armful of balloons that she was lobbing at him with peels of laughter. Watching Monica as she laughingly stared at Jack to make sure her aim was accurate, a thought crossed Kath's mind. Unless she was very much mistaken, there was love in that look! Did Jack realize? And if so, did he welcome such depth of affection from his work colleague? Was the feeling reciprocated?

Kath reeled as if she had been thumped in the stomach. Jack and Monica shared so much – their medical training, their experience as doctors, the care of their patients, life in the hospital in which they spent such long hours and, it seemed as

Kath watched the two of them now, the same sense of humour. But if Jack was falling for this vivacious, extremely attractive and capable woman, why on earth had he invited Kath along today?

Feeling awkward and superfluous, Kath slipped away knowing that Jack hadn't noticed her coming over to the stocks, and that he was definitely too preoccupied to see her making her way back over to her own table beside the sound tent. She had plenty to keep her busy as a steady queue of race organizers and stallholders came to report results to her throughout the afternoon, but the enthusiasm with which she greeted them, and the big smile pinned on her face, was at odds with her leaden heart, which was aching with a sense of something she couldn't quite identify.

At one point, Jack and Monica came across to see how she was doing, asking if they could bring her back a hot dog or some spare ribs from the barbecue. She felt rather proud of herself as she casually laughed and replied that writing beautiful italic script on award certificates might be a bit tricky if her fingers were mucky with barbecue sauce.

"Thanks, Kath," smiled Jack, putting a hand on her shoulder. "Just look at all these results and certificates. You've got everything in apple pie order, just as I knew you would. You're a star helping us out like this today, you really are!" And with that he bent down to kiss her affectionately on the top of her head. "We'll see you later, then, at the Awards Ceremony!"

"I wonder if you'll win the prize for being the wettest person in the stocks today?" grinned Monica, giving Jack a friendly dig in the ribs.

"Do you know," Jack laughed, "she brought her own enormous water gun to make sure I was well and truly drenched. Just you wait, Monica Freeman! I'll get my own back for that."

And as the two of them darted off, chasing after each other

like teenagers, Kath bit her lip and lowered her head to stare blindly at the certificate she was trying to fill in.

Yes, she thought. *Monica loves him. And even though Jack may not know it yet, my guess is that he's falling in love with her too.*

As the afternoon wore on, more results were coming in and the pace at which certificates were needed was really hotting up. Kath worked flat out until the moment the chief executive of the hospital was invited on to the platform to do the presentations. Kath handed over a clear list of all the prize winners to Joan Cusack as she stepped up to the mike to make the announcements. Then, as each winner came to collect their award and shake hands with the chief executive, Kath was standing to one side, making sure that the correct certificates, medals and cups were given to the right people. Finally, around five o'clock, Joan thanked as many people as she had time to mention, before reminding everyone that there were still a few tickets left for the Country and Western hoedown in the marquee that evening.

As the crowd dispersed, Jack came over and wrapped his arms around Kath in a great big hug.

"Do you fancy staying for the hoedown?" he asked.

"I forgot my cowboy hat and boots, I'm afraid."

"And I don't think I remembered to tell you about the dance, did I? I'm sorry, Kath. Perhaps you'd have liked to go?"

"I'm not sure my feet are up to dancing after being on this grass all day." She hesitated before going on, looking straight into his eyes before she continued. "And I think you already have a partner."

To his credit, he didn't try to bluster his way out of her challenge. It was clear that he completely understood her meaning.

"You make a nice couple," said Kath slowly.

He shrugged slightly. "We're not a couple."

"Not yet, but you're heading that way."

"We get on well, but that's not surprising, is it, when we work together and have such a lot in common?"

"You laugh with each other and, my darling Jack, I know from long experience that sometimes the responsibility of your work lays so heavily on your shoulders that you don't find much time to laugh. You smile in Monica's company and she comes to life in yours. She loves you. I don't know her at all, but even I can see that."

He looked at Kath with a growing wonder in his eyes. "Do you think so?"

"Don't you? And my guess is that you feel much the same way."

He said nothing, apparently digesting that thought.

"Is she free to have a relationship with you? She's not married or with a partner already?"

"She did have. Her divorce came through two months ago."

"Children?"

"Two: a boy and a girl, both in their teens. Her son, Jonathan, is already at uni, and providing Patti sails through her A-levels as she's expected to, she'll be off to study medicine at Cambridge in September."

"So Monica will have an empty nest."

He nodded. Kath found she had nothing else to say.

"I'm sorry, Kath," he said at last. "I've been utterly unfair to you. I didn't mean to be, because honestly I wasn't really sure how I felt about you or Monica—"

"But this conversation has helped you decide?"

"You're just being you, even now. In your usual direct and practical way, you saw what I couldn't see myself."

She sighed.

"Have I hurt you, Kath? Because that really wasn't my intention."

"I know."

"And I am truly pleased to be back in touch with you again. Apart from anything else, we were always friends first and foremost. I've missed that friendship. I've missed you."

She nodded, unable to answer.

"I think I'll go home now," she managed at last.

"Don't go. At least have a cup of tea with me before you leave."

She gathered up her pens and papers from the desk, and placed them in her leather bag. "I've quite a long journey ahead of me. Better to leave now."

"I love you, Kath," he whispered, slipping his arms around her and pulling her close. "I'll always love you."

But not enough, she thought, burying her face in his neck, breathing in the familiar scent and feel of him. Then she stepped back, picking up her bag as she started to walk away.

"Drive carefully, Kath. Let me know when you're home safely. And keep in touch. Let's always be in touch…" His voice faded as she strode off without looking back.

Later, as she drove home with the sun shooting blinding rays into the car, she found her eyes clouding with tears. She wasn't crying for Jack, she told herself, because she'd already decided that she wouldn't put her life on hold for him. And, in all honesty, the thought of Jack and Monica together was so logical and right that she simply wished them well.

But Kath realized that as the two doctors were coming together to start a new chapter of love in their lives, a door was closing in hers. Later that year she would be fifty years old, and she felt no sense of celebration in that thought. Where had her life gone? What had she achieved? Who cared, anyway? Kath found herself overwhelmed by an aching loneliness; a longing for a companion, a friend, a partner – someone who simply wanted to laugh, love and live with her.

And as the sun sank deeper in the sky, Kath reached into her bag, grabbing a paper tissue to scrape across her cheeks. The rays were really creating havoc with her mascara.

"The numbers are creeping up, Maggie!" Shirley marched into the kitchen and spread out her A4 notebook on one of the surfaces. "We've just hit eighty tickets sold, and there's still a fortnight to go until the first Saturday in June. I reckon a lot of people are more likely to book for something like a school reunion when they know lots of others have already decided to go."

Maggie looked at Shirley's notes with interest. "Well, I'm planning a buffet catering for about a hundred, so let me know nearer the time if you think the final figure will be higher."

"It's going to be so interesting to see how everyone's changed. Thirty years! A lot's happened to us all in that time."

"Did you meet your Mick at school?"

"Yes. He was one of the 'populars' – you know, the good-looking ones that everyone fancied."

"And you got him!"

"Actually," retorted Shirley, "I allowed him to get *me*. I was pretty popular too!" She threw her head back, laughing so loudly that anyone in the foyer would have wondered where on earth the noise was coming from. "Anyway, Mags, I'm on my way home now. See you tomorrow!"

That left Maggie on her own in the kitchen, clearing the dishwasher for the last time that day and setting out some of the items that would be needed for the next morning. The work required little concentration, which was just as well as her mind was still on the conversation she'd just had.

Shirley had never asked if Maggie was a former pupil of Walsworth Road Comprehensive herself, and that was a good thing. In fact, she had been three years ahead of Shirley, and studying different subjects, so their paths had never crossed during her time at the school – but in any case, Maggie had no intention of being anywhere near Hope Hall on that reunion evening. It wasn't that she hadn't enjoyed her school days, or that she'd done badly in her studies. In fact, it had nothing to do with her performance or popularity at school and everything to do with the way she was feeling about herself right now.

Glancing up towards the glass doors on the cupboards, she caught sight of her own reflection. She was *huge*. If only she were three inches taller no one would think her overweight at all, but at five foot three and tipping the scales at just over thirteen stone, she looked too short, too fat and – to her mind – just hideous.

At school it had been very different. She was never ever slim, but in fact her stocky, solid frame was a positive benefit in the school hockey team, which she really enjoyed. Then there was the kitchen and waitressing work that kept her on her feet and busy most weekends, and a mum who slowly became more disabled with MS throughout her teenage years. It all meant that the young Maggie had looked much fitter then than totally out of condition and enormous, as she felt now.

It was once she'd discovered her talent for cooking delicious cakes (which, looking back, was probably the main reason Dave had been so keen to marry her) and after the birth of their two children, Steph and Darren, that her willpower had slipped at the same rate as her waistline expanded. Well, she'd been content! She loved being a wife and mother, and had relished the ups and downs of family life. That wasn't unusual for a woman, *any* woman. Of course, it was totally unfair that some irritating, skinny-ribbed women could eat a whole loaf of white bread smothered in butter and jam and not put on an ounce, while she just had to let the *thought* of a choux bun enter her head and she'd gained a pound or two!

So, she wouldn't be reminding anyone at the reunion how she used to be a sporty teenager at school, but had since grown into this unrecognizable, wobbly blob! And although as Hope Hall's catering manager she was in charge of organizing all the food, drink and decorations for the event, she had put a note in the diary to say she had an unavoidable family event that evening, and had arranged for her assistant Liz, along with helper Jan, to hold the fort. And while they worked flat out all evening, she would be stretched out on the settee eating praline toffee ice cream and watching a Kevin Costner movie. Okay, so a lot of people thought he was old hat, but then so was she! Her divorce from Dave had left her feeling old, discarded and unlovable. So, if anyone had anything to say about her getting out a box of paper hankies to watch Kevin in *The Last of the Mohicans*, which was undoubtedly her favourite movie, they could just push off and mind their own business!

With a heavy sigh, she looked around the kitchen to make sure everything was done, grabbed her coat from the hook on the wall and a chocolate bar from the display cabinet, then slammed the door behind her.

Michael hadn't come back to the Food Bank the following Monday afternoon, even though Sheelagh had been keeping an eye open for him in case he was staying out of sight behind one of the trees that lined the pavement in front of the hall. Concerned and slightly disappointed, she really hoped he would find the opportunity, or perhaps the courage, to return.

Eventually, he did. A couple of weeks later she caught a fleeting glimpse of him hovering near the wall where she'd chatted to him on that first visit. Keeping her fingers crossed that he wouldn't disappear before she got there, she hurriedly poured out two cups of tea, grabbed the bag of sandwiches, cake and biscuits that she had already prepared in case he came, and walked as quickly as she could in a way that she hoped would appear suitably casual and relaxed.

"You do like yours with sugar, don't you?" she smiled at him.

He grunted, waiting for her to put the cardboard cup on the wall before he reached out to grab it. He immediately gulped down two or three mouthfuls of the hot liquid.

"I'm glad to see you again, Michael. How have you been?"

When he didn't reply, she opened the plastic bag to show him the selection of food she'd brought for him. "You might like some of these with your tea."

In one swift movement, he grasped the bag and drew behind the tree a little to inspect the contents. He immediately chose the sandwich, pulling the wrapper apart and biting into the BLT with great concentration.

"I see the coat fitted," she commented. "Were the other clothes any good?"

He shrugged, but she got the message that they'd been okay.

"And do you need anything in particular today? Other pieces of clothing? Shoes? Anything for where you live?"

He seemed to be too busy eating to answer. Sheelagh waited for a while, shocked at how hungry he plainly was as he devoured the entire contents of the bag. When he'd finished, she held out the second cup of tea. "I put sugar in this one too. Help yourself!"

He seemed calmer now, sipping the tea with less urgency.

"Have you got somewhere to live, Michael?"

He didn't reply, but from his body language she got the impression that he did have somewhere that he regularly stayed.

"Is it a safe place and okay for you to be there?"

Another shrug of the shoulders suggested it was.

"Warm enough?"

He shrugged again, staring down into his teacup.

"Can you tell me where it is?"

He didn't look up and said nothing, silently communicating a clear "no".

"Have you got any family nearby?"

Nothing.

Sheelagh left it a few minutes before trying again.

"I was so impressed by how much you knew about the food industry when we were talking last time."

He looked straight towards her then, a new glimmer of interest in his eyes.

"Have you worked in the food industry in the past?"

He gave a derisive snort. "You could say that."

"What did you do?"

A few seconds ticked by while he considered how he should answer. Eventually, he said, "I ran a shop."

"Oh, that's interesting – and such a responsibility. Was it a family concern?"

There was the faintest suggestion of a smile crossing his face, scornful and bitter. "A bit bigger than that."

"How big?"

Suddenly he'd stepped towards her, his face inches from her, his breath acrid, his body tense with anger. "I was the manager of a huge supermarket retail outlet. Is that big enough for you?"

Chapter 4

She might have been expecting it, but it still hit her like a ton of bricks.

The moment that large brown envelope dropped through the letterbox, Maggie knew exactly what it was. In some ways she had been looking forward to it coming – the official notification of the Decree Absolute that severed the final ties of her long marriage to Dave – but it surprised her how much the reality of seeing the statement in black and white knocked her sideways.

Her reaction had little to do with Dave. In fact, she was so angry at all the hurt he'd dished out to her and the family in recent months, he felt almost irrelevant to her now as she struggled to even *like* him. What laid her low was not the loss of her husband, but the loss of her marriage. She had enjoyed being a married woman, a wife, a mother to a growing family. She enjoyed being a "Mrs", and she'd lain awake for a couple of nights worrying about how she would fill in official forms in the future. Was she now a "Ms" – no longer a married woman, but definitely not a dainty, yet-to-be-wed "Miss"? The nearest term she could think of to describe how she felt was a widow, mourning the loss, not of the man, but of the marriage to which she had made a total commitment. And that did feel like a bereavement. It was sad and frightening and rather overwhelming to know that from now on her sentences could only begin with "I" rather than "we". There was respectability in being a couple, as if she was grown up, wanted and acceptable in polite company. A divorced woman might sound racy, desperate or even a threat to other people's marriages. She probably wouldn't be invited anywhere from now on!

But then, because of her marriage she had two wonderful children, Steph and Darren, both grown up of course, with homes of their own. In recent years, her relationship with Steph had become really close, especially when her daughter became a mum herself after Bobbie arrived nearly three years ago on Steph and Dale's first wedding anniversary. So as Maggie sat on the stairs, staring stupidly at the Decree Absolute, she fumbled in her pocket for her mobile and rang Steph.

As the phone was answered at the other end, all she could hear was Bobbie shrieking his head off in a toddler meltdown.

"Don't worry!" Maggie yelled over the din. "I'll ring back."

"No, you won't!" retorted Steph. "Dale's here and he's going to have breakfast with Bobbie before he leaves for work. Hang on. I'll shut the door and I'll be able to hear you then."

"The letter's come from the solicitor, Steph."

"Your Absolute? Well, congratulations, Mum! You're a free woman."

When Maggie didn't answer, Steph's voice was firm and commanding, as if she were talking to Bobbie. "Now, you listen to me! That man left you to go off with air-brained Mandy and her children, and he's about to become a father again at the age of fifty-one. He is no longer the dad I grew up with or the husband you loved, is he?"

"No."

"And if he came knocking on your door this morning begging for you to take him back, what would you say?"

"Well, he's not going to do that, is he? But the answer would probably be no."

"Do you respect him as he is now?"

"No."

"Do you like him?"

"No."

"Do you love him?"

Maggie sighed. "Old habits die hard, don't they, Steph? I've known that man since we were teenagers. He was my first and only love."

"Well, he won't be your last."

"Oh, don't be ridiculous! I'm forty-seven. Who's going to want me?"

"I think you'd be surprised."

"I know you're trying to be kind, sweetheart, but my relationship days are over."

"Why? You're the kindest, most hard-working, capable person I know. You always put others before yourself. That's why we love you so much."

Maggie plainly didn't think those comments merited an answer. Finally, she said, "I'm no good at change, Steph."

"You're scared, and that's hardly surprising. This is a huge upheaval for you."

"Packing up our home... It's really hard."

"But just think. Now the divorce is done and dusted, your financial settlement will come through. Has the solicitor confirmed an exchange date on the house yet?"

"They rang me yesterday. Apparently, contracts on this house and my new flat will be exchanged any day now, and completion can happen very quickly after that."

"Then you and I had better get cracking with the final boxes that need to be packed. And we'll need to go shopping to get you some lovely new things for that fantastic kitchen of yours."

Maggie smiled. "I'd like that."

"Tell you what. Dale and I will come round this evening and get all the stuff down from the attic. We'll bring fish and chips."

"And I'll make a carrot cake for Dale. I know how he'll like that."

Saying their goodbyes, Maggie switched off the phone with a smile on her face. "I'm single, I have a great job, a lovely family – and a cake to bake!" she shouted, enjoying how her voice echoed up the stairs and round the house where, in every room, there were boxes packed and ready to go. Whatever would the neighbours think?

Using her hip to push open the heavy old school door to the office, Shirley carefully balanced the two full coffee cups she was carrying until she was able to put them down on the desk. Ray's face was a picture of concentration as he stared at his computer screen, trying to make sense of a complicated spreadsheet showing all the bookings and facility requirements for events at the hall over the coming months.

"Can't all that wait until this afternoon?" suggested Shirley, pushing his cup towards him. "Kath will be back then, and she'll be able to give you the answers you need in no time."

"Whatever happened to just having a diary where everything's written down so you can find what you need straight away and understand it when you do?" Ray grumbled as he took a sip of coffee.

"It's progress, Ray. Technology rules!"

"Not for me it doesn't."

"Have you got time for us to have a chat about the final arrangements for the reunion now? It's only just over a week away, and I'd like to make sure we've got the parking planned and the hall laid out properly."

"Whatever you think is fine by me," grunted Ray, turning his attention back to the screen. "This is your event and I trust you. You say what you want, and I'll just put in place whatever you need."

Shirley eyed him thoughtfully for a while as she drank her coffee. Since the loss of his beloved wife Sara just a matter of weeks ago, Ray had allowed himself very little time to grieve, and had thrown himself back into his work as caretaker of Hope Hall with determination. Shirley had originally been taken on to lend a hand with the cleaning and general maintenance work at the hall while Ray was nursing Sara, but she soon became much more than just a work colleague to the couple, popping in most days to visit Sara at home, running the vacuum cleaner over the carpets and keeping things tidy, as well as making sure there was always a home-cooked meal in the fridge that might tempt Ray to eat.

As he finally gave a groan of frustration and pushed the keyboard away, Shirley reached out to cover his hand. "How are you doing, Ray?"

"Fine."

"Are you sleeping?"

He shrugged. "On and off."

"Did you have breakfast this morning?"

"You're nagging, Shirley. Don't!"

"I'm worried about you, and you snapping at me won't stop that."

His shoulders sagged. "The mornings are the worst. I always took her a cup of tea in bed. Did that every day for thirty-two years. Mornings never feel right now."

"I guess the evenings are much the same…"

"She always had our evening meal ready when I got back from work. I'm hopeless at cooking. That's the problem when you spend most of your life with a wonderful cook. But my job was the washing-up, and then I used to make us both a cup of cocoa. Well, it doesn't take long to wash up one plate and one set of cutlery – and I can't bear the thought of drinking cocoa on my own, so I don't bother."

"There's nothing you'd like to do in the evenings? I know you've never been one for watching telly."

"No, I can't be bothered with all those soaps and repeats they put on now. I don't mind the *Six O'Clock News*, but the TV goes off after that."

"So, what do you do all evening?"

"Not much. I think. I look at photos. I remember."

"No friends you could pop round to see, or who might like to come and join you for an hour or two?"

He smiled sadly at her. "I'm not great company, Shirley."

"Hobbies?"

"Not really. I don't mind a good jigsaw once in a while."

"Have you got any to do at home?"

"Dozens. Sara gave me a box every birthday and Christmas."

"Well, why don't you dig out one of those that you've not done for a while? That would be a very entertaining way to spend a few hours."

He sighed. "Yes, I suppose I could."

She moved her chair nearer to his so that their shoulders were touching. "You know, your emotions are all over the place right now…" she began.

"Like a jigsaw puzzle where none of the pieces seem to fit," he continued.

She nodded and leaned in towards him, tilting her head to rest against his. "Start with the corners," she said gently. "That's the way to begin. Then look for the blue sky pieces. They're all there – and with a bit of time, you'll find them."

"At the order, to the front, salute!"

This command, which came ringing across the playground, stopped Kath in her tracks as she stepped outside the front entrance of Hope Hall.

"I will call the timing!" boomed the voice, which Kath instantly recognized as belonging to Muriel Baker, the intimidating unit leader of the Sea Cadets.

"She's terrifying, isn't she?"

Kath spun round in surprise at the sound of a voice that seemed to be coming from around the corner of the hall. Curiously, she followed the sound to find the man she had so spectacularly bumped into a week or so earlier, spilling her folders all over the floor at his feet. He was leaning casually on the wall looking across the school playground at the troop of about twenty Sea Cadets who were deeply engrossed in drill practice under the eagle eye of Muriel. About two-thirds of the cadets were boys, the rest girls, with ages ranging from about ten to late teens.

"Their knees must be knocking with fear," grinned Kath. "What happens if they get it wrong? Are they clapped in irons?"

The man turned towards her then, his eyes dancing with amusement. "Or ordered to walk the plank? Nothing quite that draconian these days, I'm glad to say. And it is very character-building, training like this with the Sea Cadets. It's years since I did it, but I know it set me off on the right path."

"Did you have a career at sea after that?"

"I was in the Royal Navy years ago, just long enough to prove a point to my dad that I could stand on my own two feet. I only put in about seven years of service before I felt I had to do my duty and follow Dad into the family business, manufacturing agricultural machinery. I still enjoy sailing a bit when I can, but only as a lowly crew member when I'm sure someone who really *does* know the ropes is wearing the captain's hat. So I have to own up to being a bit of a landlubber these days."

"But you've retained your interest in the Sea Cadets?"

"That's my son standing alongside the magnificent Muriel. William is a petty officer cadet now, and he really is keen to take up the naval life. If he knuckles down and gets the A-level grades he's predicted at the moment, he's hoping to be sponsored through his degree studies by the Royal Navy."

"'Join the Navy, see the world!' Although it seems to me that it can be a very challenging and dangerous world for the military man nowadays," mused Kath.

His eyes locked with hers. "I've had that conversation with him. Whenever I mention the state of world politics and the potential danger for anyone in military service, he accuses me of being patronizing, and he's right. I can hear my dad saying exactly the same thing to me when I told him I wanted to join up all those years ago. But that's a dad's job, isn't it, to look out for his boy? You want them to learn from your experience, save them the pain of getting hurt. I remember feeling just like him, hating the way my dad always felt he knew best about anything I wanted to do. William just throws back at me that I've always encouraged him as a Sea Cadet, but he's the one who, since he was ten years old, has put the work in to move up the ranks. He's right. I have to respect that. He thinks he's going into the service with his eyes wide open. But I watch the news bulletins every day and I'm terrified for him."

"That's a dreadful dilemma for you as a parent. Of course, you only want what's best for him, and top of your list is his safety."

"I suppose it's in his genes. His mum's father was Admiral of the Fleet."

"Does that make the dilemma any easier for her?"

"We lost Elizabeth five years ago now. William was only twelve. It hit him hard."

"Oh, I'm so sorry," mumbled Kath, appalled at the thought

that her questioning might have been intrusive and prompted painful memories.

"No apology needed," he smiled. "She was a wonderful person, who approached her illness in the same pragmatic way she treated everything else life threw at her. She prepared for her own death by preparing us well too. She instilled in us both the need for courage and hard work."

"And William will need both of those qualities in his military career."

"He will, and because of Elizabeth he understands that. So do I."

Sensing a need to move the conversation on, Kath glanced out towards the cadets, some of whom were plainly struggling with the timing of the drill exercise. "That's obviously harder than it looks!"

"William will sort them out. Muriel gives the orders, but he's the second-in-command, charged with making sure the younger cadets get the one-to-one time they need."

"Do you always come to watch?"

"Heavens, no!" he laughed. "William hates me being here, but I had to be this evening. I don't know quite how it happened, but I've ended up being chair of the local trustees for the Sea Cadets in this area. It was me who had to put the rubber stamp on the unit using Hope Hall this summer while their own hut is being repaired. And it will be me paying the bills to the hall – so perhaps we should introduce ourselves properly? I'm Richard Carlisle."

"Kath Sutton, administrator here. Carlisle? You aren't anything to do with the Carlisle Family Trust that so kindly gave us a donation earlier this year, are you?"

"Guilty as charged!"

"That was very generous, and much appreciated."

"From the little I've seen of the activities here, I can imagine you've put the money to good use."

"It's gone towards our Good Neighbours scheme, so we can keep in close contact with vulnerable people in the community. That includes all sorts of folk – from the elderly who come along to our weekly Grown-ups' Lunch to the trips and outings we organize, as well as a huge programme of befriending and practical support in their own homes."

"It's a very impressive scheme. I'd been keeping an eye on it from a distance for quite a while before we made that donation. Your accountant, Trevor, has kept me in the picture."

"Oh, of course," said Kath, grimacing at the memory. "That first day when I literally fell at your feet you were going to the trustees' meeting for the Money Advice Group here. It was Trevor who *almost* introduced us, but not quite!"

"How could I forget?" grinned Richard. "That was quite an entrance. But I recognized who you were immediately from the big build-up Trevor had given you. He's always talking about how you're stretching the programme and the achievements of Hope Hall in many excellent directions."

Kath could feel the flush of embarrassment colour her cheeks. "Yes, we've got a good team here."

"A team which benefits from strong and insightful leadership from the top."

"Well," began Kath, taken aback by his compliments. "I must be going. It's been very good to see you again, Mr Carlisle."

"Richard. And it's been most enlightening to meet you properly too. May I call you Kath?"

"Of course. Hopefully our paths will cross again soon."

"I'm sure they will. Goodnight, Kath."

Smiling a goodbye, she quickly made her way out of the main gate, crossing the road towards the park through which she could

73

walk back to her apartment. Ten minutes later, as she put her key in the door, she realized she was still thinking about the disarmingly intimate conversation she'd just shared with a perfect stranger: Richard Carlisle.

"They're not dancing! Why aren't they dancing?"

Moving to stand alongside her sister Barbara, Shirley's expression was full of concern as she stared out at the crowd that had gathered in the hall for their school reunion.

"Because they're *talking*," replied Barbara. "Most of them haven't seen each other for thirty years or so. They've got a lot to catch up on."

"But they *loved* dancing. There was always music when we were teenagers and we couldn't stop ourselves dancing. Shall I ask the DJ to turn the volume up?"

"Later," smiled Barbara. "They'll dance later. I've given that DJ a complete playlist for the evening. We're going to build up slowly, but I guarantee they'll be bopping away just like they used to before the evening's out."

That silenced Shirley for a while as she scanned the faces around the hall. "Honestly, are this lot *capable* of bopping? They're all so *old*! There's a lot of very round waistlines here and quite a bit of grey hair. How come men get bald so quickly? I didn't recognize who it was when that Dennis Freeman came over to say hello. He had long straggly hair when we used to hang around together. He thought he looked like Mick Jagger back then, and I quite fancied him. I wouldn't want to get locked in a lift with him now!"

"Did you see that Marcus Williams is here tonight? I used to have such a crush on him," sighed Barbara. "Good job I avoided that one. He's just told me he's been divorced twice and he hasn't seen his two boys since they were toddlers because both his ex-wives have taken out restraining orders against him!"

"Whatever for?" demanded Shirley, her eyes as wide as saucers. "Is he violent? Or just mean and heartless?"

"Oh no, he's completely innocent and misunderstood – or at least that's what he's just told me. I think I dodged a bullet by missing out on that charmer."

"I've been looking out for Dan Marshall. Have you seen him? He replied to say he was hoping to come."

Barbara looked at her sister with a grin. "And you were *definitely* hoping he'd make it. You were soft on him for ages. It's a terrible thing, unrequited love—"

"Well, not quite unrequited. I never told you – and you must promise never to breathe a word of this to Mick – but what actually happened was that as soon Mick asked me out and we started dating, Dan suddenly found me a lot more interesting."

"Did Mick realize that?"

"He would have dumped me in a flash if he'd any idea at all I was two-timing, and he'd have punched Dan's nose as he left!"

"Did you and Dan have a bit of a fling, then?"

"Well, it wasn't even that, really. He asked me out for a walk – and we all knew what a fella had in mind back then when he said he wanted a *walk*."

"But you went anyway?"

"I had to *know*, Barb!" Shirley's expression clouded as she relived the old memories. "I'd fancied Dan for ever. If I had a chance with him, well, I didn't want to miss it. And I hardly even knew Mick; we'd only been out twice. I liked him, of course, but he was a bit shy at the start, so I hadn't really got the measure of him then."

"What happened?"

"Not a lot really."

"Was that Dan's choice or yours?"

Shirley thought about that for a moment. "Mine, actually. He was really full of himself. He started off by telling me he knew I fancied him. I was mortified. I thought I'd been really off-hand and cool. You know, treat 'em mean, keep 'em keen!"

Barbara threw her head back and laughed. "You were never cool and off-hand! If you liked someone, it was written all over your face. Of course Dan knew you fancied him. Everybody did!"

"Well, that night on our 'walk', he went in for the kill too soon for me. And I thought about Mick and how nice he was, and how I rather liked the fact that he was a bit shy, and I wondered what on earth I was doing there with Dan, who plainly thought he was God's gift to women."

"So, for heaven's sake, why are you hoping he'll be here tonight?"

There was a touch of steel in Shirley's smile as she replied, "Because I want him to know what he missed. I want him to catch sight of me in this new dress of mine and wish he'd been kinder to me. I want him to see me with my lovely Mick and know that's what relationships should be."

"Well, breathe in and put on your very best smile in that case. Isn't that Dan walking over towards the bar now?"

With a start, Shirley stared in his direction. "Do you know, I think you're right. Shall I go over?"

"Cool and off-hand, remember? Why don't you go over to the kitchen to see if Liz is ready to serve the hot buffet? Then you can stand silhouetted in the light of the kitchen hatch looking alluring and untouchable!"

"I'll laugh. I know I'll laugh."

"Then, my lovely little sis, the last laugh will be on you. What's Mick's favourite dance track?"

"'The Only Way is Up', by Yazz and the Plastic Population. He loves that."

"Once the buffet's over, I'll make sure the DJ plays that so that you and Mick can take to the floor and stun that Dan with how well you dance together."

"I don't fancy dancing all on our own. You and Stu will come up too, won't you?"

"I'm your sister. I've been a bossy dance teacher for years. If I tell them to get up and dance, they *will* all get up and dance!"

Ten minutes later, when the DJ had announced that the hot buffet was about to be served, Mary Barratt tugged at her husband's arm. "Come on, Trevor, you know how good this buffet will be. I can tell from your waistline that you don't just stick to crunching numbers when you're here supposedly concentrating on the Hope Hall accounts. You clearly sink your teeth into a fair amount of Maggie and Liz's cooking too! So, come on, let's get to the front of that queue."

"Tell you what, Mary," sighed Trevor, "you go and save me from myself. Just don't bring me all lettuce leaves! That Chinese stir-fry smelt great when Liz was cooking it up earlier. I'd like some of that please *and* some shepherd's pie. And don't forget the beans!"

Mary huffed a little as she made her way over to the buffet on her own. Trevor had made no secret of the fact that he hadn't been looking forward to her school reunion. The two of them hadn't met until university, so he knew no one here, and he hated disco music. On top of that, a big golfing tournament was being aired on one of the sports channels that evening, and Mary knew he was sulking a little because he would far rather be stretched out in his recliner chair watching TV with a couple of beers and a large packet of his favourite salted cashew nuts.

"Mary?" The lady standing behind her in the queue stared at her with open curiosity. "Mary Brewer, is that you?"

An instant image shot into Mary's mind of Latin A-level classes taught by Mrs Jackson, who had seemed to her teenage students to be so old that she might have actually been around in the time of Homer and his odyssey.

"Linda? Linda Sandford?"

"Linda *Armitage* now. You remember Bruce, don't you? Bruce Armitage from the year above us?"

A smiling man peered over his wife's shoulder. Mary's mind went into overdrive as she tried to tie up the old hazy memories she had of Bruce as a seventeen-year-old youth with the man now standing in front of her.

"My goodness! You married him!" exclaimed Mary, recalling how she and Linda had giggled when Bruce first asked her out, because, with the natural cruelty of teenage girls, they'd always dismissed him as potential boyfriend material because he was not only thin and gangly, but suffered from the double whammy of acne on his face and dandruff dotted across the shoulders of his dark school blazer. This man was tall, and his broad shoulders fitted perfectly into a smart and spotless jacket. His face looked fashionable and friendly with its neatly trimmed beard.

"I *did* marry him!" laughed Linda. "Because when I finally gave in and kissed him, this darling frog of mine turned into a handsome prince!"

There were hugs all round as the three friends exclaimed how wonderful it was to see each other again, and how none of them had changed a bit. Mary pointed over to where Trevor was sitting at their table, hoping with all her heart that he would look at least a little interested when she waved at him. Bless him, he obviously got the message because Linda and Bruce said they couldn't wait to come across and join Mary and Trevor at their table so they could catch up properly.

Twenty minutes later, Shirley checked her lipstick, sucked in her stomach, then timed her exit from the kitchen just as she knew Dan would be passing. She looked over in his direction to be sure he got a good look at her, but her gaze was lifted over his head, as if she were in a hurry, a woman on a mission.

"Well, well, well! It's Little Miss Burton, if I'm not mistaken."

Shirley looked at him without a trace of recognition. "I'm sorry, were you speaking to me?"

"Shirley, Shirley, with locks so curly, what a pretty little girlie!" Dan drawled the chant as he leaned back against the wall looking Shirley up and down, as if considering whether she was worth his attention.

"Dan Marshall. You haven't changed a bit. Still as full of yourself as ever."

"And you, Miss Burton, are looking very well indeed."

"Sorry, Dan, I can't stop. I'm busy."

"One of the kitchen staff, are you?"

Shirley crossed her fingers out of sight as she replied, "I'm Senior Manager here at Hope Hall."

"A *senior* manager, eh? At a local hall? What needs to be managed at a hall like this? A dustpan and brush? Refuse collection?"

Shirley looked at him with absolute disdain. "You plainly don't know much about the very complex and comprehensive programme here at Hope Hall, do you?"

"You're speaking to the CEO of a major import–export company. I don't think there's much you could tell me about complex programmes and management skills."

"And what do you import and export?"

"High-tech electronic components. There's probably little point in me telling you more than that."

"Why? Do you find your products so complicated you aren't able to explain them to other people?"

He laughed, but there was no humour in his eyes. "That's

what I always liked about you, Shirley. You were spikey then and you're still spikey now. I like a woman with spirit."

"And is Mrs Marshall suitably 'spikey'? I sincerely hope you married someone honest enough to tell you when you're being arrogant and patronizing."

"The present Mrs Marshall seems very happy with the manner in which she is now being kept."

"Kept?"

"She likes life's little luxuries. I make sure she gets them and in return she is most understanding—"

"Turns a blind eye, do you mean?"

His eyes twinkled with mischief. "Exactly. She's the perfect wife for me."

"Is she here tonight?"

"She would have been bored to tears. And she has a point. I hardly recognize anyone here, and those I do remember are disappointing. So mundane. So small town—"

"So leave!" snapped Shirley. "You won't be missed. I will be, though, by my wonderful husband who is ten times the man you are! Goodbye, Dan."

Just at that moment, as Shirley turned on her heel and marched away, the DJ pumped up the volume so that the sound of Yazz singing "The Only Way is Up" filled the hall.

Having kept her eye on Shirley and Dan's conversation from a distance, Barbara stood to greet her sister as she walked back towards their table. One look at her determined face was enough for Barbara to grab her husband Stu just as Shirley stretched out a hand to Mick, and the four of them walked out on to the dance floor. Barbara may have been the one who went on to become a dance teacher, but it was the sisters together who had always stolen the show as soon as any disco music started. Shirley had told her children she had been a bit lukewarm about Mick when they'd first started going out, until that magical night when he took her to a youth club disco. John Travolta had nothing on him! Mick had built on the *Saturday Night Fever* moves he'd practised when he was a young boy, adding the moonwalk and a few early hip-hop moves to his repertoire by the time he met Shirley. When he danced, the girls noticed him, and once Shirley had got over the shock of realizing that the quiet, apparently shy Mick had an animal magnetism the moment he stepped on to the dance floor, she decided he was a keeper. By the time she was twenty and he was twenty-two, they were married with their first son, Brandon, on the way.

Shirley was aware of Dan staring in amazement from the side of the disco floor as she and Mick danced with all the expertise that thirty years of practice together gave them. They twirled and dipped, bopped and boogied, until the music merged into Whitney Houston singing "I Will Always Love You", when Mick swept his wife into his arms and kissed her as if they were teenagers.

From their now empty table at the side of the hall, Trevor and Mary sat looking at the dancers. Linda and Bruce Armitage had turned out to be delightful companions as they and Mary caught up on all the years since they'd been at school together. Trevor had found them excellent company too. Bruce was the financial director of a small distribution organization, so their common interest in figures and accounting gave the two men something to talk about straight away. And then, once they'd discovered that they shared a passion for golf, the friendship was sealed. The Armitages lived in a village not far out of town, and a date to meet up for lunch at the golf club was already in discussion.

However, when the disco started in earnest, Linda and Bruce were out of their seats and on to the dance floor in a flash, keen to make the most of another of their passions – disco dancing, honed to perfection through a decade of ballroom lessons.

How Mary wished Trevor could dance! He always said he had two left feet, and he was probably right, but oh, how she wished he would give it a try. Just swaying from foot to foot and having a bit of a cuddle on the dance floor would have been enough for her.

As they sat together staring across the floor, their attention was caught by Shirley and Mick, who were ending one dance number with a surprisingly passionate kiss.

Mary leaned her shoulder against Trevor's, raising her voice so that he could hear her. "Do you think the romance has gone out of our marriage?"

He looked at her, considering his answer. "I think," he said at last, taking her hand in his, "that you and I are like a pair of comfy old slippers: warm, cuddly and nicely worn-in."

She gave his hand a squeeze before stretching across to plant a kiss on his cheek. "You're right. We make the perfect pair!"

An hour or so passed before Shirley realized that Dan had left the hall. Obviously the evening had been a disappointment to him, not interesting or successful enough. Well, good riddance! And thank goodness she had seen how shallow he was in time to save her budding relationship with Mick all those years ago. Her husband had turned out to be so much more than Dan Marshall could ever be!

As the evening finally drew to an end, Shirley went into action, organizing the clearing of tables, stacking chairs and making sure everything was locked up and secure before she left.

She was back at seven the next morning so that by nine, when the organizers of the jumble sale in aid of a local animal rescue centre arrived to set up their stalls, Hope Hall was spotless, without a trace of the wonderful event that had taken place there the evening before.

Shirley stayed on hand at the hall all morning, delighted to hear when the animal rescue volunteers eventually totted up their takings that the jumble sale had raised nearly nine hundred pounds for the cause. As soon as they'd all left, she set about clearing up the hall yet again, leaving for home at about half past one.

Once there, she made Mick a pile of his favourite ham and tomato sandwiches, then went out into the garden for an hour of much-needed weeding. Standing back to admire her handiwork, she then pulled a reclining chair into a sheltered corner of the garden, where she could stretch out in the June sunshine. She was dimly aware of the commentary from the sports channel Mick was watching in the living room beyond the open patio doors, and smiled at the thought that he was there. Then her mouth fell open, she started to snore noisily and she didn't surface again until teatime.

Sheelagh Hallam knocked and then popped her head around Sam's door as soon as she heard him invite her in.

"Sheelagh, grab a seat. I hope you're ready for a cup of tea."

"Salvation Army tea is the best," she smiled. "I'd love one. I can nip down to the kitchen and make it."

"No need. Josie saw you coming and went straight down to put the kettle on. How nice to see you! What brings you our way?"

Sheelagh reached into her handbag and drew out her mobile. Scanning through the photos for a few seconds, she finally handed the phone over to Sam so he could see the snapshot she'd taken of Michael. She had managed to get a long-distance but relatively clear picture of him the previous week when he'd come again to the Food Bank.

"I was wondering if you knew this man. All he's told me is that his name is Michael, but he keeps his distance and is very difficult to engage in conversation."

Sam peered at the photo. "What do you know about him?"

"Not much. He took me by surprise the other day when

he told me he used to be the manager of one of those huge supermarket stores, and certainly the only time he's ever been at all animated was when we were talking about food and how wasteful he feels the big food chains are. Apart from that, I know nothing about him. My guess is that he's got some sort of roof over his head, but it must be very basic because he's dirty, poorly dressed and obviously hungry. I just wondered if you could throw any light on who he is and what difficulties he's facing at the moment."

"I've not personally noticed him here, but the street teams may well have come across him. Could you forward this picture to me and I'll have a word with them? They have a good relationship with most of the homeless folk in this area, so hopefully they might be able to come up with something."

"Thanks, Sam. He worries me. He's obviously articulate and educated, but he's hit rock bottom. I don't think he's a drinker. I might be wrong, but he didn't seem like that to me. I guess he may have had a mental breakdown of some sort, or perhaps an upheaval at home or work that's resulted in him just walking away into oblivion."

"It happens," nodded Sam. "How long have you been aware of him?"

"Six or seven weeks, I reckon. He doesn't come every Monday, but he's been three times in a row lately, so I'm hoping I can build a proper rapport with him. Knowing a bit more about him might guide my conversation, because if I get it wrong, I have a feeling he'll disappear into the ether. I really don't want that to happen. He obviously needs help."

"Right, leave it to me. I'll get back to you as soon as I've had a chance to ask around."

"Thanks, Sam. Now, how are things here at the hostel? Anything I can help with?"

"We're in need of a new tuba player for the band," grinned Sam.

Sheelagh chuckled. "Well, I can give you a bit of helpful advice in return. Don't ask *me* to play. You'll be needing earplugs if you do."

Chapter 5

Maggie's feet hurt. So did her knee, from a tumble she'd taken on the tarmac. And she had a huge bruise on her right hip where she'd collided with the corner of the sideboard. Her hair hung in damp tendrils around her face, a face that shocked her when she caught sight of herself in the mirror. It was the colour of dust, with black circles of exhaustion under her eyes. Her head ached. Perhaps she was coming down with a cold. Or maybe she was just absolutely worn out and feeling her age. But none of this mattered one bit, because she couldn't have felt any happier than she did at this moment!

She was standing at the window of the back bedroom of her new apartment. Correction – she was standing at the window in her new *home*, because home this most certainly was. From the moment her daughter Steph had first arranged a viewing for her, Maggie knew this place was destined to be hers. This was a house that had always been in her life, ever since her best friend at school had lived here. She'd had scores of sleepovers here when she was growing up. She had run around the garden, eaten in the kitchen with the family, pored over homework on the old dining room table, and whispered best-friend secrets on the stairs. That had been when the house was home to a whole family. However, in the past five years, it had been split into two apartments, and the one on the top floor, the one with its familiar view of the garden and the houses beyond, had had her name on the door from the second she'd first stepped inside.

Today had been brutal, physically and emotionally. Her son

and daughter, Darren and Steph, had organized it all. Years of Maggie providing gorgeous cakes and buns to her children's friends every day after school had paid off too, because at eight o'clock that morning half a dozen of them turned up – huge young fellas who immediately rolled up their sleeves to dismantle beds and wardrobes, while their wives and girlfriends got cracking on the last-minute packing, cleaning and vacuuming, as well as manning the kettle and a non-stop supply of biscuit and snacks. Mattresses were manoeuvred down the narrow stairs. The settee was turned on its head to get it round two sharp corners and out to the van. They'd only got the fridge freezer out by squeezing it through the French doors and then the gate at the back of the garden; and they had very nearly forgotten altogether about the tumble dryer in the garage. All those boxes she'd packed and carefully labelled for each room were carried out one by one. Delicate items like glassware, ornaments, photographs and Maggie's beloved house plants were put in a variety of cars for safe passage. Electrics were disconnected, lampshades removed, carpets shampooed and dark corners that hadn't seen the light of day for years were scrubbed until they shone.

And then came the moment when everyone else had gone on, and only Maggie was left having a last check around before she locked up and dropped the key off to the estate agent. Tears pricked in her eyes as she saw the square patches on the walls where family photos had always hung. As she closed the doors to the conservatory, she had a sudden vision of the time their children's two hamsters had got out of their cage and set up home among all the clutter in that garden room. Their hamster menagerie that had started out with two soon multiplied until there were about twenty of them living in so many corners that it was impossible to find them all. Then there was the toilet door upstairs that had stuck for years – until the day four-year-old

Steph had locked herself in and Dave had been forced to get out a ladder, prise open the window and squeeze himself through to rescue her. He soon sorted out the toilet door after that!

With one last look around the hall and stairs, Maggie had walked out through the front door and pulled it shut behind her. There! She'd done it. Every step she took from now on would be a step further into her new life, and she was ready for it.

She'd almost lost her resolve when her neighbour Doreen came out with glassy eyes, a big hug and an even bigger pot plant as a housewarming gift for Maggie's new home. Doreen and Maggie had walked their children to school together for years. They'd put the world to rights over the garden fence, shared Sunday lunches, babysat for each other's youngsters and been there with casseroles and sympathy when times were difficult or painful.

"I'm only moving just round the corner," Maggie had choked, suddenly struggling to speak. "I'll always have the kettle on. Come as soon as you like. Come any time. Just come. Promise you will!"

And with Doreen's reassuring promises ringing in her ears, Maggie had climbed into her car, switched on the engine and driven away. She couldn't bear to look in the rear view mirror. She just stared ahead, knowing that whatever the coming days might bring, her future lay in that direction.

That had been at one o'clock this afternoon. Now, five hours later, she looked out over the treetops at the bottom of the garden to see the sun setting, painting the sky vivid orange and gold. It looked beautiful. She would enjoy watching that sunset whenever she could from now on.

"Mum! The fish and chips are here." Steph's voice rang out from the kitchen along the hall. "You do want ketchup, don't you? And would you prefer a cup of tea or something stronger?"

"Ooh, tea, I think," Maggie replied as she made her way to join the others sitting round the breakfast bar in the kitchen.

"Tea *and* a glass of champagne? Or just tea?"

Maggie grinned. "Tea for every aching muscle in my body, and champagne because this place is wonderful. I love it already! And I love all of you for everything you've done for me today. I could never have done this without you."

As Steph stepped forward to hand her mum a glass, Maggie heard someone on the other side of the room shout, "Three cheers for Maggie! Hip hip hooray!"

"Cheers!" she cried, holding her glass high in the air. "Here's to all of you, and here's to me! I've done it! Hooray!"

Kath took a last look at the seating she had set out in the far corner of the balcony lounge and checked everything was absolutely ready. The members of the organizing committee for the Hope Hall Centenary Celebration Day would be arriving any minute now, and she wanted to be sure all the papers were prepared, refreshments organized, and that she had an answer in mind for every question they could possibly ask. Glancing at her clipboard, she ran her finger down the list of committee members:

KATH SUTTON – *chairman, administrator of Hope Hall*

TREVOR BARRATT – *Hope Hall accountant*

MICHAEL SAYWARD – *local historian*

THE REVEREND JAMES BARNARD – *vicar of St Mark's, leading the Centenary church service*

MRS ELLIE BARNARD – *representing Broad Street Upper School*

PETER RADCLIFFE – *Public Relations Officer for the local council*

BRIAN MACK – *building contractor*

ROGER BECK – *Rotary Chairman*

BRENDA LONGSTONE – *Women's Institute Chair*

MAGGIE STAPLETON – *catering manager at Hope Hall*

RAY BROWN – *caretaker at Hope Hall*

Satisfied that all was in order, Kath smoothed down both her hair and her skirt, and set off for the foyer to await their guests. As she walked from the old school building towards the hall, she saw Ray striding across the playground towards the main entrance, where Trevor was already waiting, a file of papers tucked under his arm. Predictably, Brenda Longstone, renowned for being dauntingly efficient in her role as Chair of the Women's Institute, arrived right on time, closely followed by James and Ellie, who had walked across from St Mark's vicarage, meeting up with Roger Beck on the way. Brian Mack's van, covered in eye-catching advertising for his building services, drew up outside Hope Hall just a few minutes later.

"Why don't we all get settled up in the balcony lounge?" suggested Kath, as Maggie walked past carrying a huge tray of coffee, biscuits and cakes.

"And I'll wait for Peter Radcliffe," suggested Trevor, who for years had never known the Council Public Relations Officer to arrive on time for any meeting they'd both attended.

Quarter of an hour later, coffee served, cakes and biscuits devoured, the committee was complete and ready for business.

"Right," started Kath, "let's run through the order of the day.

The service of thanksgiving and commemoration will start at the church at eleven o'clock sharp. So, what time do we need our congregation to be in their seats before the dignitaries arrive?"

"Well, the choir and orchestra will be there rehearsing from nine thirty onwards," replied James, "and I think the general public should be in place by ten forty-five – fifteen minutes before the start of the service."

"And your school choir and performers, Ellie? What time should we expect them?"

"Oh, we'll be there from nine thirty as well."

"And they'll be in costume?" asked the historian, Michael Sayward.

Ellie smiled in Brenda Longstone's direction. "They certainly will, mainly thanks to the generosity and sewing skills of some of Brenda's WI ladies. They've produced some wonderful outfits for the children."

Brenda brushed aside the compliment, businesslike as ever. "In trying to recreate the look of a hundred years ago," she began, "we have the advantage of hearing from our most senior members, some of whom were born less than twenty years after Hope Hall's foundation year of 1920. Those ladies have been very instrumental in advising us on the styles, materials, footwear and jewellery that would have been in common use at the time. In fact, the ladies remember a great deal about the fashion of those times, because at least three of them still have coats and dresses that belonged to their mothers. They simply couldn't bear to part with them, although they have been kind enough to lend some of those original items to our staff members who will be with the children and organizing our Centenary Pageant for the occasion."

"The school choir will be wearing those costumes throughout our pageant, which will end with a medley of 1920s songs," added

Ellie. "James and I were discussing whether the children should be kept out of sight before the performance. Their costumes are going to look so striking that we feel it would make the best impact if we kept them in the vestry until they're due to sing. They won't have to wait long, because after the initial welcome from you, James, a hymn and then a few brief words from the mayor and the chairman of the council, Broad Street Upper School's performance will be the next item."

"Have all the VIP guests replied to their invitations, Kath?" asked Trevor.

"Well, Peter can bring us up to date with the council invitations, but as you know, we've tried to invite not just key members of our present-day community here, but to concentrate on the older people in the area who have memories of this hall and its role over the years. We've invited all the members of our Grown-ups' Lunch Club here at Hope Hall, as well as residents of local care homes and organizations for the elderly. Very few of them are younger than eighty, and several are in their nineties, so I think they should be thought of as the most important people taking part on the day. Good Neighbours transport has been arranged for them all and seating allocated for them conveniently near to the aisles, with the best possible view of the proceedings.

"That means they'll be near the toilet facilities too," Ellie added with a smile.

"As you know, three of them will be saying lines of prayer during the service," added James, "and one of them, Mrs Alice Mendrake, is a regular member of our congregation. She's ninety-seven years old with a memory that's still as sharp as a razor, so her contribution should be very moving."

"Peter has the list of council VIP guests," continued Kath. "Are we still likely to get the full complement of mayor and two local councillors? And have we had a definite acceptance from the high sheriff yet? He did show an interest in coming, if his schedule allowed it."

"Yes, the mayor and the councillors are confirmed," replied Peter, checking his list. "The high sheriff has agreed to come. The Lord Lieutenant, unfortunately, is otherwise engaged that day and has sent his apologies."

Kath looked over at Brneda as she asked: "And about the decoration of the church and the hall for the occasion – Brenda, I believe your WI ladies have the floral arrangements well in hand?"

"Indeed," replied Brenda. "My floristry committee has everything planned and organized. We could do with a cash float so that we can place our order for the blooms in good time and make sure we are equipped on the day with all we need at the best possible price."

"Let me have your estimate," agreed Trevor, "and I'll get that sorted straight away."

"And Roger," continued Kath, "your Rotary colleagues were such a wonderful help during our Easter Monday Centenary Fayre. I'm hoping they'll be able to work their magic again this time."

"Certainly," smiled Roger. "We all really enjoyed that Easter Fayre. We'll help out with staging, microphones, stewarding and anything else you need. Just keep me in the loop."

"Of course. I do hope, Roger, that both you and Brenda will tell your members how much we appreciate their enthusiasm and practical help in making this occasion so special. And Ray here, who is in charge of the fabric of Hope Hall, and Shirley, who I think you all remember from the Easter Fayre, will both be on hand whenever necessary to facilitate anything you require or want to check here at the hall, either on the day or beforehand. And Maggie, I've no doubt you have everything in hand for the buffet our guests are invited to enjoy at the hall after the foundation stone ceremony!"

"Even though it's technically lunchtime," answered Maggie, "I'm thinking of making it a really elegant high tea, with savouries, salads and sandwiches served at each table, as well as patisserie cakes, pastries and cream scones, with endless pots of tea and coffee served in china cups and saucers."

"I love your baking, Maggie," sighed Trevor. "Thank you for bringing along some samples this morning. They're delicious."

Everyone laughed as Trevor helped himself to another creamy cupcake, sinking his teeth into the delicacy with an expression of sheer delight.

"Well, as enticing as it is to concentrate on what we're all going to eat on the day," laughed Kath, "let's just go over our plans for when the church ceremony is over. That's the point at which the whole congregation is invited to walk across to Hope Hall for the rededication of the original foundation stone and the unveiling of the new one. You'll lead that part of the ceremony, won't you, James?"

"Certainly. Who do you have in mind to do the unveiling?"

"May I make a suggestion here?" It was the historian Michael Sayward who spoke. "I wonder if we should ask Celia Ainsworth. It was the Ainsworth family that owned the land on which the hall stands, and who also provided half of the funds needed to build the hall. The rest, as you know, was raised by the local community themselves. But Celia's great-grandfather Reginald was the owner of the mill here, which provided a lot of work for people in this area, especially just after the Great War when industry had to be built up again so men returning from the trenches could provide for their families. He was a good-hearted man who believed it was his Christian duty to make sure his employees had decent houses to live in and healthy opportunities for community life and activities. Hence his decision to build Hope Hall."

"Celia Ainsworth?" queried Kath. "Was that the lady I met with you in the foyer the other week?"

"That's right," confirmed Trevor. "We're all trustees for the Money Advice Centre, and we had our annual trustees meeting that morning. As usual, she was with Richard. They're always together, those two. You know, Richard Carlisle – remember the Carlisle Trust that gave us a generous grant at the beginning of the year?"

Richard Carlisle, Kath thought. Her "perfect stranger" at the Sea Cadets the other evening. She remembered him saying he was a widower, although it seemed he now had a new partner in Celia. He'd found happiness after the sad loss of the wife he plainly adored.

"You think Celia would be best for this occasion, rather than Douglas?" asked James.

"Well, since Douglas took over from his father as CEO of Ainsworth Mill," replied Trevor, "he's become a bit of a jet-setter, with business and public relations meetings all over this country and abroad. Mind you, he's never really been someone who wanted to involve himself much with community life. Of course, he does have a very accomplished board of directors who've overseen the business and now that company is one of the largest and most popular breakfast cereal producers in the country."

"We could ask him," Michael replied, "but even if he had time, I'm not sure this would be of interest to Douglas. He's really not the sentimental type. It's common knowledge that there's no love lost between Douglas and his sister. Celia's got a very good instinct for facts and figures, which is why she's now the director of the multi-million pound pension fund at Apex Finance. That's a huge responsibility, which she handles very well, but I think she would have liked to have had more influence in her own family business."

"Well, that's just not the tradition in the Ainsworth family," explained Trevor. "The business has always been inherited by the oldest son. Douglas may be two years younger, but he's fiercely jealous of Celia's natural business acumen and her flair for financial matters. As a family member, she's on the board of Ainsworth's, of course, but Douglas won't let her have any say in its operation or future plans."

"And I really don't think he has much interest in anything to do with the past, even within his own family," added Michael. "It's the future he has his eye on. I've tried to engage him with a few local history projects that have involved the activities of his family members in years gone by, but he's basically told me to go away."

"So you think Celia may be quite sympathetic to what we're celebrating here at Hope Hall?" asked Kath.

"Yes, I think she would be," replied Trevor thoughtfully. "In fact, I'm sure she'd be delighted to be asked."

"Should I write to invite her, or should you have a quiet word with her, Trevor, as you already know her through the various committees you both sit on?"

"Yes, let me ask her. I'll call round and see her later this week. I think she'd be pleased to come if she's free, and she'll have a real sense of occasion for the whole event."

"Good!" said Kath, quickly scanning the list of matters to be discussed. "Brian, I think that brings us to you. The ceremony here at the hall not only rededicates the original foundation stone, but also commends the plaque we've planned to mark the hall's hundredth birthday. How are your plans coming along for the new plaque itself?"

Brian Mack pulled out a piece of paper from his file and laid it on the table in front of them. "The stonemason is ready to start work, assuming we are now completely agreed on this wording:

'FOR ALL WHO HAVE ENJOYED HOPE HALL

THROUGHOUT ITS 100 YEARS,

AND FOR ALL WITHIN ITS WALLS IN YEARS TO COME,

WE ASK YOUR BLESSING, LORD.

28TH AUGUST 2020'

Do we still approve that wording?"

Everyone around the table nodded in agreement.

"And are we still putting a time capsule behind the plaque? How's the content coming along?"

"The children have done some wonderful work on the plaque," explained Ellie, "and we've chosen four of their pieces to be included. They talk about the town, their school, their families and what they appreciate most about the hall. Those children will be reading out their contributions during the ceremony as the new stone is laid."

"And the council is preparing a commemorative programme of our Centenary Day events. Isn't that right, Peter? A copy of that will go into the time capsule too."

"That's all ready. We're putting in quite a lot of paperwork relating to specific plans, decisions or events in the area, and a memory stick that explains and illustrates how the town has developed since Hope Hall was built. We plan to place it all in a metal tube so everything will remain in pristine condition for the moment it's opened, probably a hundred years from now."

"And the old foundation stone?" asked Kath. "That's beginning to look a bit jaded, so I know you mean to give that a bit of a facelift before the big day."

"That's the plan," answered Brian. "We do need to get some basic renovation work done on it before we replace it on the wall next to our new commemorative plaque."

"And of course," interrupted Michael, "there's every chance the community which laid that stone a century ago also left some artefacts inside for us to open now. I'm assuming some of you would like to be present when Brian's team takes the old stone out to see if there *is* anything in there?"

There was enthusiastic agreement all round, and diaries came out as discussion followed to decide a date at the start of July for the removal of the old foundation stone.

"Well, that will certainly be something to look forward to," commented Kath. "Does anyone have any other questions for us to consider today?"

Once they had all agreed that the meeting had covered everything, the group members gathered up their notes, said their goodbyes and started down the stairs – except for Trevor, who helped himself to one more strawberry cream scone before he too got up and followed them.

"There she is!"

Terezka was the first to spot Mariana waiting for them on the steps of the main entrance to Hope Hall. Mili had to quicken her pace to keep up with her room-mate as Terezka strode off ahead of her.

"We are late?" asked Mili as the three girls met up.

"I like to get here early," smiled Mariana, "so I can spend a bit of time with Carlos before the band starts playing. I've saved us a table right near the front."

Glancing over to the stage just in case she could catch a glimpse of Andy, the keyboard player, Mili saw that the band's equipment was already set up and ready to use.

"Carlos is up there?" she asked.

"Well, the rest of the band are, but I couldn't find him. I think he must be running a bit late."

Remembering what Andy had said in the café about Carlos leaving all the setting up of equipment to the other band members so he could make a big entrance, Mili bit her tongue and said nothing.

"Come on," beckoned Terezka. "Let's grab that table before someone else does!"

As she walked through the gathering crowd, Mili was pleasantly surprised by how popular these once-a-month dance nights at Hope Hall seemed to be. Andy had warned them to get there by seven fifteen at the latest, ready to sweep in through the door the moment it opened. He'd explained that a DJ played a good selection of disco music between seven thirty and eight fifteen, before the band took over for its first set, which lasted an hour. At a quarter past nine, a buffet was served while disco music played for forty-five minutes, and then the band performed the second set between ten and eleven. After this people dawdled and chatted until finally the hall was cleared about half past eleven.

Taking a seat near the wall, Mili scanned the rest of the crowd. It was a mixed group, from middle-aged couples and even older, right down to people of her own age. In fact, she wondered if she might be the youngest there. The men were mostly casually dressed, although some of the women were surprisingly glamorous, with sparkling tops and very high heels for dancing. Mili looked down at the customary jeans she'd teamed with her favourite blouse from home, which was hand-embroidered with flowers across the shoulders and neckline. She was suddenly embarrassed to be wearing something so obviously old-fashioned and home-made, and tried to slide even further back into her seat so she could hide in the shadow of the wall.

"Mili, you came!"

She looked up to see Andy coming down the stairs at the side of the stage and heading towards her. Her stomach knotted with nerves. They had shared several lovely conversations in the café, but this felt different. Perhaps he would take one look at how unfashionable she was and wish he'd not invited her. She hesitated as he made his way over to her chair, and it seemed he picked up on her reticence, because he simply sat down on the seat next to hers so that their shoulders and knees almost touched.

"I'm so glad you made it," he whispered in her ear. "I'll have to get all the notes right now!"

She smiled then in the warmth of his welcome. "I know you get notes right."

"Ah, but *how* do you know? You've only ever heard me talking in the café about playing the keyboard. Perhaps I can't play at all."

"No matter!" she laughed. "I'm sure I like it."

"Well," he said, leaning his shoulder closer to hers. "It matters to me that you do like it. I want to make a good impression."

She looked puzzled as she tried to remember what the word "impression" meant.

"It means," he said softly, his gaze holding hers, "that I like you, and I hope that after tonight you might like me too."

Unable to find the words to describe the flutter of excitement that coursed through her, Mili simply nodded and grinned at him.

Two other girls joined their table and were greeted by Terezka and Mariana, who clearly knew them well.

"Those two always come," explained Andy as he followed her gaze. "Jayne, with the long blonde hair, is married to the drummer, Nigel; and the other girl is Ali, Graham's girlfriend. He's very talented. He plays the guitar and sings really well – when Carlos lets him, that is…"

Mili felt a little shy when Mariana introduced her to Jayne and Ali, but as the two newcomers waved a hello in her direction, Mili gradually felt herself begin to relax in their friendly company. Andy reached across to give her hand a squeeze.

"So, now you've met most of our crowd. Jake's up there giving everything a final check. He hasn't got a girlfriend; he's just here for the music. I'll introduce you when he comes down for a drink. Anyway, I know the girls will look after you while we're up on stage playing. I hope to see you dance."

Mili grinned. "My mother taught me dance. I don't think my dance is good here."

Andy laughed. "I can't dance at all."

"You play music. Everybody dance!"

Suddenly, the hall was filled with sound as the DJ burst into action with a pulsing beat that provided a backdrop as he welcomed everyone to the great evening they were about to have. And as he lined up the first track, at least a third of the crowd now sitting at tables around the edge of the hall leapt to their feet and made their way on to the dance floor. There were so many different styles of dancing that Mili's head was spinning. There were groups of girls bopping around their handbags, four young men doing some sort of line dance, which others joined in with once they'd worked out what the steps should be, and several couples doing a series of impressive and complicated jive moves that cleared a big circle around each of them. When she looked back towards the entrance of the hall, she could see three older couples doing some sort of ballroom dancing.

"Are you coming?" yelled Terezka from the other side of the table.

Mili shook her head with alarm.

Shrugging, Terezka marched on to the floor herself, grabbing Mariana's hand as she went.

"No Carlos yet," Andy shouted into Mili's ear.

Her eyes widened. "No? Where he is?"

"Who knows? He just hasn't managed to join us yet."

"He's coming?"

"Probably about five minutes before we're due to play."

"Is a problem he's late?"

"We've had no sound check. We can't do that without our singer."

"But it will sound okay?"

"Yes, it will, because we know what we're doing. It's annoying, though. He should be here."

"*Whoosh?*" Mili clapped her hands together, her eyes dancing.

Andy laughed his agreement. "Yes, *whoosh!* Friction!"

Just ten minutes before the band were due to start playing at eight fifteen there was a bit of a stir as Carlos walked straight through the dancers in the middle of the hall, acknowledging greetings and stopping every now and then to shake hands with a friend here or to hug a pretty girl there. Mili caught a glimpse of Mariana's expression as she watched Carlos gaze lovingly into the eyes of one girl for whom he'd diverted his route to make sure he had a chance to embrace her. But the Spanish girl's eyes lit up when he finally made his way over to their table, where he put one arm around her waist, pulled her roughly towards him and kissed her passionately. While Mariana's eyes were still glassy with emotion, Carlos moved away, clicking his fingers towards the rest of the group.

"Ready, boys? Shall we make this place rock?"

Mili felt Andy stiffen with resentment beside her, and she leaned in towards him in silent support. He turned to gaze at her, his eyes warm with thanks.

"Showtime!" he said quietly before getting up to follow the rest of the band on to the stage.

It didn't take more than the first song for Mili to realize this band was good, *really* good. Each player was a great musician in his own right, especially Andy, who was obviously the musical leader, almost imperceptibly controlling all the starts and finishes, and setting the tempo for each song. And even though she hated herself for thinking it, she had to admit that Carlos was a magnet for the eye. The undulating rhythm of his moves, the expression he put into each line, the way he held the mike as if it were a woman he loved – everything about him enhanced the fact that he had a strong, raspy voice that could punch out rock rhythms one minute and melt your heart with emotion the next. He was good and he knew it. There was an arrogance about him that seemed to demand recognition and admiration from his audience. Mili could see exactly why the rest of the band were in a quandary when it came to Carlos. Without a doubt he was an asset to the group, but he treated the others as if they were there simply to support Carlos the Star.

For Mili, though, the real star on stage was Andy. From the side of the hall where she was sitting, she could see his fingers moving across the keyboard with skill and ease. Sometimes his face was full of concentration as he played. At other points, he was animated and involved as he sang backing harmonies, his thick brown hair sliding down over his forehead as the music became more lively and animated. And every now and then, he would catch her eye and smile across at her, and she felt something deep and exciting churn in the pit of her stomach. If only Father Peter could see her now. He might regret encouraging her to leave the safety of home for excitement like this.

The first set of music came to a spectacular conclusion as the group performed their version of Queen's "Bohemian Rhapsody", during which it became abundantly clear that Carlos was not the only great singer. Every member of the band sang those famous harmonies with sweet precision, especially the guitarist, Graham, whose voice was superb. His style was very different from Carlos's, but his intonation and clear purity on the long notes was stunning. The other guitarist, Jake, was deeply into the music, his face a picture of concentration and emotion. Nigel, the drummer, skilfully altered the tone and atmosphere from dramatic to softer sounds by adding his own deep voice with intricate rhythms that didn't always come from the drum kit, but often from an array of smaller percussion instruments. Andy too had a soulfully expressive voice that enhanced the emotion and meaning of each word and verse. This band was brilliant!

After what felt like minutes of applause, the band members made their way down to their table, except for Carlos, who sat on the edge of the stage surrounded by a crowd of adoring girls. Meanwhile, the rest of the people in the hall helped themselves to the buffet that had just been served. Mili's heart went out to Mariana, who was visibly unhappy that her boyfriend was ignoring her for so long in favour of his devoted fans. In stark contrast, Andy had arrived at Mili's side minutes after the band finished.

"So?" he asked anxiously.

"So," she began, taking his hand, "your notes very good. Your voice very, very good. You – I think very good for me."

And right there, with the hall crowded with people around them, Andy leaned forward to plant a soft kiss on Mili's lips.

Maggie had barely reached home, dropped her bag and switched on the kettle before she heard a key in the door. Alarmed because she wasn't expecting anyone to visit, she was surprised to see her daughter Steph walk into the hallway with grandson Bobbie squirming in her arms.

"Hello! This is a nice surprise," smiled Maggie, stretching out her arms to claim and cuddle the wriggling little boy. "I've got a chocolate cake for you, young man; your favourite with sprinkles and Smarties on top!"

At that moment, Maggie caught sight of Steph's expression and realized with alarm that this was not just a social call.

"Are you okay? What's happened?"

Without a word, Steph walked across to put an arm round her mum's shoulders as she held out her phone so that they could both clearly read the message displayed on it.

> *Great news! Our daughter Aurora Giselle was born at 2.24 pm today, weighing 8lbs 3ozs. Mother and baby are doing well, and our whole family is delighted at the news. Please feel free to come and meet your new sister as soon as you can. Love, Dad and Mandy xxxx*

Slumping back against the kitchen work surface, Maggie drew in a deep breath. "So, are you going over?"

"Nope."

"He's right though. She is your sister."

"My sister, and my son's auntie – and she's two years younger than him. How insane is that!"

Maggie said nothing. There was nothing to say. They stood in silence for a while, each absorbed in her own thoughts.

"Aurora Giselle. Only Mandy could choose Disney names for all of her children."

"Has she really?"

"Disney princess names for both of the girls, and the boy, Marlin, is named after Nemo's dad – a stripy orange clownfish!"

Suddenly, laughter bubbled up inside Maggie until she was almost crying, not out of distress, but with sheer delight at the ridiculous idea of Dave, *her* Dave, having a daughter named after not one but two Disney princesses. Dave hated cartoons. He always had, even when the kids were small, and he would stomp out of the room if they wanted to watch Mickey Mouse or any sort of animation. This couldn't be happening to a nicer fella! As the same thought obviously hit Steph, a rather bemused Bobbie looked on with curiosity as his mum and nan hugged each other, crying with laughter.

Chapter 6

"I don't care, Tyler!" Shirley's voice echoed around the house so the whole street could probably hear it. "I'm not having you lying around playing games on your phone all day long while your dad and I are out slogging to pay for everything. If you're going to stay here, you've got to work!"

"But what if Jasmine decides she wants me back again? I'll be out of your hair and then I'll get a proper job."

"Jasmine threw you out because you've been worse than useless at finding a proper job, so she was the one doing all the work. That girl always was too good for you. She's far too sensible to take back a good-for-nothing layabout who just wants to play computer games day and night."

Tyler grinned at his mum. "Oh, you don't know. I might have other qualities she finds very endearing—"

"What's most endearing in any relationship is to have a partner who helps pay his own way. Grow up, Tyler!"

"I will work, just as soon as I find something I *like*!"

"Well, until you find a job you like for someone daft enough to employ you and pay you wages, you'll do as you're told, especially if you want to live and eat in this house."

"Look, I'm no good at gardening. You know that. I've always hated weeding and mowing the lawn."

"Everyone hates weeding and mowing the lawn. It's hard work, but it's got to be done. Ray has a busy job at Hope Hall, and he needs to have his lawn cut because he hasn't got time to do it himself. And he wants the flowerbeds weeded, and a few overhanging branches sorted out. He's expecting you this afternoon, so get up off that settee, get yourself dressed and get round there. And if you don't, you may as well pack your bags, take all your rubbish with you and find somewhere else to doss."

And so it was that half an hour later a stony-faced Tyler was standing on the doorstep when Ray opened his front door.

"Hello, Tyler. Your mum just rang. Gave you a hard time, did she?" asked Ray, standing back to let him in.

"You could say that."

"Don't you think she's got a point? You are living off your parents at the moment. Is that fair?"

"No, but I'm so fed up with the way she talks to me as if I'm a little kid."

"Can you blame her?"

"Yes! Why can't we just have a normal conversation? Why does she have to shout all the time?"

Ray chuckled. "Well, our Shirley does have a voice like a foghorn—"

"When we were kids, our next-door neighbours used to be so scared when Mum was yelling at us at bedtime they'd rush upstairs to clean their own teeth and get into bed!"

Ray threw his head back and laughed. "That's our girl!"

"That's my mum, and I've had enough."

"So, what *do* you want to do? What are you good at?"

Tyler perked up at this question. "Computers. I'm good at technology. I did really well with it at school, and I've always found it makes sense to me. It's the logic of it that I like. Do everything in the right order and you get the right result."

Ray huffed. "Not for me. My computer hates me."

"What sort have you got?"

"I've got two – a PC in my office upstairs and a laptop I keep down in the lounge. And, of course, there's the other one at work that has me completely foxed."

"Want me to look at the ones you've got here?"

"I'm not even sure how to explain what's wrong. Half the time I can't get the internet on my laptop. And then when I try to write letters and documents on my PC I can never work out how to get diagrams and pictures where I need them. And I've got dozens of adverts popping up all over the screen, which really gets on my nerves when I'm trying to think what to say. It drives me crackers!"

"I can fix all that."

"Really?" Ray eyed Tyler with suspicion.

"Try me!"

"Does that mean I won't get my lawn cut?"

"Mum always says you are one of the most capable and efficient workers she's ever met. We both know you're perfectly able to cut your own lawn. You've only got me here because Mum asked you to do her a favour and give me some jobs to do. Am I right?"

Ray's noncommittal shrug spoke volumes.

"So, why don't you try letting me provide a service you *can't* actually do yourself?"

"You promise you won't break the computer or make it even worse than it is now?"

"I need to know what's wrong before I have any idea how to answer that. I just know I'm good with computers. Do you want my help or not?"

An hour later, Ray's PC was purring with contentment. All the irritating adverts had been sent packing, and the whole system was tidied up. Ray even found that his laptop was happily connecting to the internet first time *every* time.

"Well, young man, you've done a very good job. What do you charge for computer repairs?"

"I've no idea," replied Tyler. "What's it worth to you?"

Ray thought for a moment. "I know that when I've taken my laptop down to the computer shop in town – as I have on far too many occasions in the past – they've charged me £50 an hour. You've accomplished more in one hour this afternoon than they ever did."

"Oh!" Tyler plainly didn't expect such an enthusiastic assessment of his work. "What do you think I should charge then?"

"How much would you have charged me to cut the lawn and weed the flowerbeds?"

Tyler glanced through the French doors towards the garden. "That would have taken me a while, probably four hours. Mum says you were thinking of paying £10 an hour, so probably about £40?"

"Well, young man, I'm going to give you that £40 for the excellent job you've done for me today, and the work in the garden is still up for grabs if you fancy a bit of extra money during the week. But I think you should consider very carefully what you'd like your future to be. It's clear you've got a natural instinct for this electronic technical stuff, but it's a huge subject, and if you're going to make a career of it, you need to study and practise at a much higher level than you are now. Have you thought about going back to college?"

"I'm twenty. Aren't I too old?"

"I would have thought you were just the right age. There's an excellent technical and vocational college down in Portsmouth, and you can get there easily enough from here. Why don't you do a bit of research to see if you could get a place on a course you'd really enjoy, starting in September?"

"Mum wants me to work."

"Your mum wants you to have the ability to work and earn

money; not just for this week or month or year, but for the rest of your life. Then you can do the proper, decent thing and marry a girl like Jasmine, knowing you can support your family properly."

For once, Tyler seemed lost for words, his mind whirring at the possibilities he was considering. "Maybe I could even get a grant."

"That would be worth looking into."

"And perhaps I could do some work on the side to help pay my way?"

"I'd say that was highly possible."

Tyler grinned. "I could come and cut your lawn…"

"And you could keep my computers in excellent running order."

"What do you think Mum will say?"

"Why don't you ask her?"

Tyler took a breath, then straightened up his shoulders with determination before heading for the front door. "Wish me luck!"

"Oh, I do," smiled Ray. "I most certainly do."

"Oh, I'm glad it's Southsea," enthused Doris when the announcement had just been made to all the members of the Grown-ups' Lunch Club that their summer outing in the second week of July would be down to the well-known seaside resort on the South Coast. "I don't think that funfair's changed a bit since I used to go there as a teenager. My mum said I shouldn't go at all because it was a dangerous place full of unsavoury types—"

"Boys, you mean?" grinned Flora. "I remember my mum saying the same thing. It only made me want to go more!"

"I always thought it was a little common," sniffed Ida. "The funfair, I mean. Southsea itself is glorious for its place in history, and that magnificent harbour it looks out over. If those sea walls could only speak—"

"They'd say that this is a great place for sitting on the wall eating a pennyworth of chips smothered in salt and vinegar, all wrapped up in newspaper!" laughed Doris. "Was it only me, or did we all do that?"

"My brother used to take me," said Flora. "Mind you, he'd find a girl he liked and leave me to my own devices until it was time for us to get the bus home."

"And what did you get up to while he was gone, you saucy minx?" chuckled Doris.

"Actually," said Flora, her eyes suddenly misty with memories, "my best friend Maureen and I used to like those sound booths there where you could go in and make your own recording. We used to sing whatever record was at the top of the pop charts at the time. No one ever offered us a recording contract, so I guess we were terrible."

"And candyfloss!" Betty had come to join the conversation. "That pink fluffy stuff ended up all over my face, and even my hair, but I didn't feel I'd really been to the fair unless I had some."

"Oh, I liked toffee apples best," sighed Doris. "They still sell them, don't they? I know I'll see them and want one when we're there, but my teeth won't like it. In fact, I probably wouldn't have any teeth left at all if I tried sinking my choppers into a toffee apple nowadays."

"I gather," interjected Ida, "that there will be no need for fish and chips or anything like it that day. We're having afternoon tea at an extremely nice hotel on the promenade. It'll be very elegant."

Flora and Doris exchanged a glance. Whoever wanted to be elegant? It was a day out at the seaside – and that meant buckets and spades, fizzy drinks and sugary doughnuts. Elegance wasn't likely to get a look in.

"So, ladies, have you decided to pack your bikinis for your dip in the sea? We gents were thinking that a bit of skinny-dipping would be fun!" Percy Wilson's eyes were sparkling with mischief as he came to join them, feeling rather pleased as Flora and Doris giggled good-naturedly at his suggestion.

"I hope, Percy Wilson," said Ida, disapproval evident in every fibre of her body, "that you will show a little decorum and take your lewd, childish suggestions elsewhere. There are ladies here!"

"Are there really?" Percy retorted. "Where?" Then, with a cheeky wave and a wink, he strode off to join his old friends John and Robert, who were standing a safe distance away from Ida's icy glare, uncertain whether to join in or to just leave Percy to it.

Sheelagh's house phone rang just as she was about to leave home the next morning. She recognized the voice of Salvation Army Captain Sam Morse the moment he said "good morning".

After a bit of friendly chat about the weather, which seemed to be stuck in the typical British late spring mix of downpours one minute followed by blue skies the next, Sam came to the point that had prompted him to ring.

"Your friend Michael," he started. "He's a bit of an enigma really."

"Oh, so your team does know him, then."

"Not very well. Once in a while he's come here to the citadel for something to eat. He doesn't like coming inside, though. He does the same thing here as he does at Hope Hall – hangs around outside trying to keep hidden, but at the same time obviously hoping either that someone will hand him some food or that he can find a chance to grab something and slip away without anyone really noticing him."

"He devoured the sandwiches I gave him last time he came to our Food Bank," agreed Sheelagh. "I remember thinking how thin his arms were."

"Well, we don't think he's eating much at all."

"How long have you been aware of him?"

"Jackie thinks she first saw him about two months ago, but he could have been in the area before that and just managed to stay under the radar."

"Any idea where he's living?"

"We do know he's not hanging out in the usual places on the streets, so he's obviously found somewhere he feels safe, away from prying eyes. When Jackie asked Ben, one of our regulars, about him, Ben said he thought he walked a fair distance to get here, and that he might be holed up on farmland somewhere, perhaps in a barn or disused outhouse."

"Was Ben able to shed any light on who Michael is, or what's happened to him to bring him to this state of affairs?"

"I'm afraid not."

Sheelagh sighed. "So, what can we do?"

"Well, Michael seems to have a past that might be traceable. He told you he was the manager of a big supermarket. My guess is that he had a bank account, a car, a National Insurance number, probably a mortgage – and maybe a wife and family. There's no knowing if he's a local man, but the chances are that there is some logical reason for him choosing to be here. You know the Salvation Army has a Family Tracing Service, which often has a lot less to work with than that."

"Could they help us in Michael's case?"

"I've got a good contact there. I'll give him a call. Of course, you did get that long-distance snapshot of him, but a better photo would be handy…"

"You're right, but I wonder what chance we have of getting one without scaring him off completely."

"And we have to consider the possibility of infringing his rights if we take a picture without his permission – which you've already done."

"Point taken, but he's obviously in trouble to the degree that his life might be in jeopardy if we don't do something. I don't know what it is that's made him want to hide from the world, but what could be so terrible that he'd prefer starving to living?"

"May I suggest," said Sam, "that Jackie just happens to be around during your Food Bank at Hope Hall next Monday afternoon? If Michael turns up, the two of you might be able to think of a way of drawing him out enough to discover a bit more."

"That would be great. Thanks, Sam."

"And thank God you noticed him. I just pray we can find a way to give him the support he needs."

At that, Sam said his goodbyes, but long after the call was over, Sheelagh found herself thinking about Michael. Who was he? What was his story? Was there a family who missed him? A partner who loved him? Or was it those very people who had made him want to run and hide in the first place?

Trevor whistled softly under his breath as he turned the car off the main road in the direction of Celia's home, then drove up towards the front door along the wide drive lined by tailored lawns and mature flowerbeds. The name "Ainsworth Cottage" was a modest understatement for the imposing Georgian house with its large bay windows on both the ground and first floors neatly positioned around the elegant front porch. But then this house merited little more than "cottage" status in the Ainsworth family, he thought wryly, because Ainsworth *House*, the sprawling country estate that had been in the family for centuries, had a baronial hall, more than twenty bedrooms and a dizzying collection of living rooms, where family members had been waited upon hand and foot upstairs by an army of staff who traditionally worked down below. That family seat was now home to Douglas Ainsworth, his wife Diana and their two young sons, and although the staff no longer lived in the shadows below stairs, Douglas felt it was important that he always acted with the decisive authority that was surely expected from the Lord of the Manor.

Trevor remembered Douglas and Celia's father, James, very well. He had been a kindly man, who led his workforce both on the estate and in the family's cereal mill with a spirit of teamwork and shared purpose. It was James who had first seen the potential for expanding the scope of work at the mill to cater for the modern breakfast cereal market. His entrepreneurial vision and enterprise saw the erection of rows of gleaming new preparation and packaging warehouses that employed a large local workforce. The reputation of Ainsworth's Mill went from strength to strength, so that by the time James decided to retire and allow his son and heir, Douglas, to take over as CEO, Ainsworth's Mill products were familiar in homes not just across the British Isles, but in many other countries around the world.

James had worried about his son taking over. Douglas had shown little interest in the operational procedures, mechanics and challenges of growing the business. In fact, he had made it clear while growing up that figures bored him, and his attention span for anything that really didn't interest him was dismally short. He had dropped out of university, saying that his tutors knew nothing he'd benefit from knowing, and that world travel was the best way to learn the true lessons of life. Three years later, after stints of living in a surfing community in California, a vineyard in France, and with a Japanese girlfriend from a very wealthy family in Tokyo who, it seems, finally paid him well to go home to England and never darken the door of their daughter again, Douglas landed back at his parents' house, demanding his rightful place on the board of the family business.

His mother Frances had begged her husband to encourage their wayward son to learn the ropes in the company he would inherit, but James was no pushover. He insisted that Douglas work his way up from the mill floor, through the different sections of the milling and packaging process, until he had earned his place on the top corridor of executive offices. His father was astute enough to recognize that Douglas was no team player. He had thrown his weight about and snapped unreasonable orders to his work colleagues at every stage of his journey to the boardroom. Eventually, when James finally admitted that he was growing weary after his lifetime at the mill, he retired on his seventieth birthday, leaving Douglas as CEO of the Ainsworth empire and hoping that the excellent board of directors he'd put in place would be able to guide his son wisely.

How often James had wished his son had the work ethic and natural business flair he saw in the older of his two children, Celia. She had spent many childhood hours at the mill, watching the workers, asking questions and helping whenever she could. In the evenings, she would quiz her father about the accounts he was working on, querying the titles and descriptions, and totting up the lines of figures to see if she made the total the same as her father did. James knew Celia would have been a wonderful company head, but the family tradition of the first son inheriting stretched back into the mists of time. Besides, Douglas had ridiculed his younger sister's interest in the mill earlier on, then resented any official part she had tried to play as he moved up the ranks. As soon as his route to the CEO's office was assured, Douglas made it perfectly clear that he wanted sole control of the business, and that his sister's contribution and interest were not welcome in any way. Celia had expected as much, but was still gutted not to be allowed to take more than a passing interest in the family business she had always loved. Her father had insisted that she remain a lifelong member on the board of directors, and Celia never once missed a meeting.

However, she soon accepted that any suggestion she made, however innovative or practical, would be greeted with spite and dismissal by Douglas. With a heavy heart, knowing her father would turn in his grave at the autocratic and often ill-informed decisions taken by her brother in recent years, Celia had no choice but to leave him to it.

From conversations Trevor had had with Celia over their many years of friendship, he knew how much the situation not only hurt her, but worried her too. There was added aggravation when Douglas's wife Diana entered the scene. In Celia's opinion, Diana was simply a society trophy to her brother – the privately educated daughter of a long-established titled family with a large estate in the Home Counties. Her only interests seemed to be dressage, showy charity garden parties, and coffee mornings with her well-heeled friends, at which they would bemoan the falling standard of nannies, stable staff, cooks and housekeepers. Diana had worked her way through many of each, especially once she'd obediently given birth to an "heir and a spare". Duty done, she expected a life of privilege and pleasure – and whatever Diana wanted, Diana got!

Celia had seen Trevor's car coming up the drive and was waiting at the door to greet him. She led the way into the large kitchen, where a rich aroma of coffee wafted on the air. They sat on high stools around the breakfast bar, where they could spread out the papers they needed to discuss and still leave room from for a large plate of delicious biscuits, which only Trevor dipped into.

"Don't tell Mary," grinned Trevor as he helped himself to yet another melt-in-the-mouth piece of shortbread.

Celia laughed. "My lips are sealed."

"Mary would say mine should be too."

"Your secret is safe with me!"

"How are things at Apex?" chuckled Trevor, wiping away the crumbs from his biscuits that had fallen on to the surface in front of him. "Is business booming?"

"It certainly is. The pension fund's really flourishing at the moment, in spite of the peaks and troughs in the market."

"Those are the times you enjoy most of all, though, aren't they?"

She smiled in mutual understanding. "Well, you know me, Trevor. When it comes to work, the more difficult the task, the more I enjoy it. I earn my salary by making a good profit for the people whose pensions I invest, and for the company that employs me. I'm the head of the UK pension fund for an international financial institution, and it's a matter of pride to me that I do my job well."

"Has the takeover by that American corporation made much difference to you? I assume they have an overall strategy you have to adhere to in spite of the fact you are operating in a very different part of the world. Has that made your role more difficult?"

"In some ways, yes, but the takeover was five years ago now. And the money market at this level is completely international – and constantly changing, so I have to make sure we keep at the top of our game. The more complex and intricate it is, the more I enjoy the challenge! And to be fair, they do allow me a great deal of autonomy when it comes to our pension investments here in the UK."

"As long as the returns are good?"

She smiled. "Exactly. And they are."

Trevor chuckled in agreement. "Well, Apex is lucky to have you. How about Douglas? Have you seen him lately?"

"At the Ainsworth Mill board meeting last month, but not since then."

"Are they doing okay?"

"Well, Douglas certainly is. He doesn't let work get in the way of a very nice lifestyle."

"And Diana..."

"...is Diana. Spoilt, ineffectual and empty-headed."

"Just say it like it is!" laughed Trevor.

"I wish it wasn't so serious, though," replied Celia. "The board members try their best to keep him in check, and when it comes to the day-to-day work of the company, they've got that under control. But it's those mad, impractical schemes he keeps coming up with – you know, the ones that involve lots of money and as many celebrity names as he can fit in. He just likes having his face in the society columns, I think."

Trevor looked at her thoughtfully. "How can a brother and sister be so different?"

"Well, we were never really close. The distance between us has just grown over the years."

"Which brings me to the main reason for my visit today. I come bearing an invitation to something that I'm sure would bore Douglas to tears, but it might just strike a chord with you."

"Sounds intriguing!"

"Your great-great-grandfather Reginald Ainsworth donated the land Hope Hall was built on, and he contributed half of the money needed to complete the building work too. Hope Hall is marking its centenary this year on August 28th."

"I knew about the anniversary, but didn't know exactly when it was happening."

"Well, the Hope Hall Centenary Committee would like to invite you to unveil the new memorial plaque, which will be placed alongside the original foundation stone from a hundred years ago."

Celia's face lit up with pleasure. "I'd absolutely love to! That will be quite emotional, I should think."

"That's settled, then. I'll get the committee to send you a formal invitation, and I'll be in touch again nearer the time so we can explain exactly what's required."

"I'll look forward to it."

"Heavens, I must be off!" Trevor glanced at the kitchen wall clock before gathering up his papers in a rush.

"Have another biscuit," invited Celia, her eyes shining with mischief.

Trevor didn't need to be asked twice as he reached forward to claim the last two cookies on the plate. "I don't mind if I do!"

Andy and the other members of Friction had a long-standing arrangement with Stan, the landlord at their local, the King's Head, to borrow the pub's back room every alternate Tuesday evening for band rehearsal. In return, the group donated their services for several music nights at the pub throughout the year, which pleased Stan because these events always drew in big crowds.

That Tuesday evening it was Andy, drummer Nigel and the two guitar players, Jake and Graham, who arrived in good time to set up all the equipment so that they would be ready to start playing at half past seven. There was no sign of Carlos, so the four musicians – who simply jumped at the chance for an impromptu jamming session when they could try out new rhythms, riffs and lyrics – just began playing. Without Carlos, Graham naturally stepped up to lead vocals, his voice mellow and versatile, enabling him to sing thumping rock songs or heartfelt love ballads. Watching Graham from his place at the keyboard, Andy marvelled yet again at his musical skill, not just vocally, but as an instrumentalist too. He was a natural musician, able to play just about any instrument he picked up. He was always happy slipping between rhythm and lead guitar as required, but was equally at home on keys or drums.

It was gone eight by the time Carlos appeared, his arm casually draped over Mariana's shoulders. Before even acknowledging his fellow band members, he turned to give her a lingering kiss.

"*Hasta luego mia adorada*," he drawled, gazing deeply into her eyes. "Tell Stan to give you whatever you want from the bar. It will be free. Carlos said so!"

"You're late." There was a hard note to Andy's voice.

Carlos took his time turning around to acknowledge the rest of the group. "I was busy."

"So were we. We've been working on new material."

"No point," shrugged Carlos. "The crowds come to see me. They like how I sing. I choose the songs. I decide."

"We are a group of equal members," stated Andy, aware that the other players were bristling with indignation beside him. "We *all* decide on the style and the material. You are just one member of this band."

"The most talented member," snapped Carlos. "Without me, this band is average. I make it great."

"This band will never be great if we don't keep up with rehearsals. This practice session starts at half past seven. If you can't be bothered to get here on time, we'll find another singer."

Carlos snorted with derision. "There *is* no other singer like Carlos!"

"That's absolutely true. Most singers have a more professional attitude and recognize the value of rehearsal."

"Other singers *need* to rehearse. I *am* professional. I need no rehearsal."

"Every band needs rehearsal. If Friction is ever going to get anywhere, we've got to put the work in. We want to go places with this band, not just in the local music circuit, but hopefully across the wider music industry. Other bands with much less

122

musical talent manage to get recording contracts. Why shouldn't we – with our own material?"

"Your own material?" sneered Carlos. "People don't want to hear your own material. They want to hear the hits. They want to dance and sing along to their favourites. And they want a fantastic singer at the front of the group – me!"

"When all we're doing is local gigs, it's probably true that playing nothing but cover versions of popular hits is what the punters want. But is that where Friction should be content to stay? Playing at weddings and monthly dance nights? We've got to move on. Yes, we need to keep the money coming in with minor bookings like that, but let's use our rehearsal time to work up to the next stage."

Carlos stepped forward so that he was looking down at Andy, who was sitting at the keyboard. "You have big ideas, my friend – too big. What this little group has here and now is a few good musicians and a great singer. And if this little group is ever going to become big, it will be because *I* make you famous. The crowds love *me*. *I* am your magic!"

The other group members were so astonished at this outburst that words failed them.

"*I* choose the songs. And I say: none of your stupid little songs. We play big hits selected by your magical singer. That's how we're going to be recognized. *I* will bring in big crowds. Then we become famous."

There was another stunned silence, which Carlos noted with satisfaction before he continued.

"But the name of the band is wrong. Friction – what does that mean? It says nothing. It doesn't say what people like most about us."

"So, what do you think we should be called?" asked Andy coldly.

Carlos's face suddenly lit up with enthusiasm. "Look around us. We rehearse in the back room of a pub. This is where the magic happens. The band should be called Carlos and the Backroom Boys!"

The following day, on Wednesday evening, Kath put in a couple of hours' extra time on the plans and invitations for the Centenary Celebration before deciding she'd had enough and packed up to go home. As she walked from her office in the old school building back towards the main entrance of Hope Hall, she saw there was great activity going on in the playground, so she took a detour through the side door in order to take a closer look.

The Sea Cadets were hard at work passing out pieces of sea-faring kit, life jackets, wetsuits and other sealed boxes of different shapes and sizes from the storeroom in which they had been keeping their equipment. Shouting instructions from where she stood beside the open back door of their minibus, Muriel Baker was being ably assisted by Petty Officer William Carlisle, who was organizing the collection and stacking of each piece so that it could all be put into the van in the correct order. Watching from the sidelines with an expression of affectionate amusement was William's father Richard, who glanced up and smiled as he saw Kath approaching.

"They're heading down to Portsmouth for a week of training. I came to see if I could help with the preparations," he grinned, "but William will never forgive me if I interfere."

"Does he mind you being here?"

He eyed her thoughtfully. "You know, Celia asked exactly the same question. She thinks I'm too protective of him, but he's been through a lot with his mum's illness and then losing her when he was still so young. Celia loves William so much, and tries to fill that gap for him however she can, but there's no one like your real mum, is there?"

Kath took a few seconds before she answered. "That's true, but it seems William has a loving family around him, and I guess that security will give him confidence as he plans the life he'd like for himself."

"You think I'm crowding him, don't you?"

"Are you?"

"I hope not, but you do have a point. I tell you what, they're going to be here for the next couple of hours, and you and I do have to settle the details of the Sea Cadets' ongoing arrangements at Hope Hall. Could we have a business meeting at the King's Head, when we could also grab a bite to eat and a quick drink? It would give us chance to chat, and I don't know about you, but I'm starving!"

For a split second, an image of the remains of a chicken casserole sitting in her fridge from the night before flashed across Kath's mind. Then, before she had time to think better of it, she nodded agreement. "Starving, thirsty and ready to talk business. Lead on, Captain!"

The King's Head was always popular, with plenty of bustle and chatter as drinks were ordered and meals served. Still, they managed to find a quiet corner where there was a chance they might be able to hear each other. The menu wasn't extensive, but it covered all the favourites so well that the pub had a good reputation for the meals it offered. Kath toyed with the idea of ordering salmon salad, which seemed ladylike and fitting to choose in the company of an influential business acquaintance she hardly knew. But then Richard enthused about the big bowls of spaghetti bolognaise they served, which he said was the best he'd tried anywhere, so when he suggested with a grin that she might just enjoy that too, she agreed in an instant.

He was easy company. The conversation started with the necessary discussion about the financial arrangements for the Sea Cadets' use of Hope Hall, but then flowed comfortably between them as Richard asked about her role at Hope Hall, and the range of activities on offer there. They spoke about each one in some detail and Kath was impressed by the questions he asked, which suggested not just a genuine interest, but an informed knowledge of the aims, pitfalls and challenges facing each club and function. They had to halt their discussion about the financial issues facing an enterprise like Hope Hall when two steaming bowls of bolognaise were delivered to their table.

As they ate, they laughed over the wily antics of some members of the Grown-ups' Club, groaned at how difficult it would be to do the movements taught in the street dancing class, and discussed how to handle groups of teenagers using the hall then leaving a trail of litter behind them as they made their noisy exit. And as the plates were cleared away, they shared their genuine concerns for the vulnerable people who often had to find real courage to come along to the Food Bank in order to feed their families, or to access the Money Advice Service when debts were confusing and frighteningly overwhelming.

"What made you take on the job at Hope Hall?" he asked as coffee was served.

So Kath told him about this being the town in which she'd grown up, but that she'd chosen to do her degree in Business Studies at a London university, which led to her staying on in the City as she started her working career. She explained how she had been drawn to the complexity of hospital management, where her natural wish for organization and order were stretched to the extreme. And how, faced with all the various challenges of personalities, equipment failures, financial restraints, political manoeuvring and unpredictable medical emergencies that were involved in the running of an inner-city hospital, she'd happily given her heart, soul and probably her health to her job as Senior Administrator.

She explained how her resolve had been reinforced every morning as she'd walked through the main entrance and passed all the various departments where patients were waiting with an air of trepidation in rows of seats lining the walls. Or as she'd picked up a coffee in the small restaurant where groups of family members often huddled around a table, anxiously discussing the failing health of a much loved mother or son. Or as she'd visited the wards to try and grab a word with staff who were run off their feet as they struggled to do their best for too many patients with too few resources and on too little sleep.

"You have a real heart for people," Richard said softly. "That's plain to see from the way you work at Hope Hall. But you were clearly at the top of the tree at that London hospital. Why would you leave that when you found such fulfilment in your work there?"

"My mother developed Parkinson's disease. Dad had died some years earlier and she was alone here. She'd always been such a powerhouse of energy and activity, and it broke my heart to see her health deteriorating, so I left London and came back home."

"When was that?"

"More than four years ago now. I nursed her for two years until she died, but it didn't take long for me to feel a bit rudderless when I no longer had Mum to look after. Then Ellie, the vicar's wife, mentioned the administrator's job here. I applied for it, and the rest you know."

"Any regrets? Do you ever wish you were back in London keeping that hospital in good working order?"

She smiled, stirring her coffee as she considered the question.

"No regrets. I did love that job, but I enjoy this one even more. I don't miss the brashness and mess of London. I like the whiff of sea air here when I go running in the morning. It's been good to be aware of the changing seasons again and the friendliness of community life. This is home now."

"I'm glad to hear it," said Richard, touching her arm lightly as he spoke. "We need you here."

"Heavens, look at the time!" exclaimed Kath as she caught sight of a huge wall clock. "When's William likely to finish?"

"About now, I reckon," said Richard, getting to his feet.

"Well, thank you for this unexpected treat. It's been good to meet you properly."

"Not just while I loiter with intent up against the playground wall, you mean?"

She laughed. "Think how many people must have done exactly that over the past hundred years at Hope Hall. You're in very good company."

"I certainly have been tonight." His eyes were warm with humour. "Thank you, Kath."

And with that they went their separate ways – Richard towards the bar after insisting on paying the bill, and Kath out of the back entrance of the pub so that she could head across the park to her apartment. As she walked, she mulled over her conversation with Richard, finally considering the things that *hadn't* been said.

She hadn't mentioned Jack's part in her decision to leave London, nor that he was now living and working only an hour's drive from where she lived. And why should she? That wasn't at all relevant to the conversation between business acquaintances like her and Richard.

Nevertheless, Kath thought, as she opened the door to her apartment, Celia Ainsworth was a very lucky lady.

Chapter 7

"No sign of him at all," sighed Sheelagh, as she peered out of the window at the front of Hope Hall just in case she might catch a glimpse of Michael trying to keep out of sight behind the trees that lined the road.

"Usually there's a queue round the building whenever we open up the canteen at the citadel in the evenings," said Jackie, who had arrived that afternoon in her usual Salvation Army uniform. "Is it the same here with the Food Bank?"

"There are definitely a few stalwarts who clearly feel they'll only get the pickings of what's on offer that week if they get through the door quicker than anyone else. It's shocking how cut-throat they can be, but who can blame them when they badly need food and clothes for themselves and their families? But I've only ever noticed Michael much later in the session, although it's possible he could've been hanging around outside for a while before I've spotted him."

"Well, there's another thirty minutes before the Food Bank closes here today, so he may still make an appearance."

"I really hope he does. He was pretty desperate for food both times I've seen him. I wonder how he's managing. Have your teams come across him at all in the last week or so?"

"Not exactly," replied Jackie, "but I had a cup of tea a couple of nights back with one of our regulars, Frank, who's been coming along to our soup kitchen for about a year now. He's a nice man who's fallen on hard times, a bit of a grandad figure for some of the younger people we meet."

"An elderly man sleeping rough? I don't like the idea of anyone's grandad having to do that."

"He gets a bed in our hostel most nights for just that reason. The places are allocated on a first come, first served basis, but Frank usually makes sure he's at the front of the line. He's very sensible that way."

"Is there any chance of getting him a permanent home?"

Jackie smiled ruefully. "He doesn't seem to want one. He's quite happy with the life he has now."

"That's really not a lifestyle you'd expect anyone to choose. It seems an impossible choice for someone like me to understand, but then I'm fortunate enough to live in a comfortable, settled home."

"Well, we're keeping a close eye on Frank. If his health becomes an issue, or if he changes his mind about the outdoor life once winter comes, we'll sort something out."

Sheelagh nodded thoughtfully.

"Anyway," continued Jackie, "it seems that Frank has come across Michael. They've chatted every now and then over the past few weeks."

"That's wonderful news! Where does Frank meet him? Did he say?"

"One of the cafés in town often puts out whatever food is left over at the end of the day just as they're about to close up. Michael sometimes shows up there."

"So, what did he say? Anything that might give us a clue about who he is or what's happened to him?"

"Frank said Michael had made a few odd comments about his job as a supermarket manager, but he didn't take much notice. We often find people create a fictional story about their past because they have good reasons for wanting to keep their actual circumstances to themselves. Frank initially thought Michael was just trying to give the impression he'd been a big shot in the retail world. But then apparently Michael started talking about the café they were getting the food from, and the ways in which they could improve their business strategy, and Frank found he was quite impressed. He thinks Michael is the genuine article."

"He didn't let his surname slip to Frank, did he?"

"I'm afraid not. What Frank did say, though, was that Michael might have been very efficient as a shop manager, but he's not managing well at being on the streets. He's trying so hard to keep out of sight that he's missing information about how and where to get the help he needs. He gets most of his food from people's dustbins, and his clothes and shoes are in a real state, apparently."

"Does he have any idea where Michael's living?"

"Only that he thinks he's got a bolthole somewhere. It sounds as if it might be an old farm building. Frank is going to try and find out more if he sees Michael again."

"That's great information, although it doesn't actually give us much to work on right now, does it?"

"Well, there was one detail Frank did remember. Michael mentioned that the superstore he managed was the biggest in the town."

"Which town? Did he say?"

"Yes. Basingstoke. Quite a long way from here, but that could have been his home for some time. Anyway, I've passed that on to our contact at the Family Tracing Service, and he's going to follow up on it. Hopefully that will throw some light on who Michael is and what he's been through. Then we might be better placed to find him help."

Kath was deeply engrossed in organizing the volunteer rota for the Good Neighbours scheme when a quick knock at her door heralded the entrance of Trevor, a file of papers tucked under his arm.

"I was just about to call you," smiled Kath. "Brian Mack has been in touch. He's got a stonemason lined up, along with a couple of his best builders, for the removal of the original foundation stone next week. They're planning to start work at nine on Monday morning, but they say it will take a couple of hours at least before they are ready to pull the old stone out."

"I suppose they've got to do everything very carefully to make sure they don't damage the surrounding brickwork. That might spoil the effect when they replace the stone again."

"That's right. So Brian says that if the people who need to be there could turn up around eleven, everything should be ready then for the great unveiling of whatever may have been left behind the stone."

"That sounds exciting. Will it be okay if Mary comes along? Say no if you think that might be one person too many."

"Of course Mary's welcome. I know how interested she's always been in the history of this building."

"I'll give Celia a ring as well to let her know what's happening," added Trevor. "I'm sure she'll be too busy at Apex to come along for this initial stage of the operation, but she's asked to be kept in the picture about anything we find."

"Michael Sayward wants to be present, of course," said Kath, looking down her list. "He might even want to bring along a few other key members of the Historical Society, because this is a big moment in our town's history. Roger from Rotary and Brenda from the WI showed an interest in coming too, and I'm not sure whether or not Peter Radcliffe from the council plans to be there. I'll drop each of them a note to make sure they all know what's happening on Monday."

"That reminds me of what I actually came in to tell you."

Trevor sat down on the chair on the other side of Kath's desk so that he could rummage through the papers in the folder he was carrying. Finally, with a note of triumph, he pulled out a thick, cream-coloured envelope on which Kath could see her own name written in beautiful italic script. Carefully, she drew out an elegant card embossed in gold lettering.

"A charity garden party!"

"And look which charity is being supported – Hope Hall's Good Neighbours scheme," beamed Trevor, leaning across to point out the small print at the bottom of the invitation. "Mary and I have been invited too."

"Who's organizing this?"

"Celia Ainsworth. She always opens her garden up one weekend in July, but changes the charity she supports each year. She must have been impressed by what she saw here when she came along to the trustees' meeting for the Money Advice Service the other week. I remember how interested she was in hearing about all the activities going on at the hall, and she asked a lot of very pertinent questions about the Good Neighbours scheme then."

"I see the event is being held at Ainsworth Cottage. I guess not a lot of people are expected then, if it's in a cottage garden?"

Trevor chuckled. "Just wait till you see Celia's home! Believe me, that house name is quite an understatement."

"So how many people usually go along to these parties?"

"No more than sixty, I should think, but it's the quality rather than the quantity that counts. Celia has some very well-heeled, charity-minded contacts. She always organizes an auction of wonderful gifts – holidays, opportunities to meet VIPs, visits behind the scenes at big football matches or concerts, perhaps even the chance to bag a couple of tickets for Centre Court at Wimbledon. And there's always some artwork there, because that's a passion of Celia's. She picks out pieces that will definitely gain in value, so that those in the know can make a grand public gesture of donating to charity with the certainty that, in time, they'll get their money back from their investment.

"But then investment is Celia's area of expertise. You know she's Director of the UK Pension Fund for Apex Finance; it's a massive international financial institution with its parent company based in New York. In fact, this whole charity event is sponsored by Apex, who consider it a valuable PR exercise. That means Celia can approach a few choice individuals among her Apex business contacts and persuade them that it would be equally good PR for them if they were seen to donate an impressive auction item or two."

"Wow! What a wonderful opportunity for us. How very kind of her. Does she require any help from us, perhaps with the publicity?"

"Oh, my dear," drawled Trevor in the poshest accent he could muster, "this is an *invitation only* occasion. Only the crème de la crème are invited. The publicity comes *after* the event, in the society columns and *Hello!* magazine."

"My goodness, how wonderful to think our lovely old Hope Hall might be mentioned in a magazine like that! What about the catering then? Could our team help out? I know Maggie would love to be involved in planning an occasion like this."

Trevor guffawed with delighted laughter. "I can assure you that no help will be required from us at all. This is a high-class charity event for high-class worthies who expect high-class catering."

"Don't say that in Maggie's hearing."

"Oh, you know I could eat Maggie's cakes all day long, but this is a world away from that."

"Champagne and ice sculptures then, is it?"

"Absolutely! A chocolate fountain, endless varieties of canapés, crusts cut off the caviar sandwiches, bone china cups and saucers, and pinkies up!" beamed Trevor.

"My!" breathed Kath. "It sounds very grand."

"And very lucrative. This could double the Good Neighbours reserves in just one afternoon."

Kath sat back with a smile as she watched the expression on Trevor's face. "I'm not sure whether you're more delighted about this as Trevor the Hope Hall accountant, or Trevor who loves nothing more than a posh cream tea."

"Both," he replied, rubbing his hands together like an excited child. "This will be a red letter day in my diary!"

At that, Kath drew out her own diary from the top drawer and wrote in the details of the garden party for the second Saturday in July. As she wrote, she thought about her first impressions of Celia when she'd arrived at Hope Hall on the morning of that trustees' meeting. She'd been the picture of elegance, expensively dressed, confident and completely aware of her impact on the people around her. She had shown no interest at all in Kath, even though she was standing alongside the other trustees. In fact, Kath still remembered the only recognition she'd had from Celia was when she threw an off-hand instruction in her direction asking for a decaf coffee with one sweetener and almond milk!

But this was the woman who had claimed Richard Carlisle's heart, and who loved William very much too, from all he'd said about her. It was a happy solution to a very sad situation.

And this offer from Celia to organize such a prestigious event to raise funds for Hope Hall's Good Neighbours scheme would bring so much benefit to elderly and isolated members of this community. It was kind of her, and kindness was obviously a quality that Richard would appreciate in his choice of partner.

Kath was glad for him. She really was.

"Right, listen up, you lot!" Shirley's voice boomed across the foyer so that even the most hard-of-hearing members of the Grown-ups' Lunch Club looked up from their dinner plates in alarm. "This is the last day for letting us know if you want to come to Southsea on our summer outing. It's two weeks on Saturday. Make sure you put your name on the list pinned up on the noticeboard over there before you leave today if you plan to come with us."

"How much is it again?" asked a lady who was still wearing a neat mauve hat with a flower on one side of it, even though she'd taken her coat off at least an hour earlier when she'd arrived at Hope Hall.

"It's all subsidised," bellowed Shirley, "so it won't cost you anything for the trip, or for the lovely tea we're all going to have at a big hotel right on the front. But if you want to bring back any souvenirs, or plan to have a flutter on the bingo, or buy a Kiss-Me-Quick hat while you're there, you'll have to bring your own money for that."

"You'll be needing one of those hats, Percy!" giggled Flora.

"Well, I'm not kissing him," shuddered Doris, trying rather unsuccessfully to keep a straight face. "Perish the thought!"

"Ladies!" announced Percy. "Please don't fight over me. Just form an orderly queue."

A squeal of indignation went up from the ladies, while the gentlemen nodded approval in Percy's direction.

"Actually, ladies and gentlemen," announced Percy once the noise had died down, "when it comes to headgear, I plan to pay homage to my nautical past."

"It's going to be a Hello Sailor hat then, is it?" asked Flora.

Percy gazed over in her direction with an expression of disdain. "Actually, I was thinking of something more classy and to the point. I think my hat should simply say 'The Captain.'"

136

While laughter and a variety of comments rippled around the hall, Ida sat bolt upright in her seat at Flora and Doris's table, her face totally without expression. "How common!"

It was only when the noise had died down to the level of general chatter that her own comment was heard, loud and clear, by everyone sitting at the adjoining tables. Some ladies looked embarrassed. Percy spluttered with laughter.

Then Shirley stepped in to remind them all of the original message. "So, names on the board today! Understood? Anyone got any questions?"

"Should we bring our own sandwiches for the journey?" asked the lady in the mauve hat. "Only I have a condition. I need to eat a little and often."

"Then be sensible and bring along whatever you particularly need to keep your strength up," replied Shirley. "And if any of you have medication you should take, please remember to have it with you. We don't want any unscheduled trips to the Queen Alexandra Hospital in Portsmouth!"

"I know we're having tea," continued the lady, "but that's at tea time, and I'll be really hungry by then. I need to know when we're going to be eating. It's important that I know."

Around the foyer, ears pricked up with interest to hear the answer to this question.

"We'll be bringing along packed lunches for everyone."

"One of Maggie's packed lunches?" enquired Flora. "With cakes? Are we going to have some of Maggie's cakes?"

"The lunches will have everything you need. They'll be wholesome and nourishing."

"Can we have sausage sandwiches?" asked Robert. "I love Maggie's sausage sandwiches."

"And some of those cheese biscuit things she makes?" suggested John, who was sitting next to Robert.

"And will there be any fresh fruit?" asked Connie. "I have to have fresh fruit every day. My doctor says so."

"Oh, for heaven's sake!" exploded Shirley. "The packed lunches will be wonderful. You know they always are when they come from Maggie and the kitchen team here. But if you need anything special for your own particular diet, then let me know today and I'll make sure we do our best to provide whatever you require."

"Don't bother with a packed lunch for me," called out Percy. "I'm going to have a bag of chips sitting on the sea wall."

"Ooh, that's what I'd like to do too!" enthused Betty.

There were comments of agreement from all around at that idea.

"Listen!" cut in Shirley. "You will each be given a packed lunch which you can eat and enjoy or feed to the seagulls for all I care. Just do your own thing. It's your holiday outing. We're all going to have a great day by the seaside at Southsea. If having a portion of chips smothered in salt and vinegar is what you fancy, or if you'd rather get your choppers around a stripy stick of seaside rock, then do it! Enjoy yourselves. That's all that matters."

"What happens if it rains?" asked the mauve-hat lady. "I've got a Pac a Mac. Will that do, or should I bring my umbrella as well? Oh, and will we need our wellies?"

"Well, I'm going to have a paddle," announced Percy. "But not in my wellies."

"So childish," snapped Ida. "It's like having a five-year-old in the room."

With a withering look in Ida's direction and a huge sigh, Shirley simply turned on her heel and headed out through the foyer towards the main hall.

Further down on the left-hand side of the hall, the door that led to the old school building burst open to reveal Shirley's son, Tyler.

"What on earth are you doing here?" demanded Shirley. "Have you cleaned your room and run the vacuum over it like I asked you?"

Tyler smiled in a way that immediately irritated Shirley.

"Look, Tyler. This is my place of work. If you've come here to see if you can wheedle any more money out of me, forget it. And what are you doing coming out of the old school building anyway?"

"I've been to see Ray."

"What?"

"I'm working in Ray's office. He's having trouble with his computer."

Shirley fell into uncustomary silence as her jaw dropped at this news.

"Actually," Tyler continued, "there's nothing wrong with his computer. He just doesn't know how to use it."

"And you do? Are you sure? There's a lot of valuable information on that computer, Tyler. Don't you dare lose it!"

Tyler shot his mother a pitying look. "The only danger to the computer in that office is Ray himself. He's got no idea. Half the time he forgets to save things he's written, and he's obviously never worked out how to compile charts and graphs, because a lot of the information he needs would be much easier to access in chart format."

"And Ray's okay with all this, is he?"

"He's ecstatic about it. He says I've set up the easiest and most efficient system he's seen in years."

"Are you sure? I'll be checking with him, you know—"

"Mum." There was a steely note in Tyler's voice as he stared directly at her. "You're hopeless with computers. I, on the other hand, am really good. Ray recognizes that, and he trusts me to help him. And he's right to trust my work and my judgement, because I really do know what I'm doing. The only person who doesn't recognize how good I am with computers is you!"

Shirley stared back at him, her mind obviously whirring. Then a slow smile of pride spread across her face. "Good. That's very good. Well, I'll leave you to it then."

"I'll see you later, Mum, okay?"

"Okay," she agreed, still grinning as she continued her journey out of the side door and into the old school building.

Because Maggie so often had to work at the weekends at Hope Hall, she usually tried to keep Thursdays as a day off in the week. Since moving into the flat, she found she enjoyed every moment she spent in her new home. She'd whiled away many pleasant hours rearranging the furniture, first in one layout and then another, until she was absolutely sure that the sofa and chairs, the sideboard and the rugs, the dressing table and the coat stand were all just where they looked at their very best.

As she laid out her favourite ornaments and family photographs on the shelves and windowsills so that they were shown off to their full advantage, she smiled to herself at the memory of the ornaments and pictures that had been on show at the old house, and how wonderful it had been to get rid of the ones she had never really liked. That was the compromise a wife made when her husband insisted on displaying every photo ever taken of him in either a football or a darts team since he'd been in short trousers at school.

He'd had so many collections that he couldn't part with. High on the list were his old albums from the nineties (lined up along the floor on his side of the bed), his beer mats (displayed on a specially built shelf in the dining room), and his ornamental bottles of liqueur from various Continental destinations that he'd brought back from their many family holidays. These liqueurs were never drunk, never even touched, but the variously shaped bottles had still been lined up along the windowsill in the conservatory for years on end.

The feeling of relief and freedom was exquisite when she finally packed the whole lot up and sent them round to his new home with Mandy. Dave was the man with whom that floozy had decided to share her life. Let Mandy find room for them on the shelves and walls of *her* house. Good riddance!

And for Maggie, there was huge enjoyment in planning the furnishings and decoration of her very own home. For the first time in her life, she didn't have to allow for the tastes and habits of other family members, first her parents and then her husband. So now, in her new home, her windowsills were adorned with pots of lush plants with variegated leaves and vibrant blooms that she watered, fed and sprayed with tender care. Everything felt fresh, and lighter.

Obviously she still wanted her family to be on display, though. Every single one of the scribbles, Mother's Day cards and cardboard creations made by Steph and Darren during their schooldays was now lovingly stacked in a box in the top section of her wardrobe, and it was grandson Bobbie's creations that were proudly on view on her fridge door.

The final touches were put in place when her son Darren helped her hang some new pictures and prints on the walls. She had treated herself to several that had caught her eye. There was one that showed a woodland scene of a small wooden bridge stretching over a bubbling stream. Any walker coming to that bridge would be faced with a choice. Should they take the path to the right on this side of the stream, or the one to the left? Or did they have the courage to step out across the bridge and follow the path that stretched ahead into the distance, destination unknown? She knew which choice she had already made. This move into a new home meant that she had crossed that bridge towards whatever lay ahead. At times it was daunting, but the knowledge that the future was hers to discover and make her own was exhilarating too. With a warm sense of satisfaction, she realized she wouldn't turn the clock back for anything now this huge upheaval in her life was behind her. This flat was testament to the fact that she was beginning to enjoy herself.

Some of the items she'd bought for the flat were out of necessity rather than desire. The only mirror in the place when she'd moved in covered the full length of the door in the bathroom. She was appalled by it. The bathroom was the very last place she wanted to catch sight of every generous inch of herself! Her body always looked dreadful in the mirror – short, dumpy and far too round. It was true that the scales told her she'd lost a few pounds during those manic weeks when she'd been racing around packing up the old house, but wherever those pounds had previously been, their loss didn't seem to have had a noticeable impact on her silhouette. She was still fat, and she still hated it.

And it was that thought that led to her considering again the email that had arrived in her inbox the evening before. It came from one of her oldest friends, Sylvie, who had lived next door but one when they were growing up. Sylvie and she had walked to school together in the mornings, and waited for each other to make the return trip every afternoon. Sylvie eventually married Bill, an electrician who'd opted for a full-time job with a building firm in south London. They'd moved away shortly after their wedding, thinking quite rightly that a permanent position in a busy and established building company would give them the financial stability they needed in order to start their own family. It had been a good choice. Three children, four grandchildren and twenty-seven years later, Bill had just retired as a director of the company with a generous pension and a holiday home in southern Spain.

Distance had never dimmed the friendship between Maggie and Sylvie, though. At first, they'd kept in touch via regular phone calls and even the occasional newsy letter, but in latter years the technology of internet and mobile phones meant that rarely a week went by without the two of them being in touch.

But yesterday's email from Sylvie had sent Maggie's mind into a whirl.

> Hi Mags. How are you doing? Have you got all that painting done in the new place yet? And have you sorted out how the central heating works? Although you won't need it for a while, with all this lovely weather we're having. My advice to you is to ask an eight-year-old. They know everything these days!
>
> How's Steph? Is Dale's work still going well? Bobbie okay? He must be growing up so fast. Send pictures! How old is he now? Is he three yet? I lose track of birthdays with all these youngsters to remember. And are Darren and Sonia still going strong?
>
> All my lot are fine. We love seeing Carol's two girls every day after school. I always do tea for them, and give them time to play in our garden, which is much bigger than theirs. It may be a bit naughty, but as Nanny I think it's my job to spoil them a bit, and I've always got ice creams in the freezer and their favourite pizza or pasta for tea. Mind you, Bill's showing his age, because I can tell he finds two small girls a bit of a handful. He usually arranges to have urgent jobs he's just GOT to do in the greenhouse when they arrive. The trouble is that the more he disappears, the more desperate they are to see him! And just to be helpful, I always point the girls in the right direction to find him.

That will teach him to duck out of his responsibility as Grumpy Grandpa!

Anyway, love, ignore my ramblings because I've got a message to send on to you. My brother Joe rang me last night, which as you know is a rare treat. It's the first time I've spoken to him since that school reunion. We should have gone, shouldn't we? At least I had an excuse because I live miles away, but I'm still cross you didn't go along to spy for both of us! I'd love to have seen pictures of some of our old classmates. I bet that would have given us a right giggle. Anyway, I'm teasing. I know you had a lot on your plate at the time.

So, coming back to the point, Joe went along and met up with quite a few of his old friends. He really enjoyed himself, and said they all had great fun talking about the teachers and the pranks they got up to and which girls they fancied. Like nothing had changed really!

Now, do you remember that when Joe walked to school with us, his friend Phil sometimes used to join us too? He lived in Bertram Street, right at the bottom – can you picture him? Well, Phil and Joe have kept in touch every now and then, even though it's been years since they actually saw each other. Phil has been working along the coast somewhere near Chichester.

Anyway, Phil's a nice bloke. At least, he always was a nice bloke when he lived around the corner all those years ago, so I guess he's still quite nice now. And he asked about you! When he discovered you weren't at the reunion, he asked Joe if you and I had kept in touch. Joe told him I had your email, and he said he'd like to drop you a line. I didn't think you'd mind, so I've passed it on to him. You could just ignore his

*email if you'd rather not write back. Let me know what
happens!*

   *Must go. I've got a cottage pie in the oven and Bill is
waiting for his tea.*

   Loads of love, as always,

   Sylvie

   Xxx

Maggie had read the email through so many times, she practically
knew it off by heart.

Phil Coleman! Just his name sent her reeling. She couldn't
believe Sylvie had asked her if she remembered him. She must
have kept her adoration of Phil a very close secret if even Sylvie
hadn't realized how the presence of Joe's friend as they all walked
to school together had catapulted fifteen-year-old Maggie into
a heady mix of devotion and terror. Phil Coleman was the most
beautiful boy she had ever seen. "Beautiful" wasn't really the right
way to describe a young man, but it was the only word she could
think of to do justice to the way he looked. He had thick dark-
brown hair, and eyes that she thought were probably hazel, though
she'd never really been brave or close enough to check. He wasn't
particularly tall, and yet there was an air of strength in his broad,
sturdy frame that translated into real talent on the rugby field. Lots
of the girls in her year liked him. He was two years ahead of them
and had seemed out of reach and glamorous. He had always been
so well at ease with girls and she had often seen him around the
school at break times chatting to one leggy beauty or other.

Maggie sighed. She had never been leggy. She reckoned her
legs were about four inches too short for her to be average, let
alone leggy. But those short, strong legs of hers had made her
a natural on the hockey field, and quite early on in her school
career she got a reputation for being the fiercest member of

the girls' hockey team. But then what teenage girl wanted to be known for her thick, muscly legs and her ability to pack a punch on the hockey field? She'd wanted to be leggy. She'd wanted to be popular. She'd wanted boys to notice her for the right reasons, especially Phil Coleman when he walked in the same group as her to school every morning. Surely he just viewed her as Joe's younger sister's dumpy, irritating friend? How could he ever have seen her as anything else? She'd never made the butterfly stage. In fact, in her mind, she'd not moved on from being the equivalent of a short, round, hairy caterpillar.

And now here was Phil Coleman, invading her world again! Just his name brought back all the feelings of insecurity and angst that had coloured most of her teenage years. Even now, after years of marriage, running a busy family home, and then going on to establish her own baking business with such success that she now held the extremely responsible and challenging role of Catering Manager at Hope Hall – even *now*, she recognized that her body shape, and the way she knew she looked, undermined any positive thought she ever had about herself.

It was her own fault. She was a baker. She loved baking, and all good cooks had to test whatever they produced! How else could she be sure that the flavours were just right and the quality of the bake was up to scratch? And, of course, her dilemma wasn't helped by her complete lack of willpower when it came to sticking to any diet regime. She'd tried dozens of them over the years. She'd given up carbs, then meat, then both for a very short time, until she swore she would never eat a lettuce leaf again. She tried starving herself for five days each week, but then stuffed herself with so much food on the other two that she'd defeated the object of the exercise.

She had tried exercise too, of course. She'd always enjoyed sport, so she'd taken herself along to the local gym only to find that she was so embarrassed by the way she looked in tight-fitting sports leggings and skinny top that she'd scuttled out again, despite having paid more than two hundred pounds for a whole term! She'd never told Dave about the money. He'd have been furious if he'd known she'd plundered their holiday savings to pay for the gym fee. But then she hadn't even told him she was planning to try the gym, because she knew he'd say she'd never stick at it, and he was right.

Now, however, so much had changed for her. She was no longer married to a man who didn't understand how low her self-esteem was when it came to how she looked. Dave had never encouraged her to stick to any healthy regime. He had simply said "I told you so!" whenever she failed. But she didn't have to put up with unhelpful comments from him, or anyone else, from now on. She was her own woman, living in a wonderful flat and holding down the job she loved. The last thing she needed was Phil Coleman coming back into her life, dredging up painful memories. So if he did send an email, she wouldn't even open it. She'd just remove it from her inbox. That's what she'd do.

Probably...

Chapter 8

Terezka and Mili walked into Hope Hall together on Monday morning, ready for their English as a Foreign Language class. Mili tried to go along to at least three sessions a week, because she found the grammar tuition and the help with colloquial English extremely useful. Terezka had been in England for nearly eighteen months, and while her English speaking was not always completely fluent, it was certainly very good. Mili felt she had a long way to go before she was as comfortable with the language as Terezka, but she was aware that it became easier every day. She also suspected that sometimes she was dreaming in English rather than her native Czech, which must be a good sign!

Mind you, her father wasn't so sure. Mili linked up with her family through the computer at the language class once a week, and her father was very concerned that his beloved daughter was becoming far too comfortable away from home. She was longing to tell her mother about the fun she was having at The Bistro, about the band night she'd been to, and most of all about Andy's company, but she was aware that her father would also be listening. He might insist on rules that had to be obeyed whether he was there to check or not. Like expecting her to be home by nine every evening, because he'd seen too many TV dramas about England, and feared that she might be frightened or even attacked. There's no doubt he would frown when he heard about the sort of music played by Friction, worrying there would be alcohol at these dance nights, which might *also* lead to her being frightened or attacked. And if she ever made the mistake of mentioning that she had a boyfriend – even a perfectly nice, wonderfully kind and talented young man like Andy – her father would worry about that more than anything else. For if his daughter with her sheltered, respectable upbringing had found herself a boyfriend, then she would *definitely* be frightened and probably attacked too!

Sometimes her mother would come on to the screen, stare straight into the lens and ask quietly how Mili was *really* doing. Mili would nod with understanding and answer in a way that allowed her mother to read between the lines enough to recognize that her daughter was actually settled and very content. And when her mother asked her if she had made any particular friends, Mili mentioned Terezka, Mariana and all her fellow students at the English class. Then she spoke of Martin, her boss at The Bistro, and finally she mentioned Andy, a very nice musician who came to the café to write his new songs. Her mother watched Mili's expression closely, and although nothing specific was said, she knew that the young man in question was probably the most significant reason for her daughter's happiness in England. She smiled with understanding, and Mili thought that she had never loved her mother more dearly nor missed her so much.

"How come your Carlos has such a big head?" Terezka demanded when Mariana came into the class to join them. Because of their work schedules, and because Mariana was often hanging around waiting on the off-chance that Carlos might want to see her, this was the first occasion that all three girls had been together since the dance night. Terezka had nothing to do with the group, but she had picked up on the frustration of the other band members that evening and quizzed her flatmate Mili to give her every single detail. There was nothing Terezka liked more than a juicy bit of gossip and the possibility of trouble in other people's paradise.

Mariana bristled at the question. "Carlos is allowed a big head. He is a star. He has the best voice. Because of him the band is allowed to play."

Terezka huffed with indignation. "All the band members are good. Nigel is great on drums, Jake on guitar, Andy runs the show from his keyboard, and Graham has a better voice than your Carlos!"

The Spanish girl's eyes flashed with fury. "So why do all the people cheer when Carlos comes into the hall? Why do they ask for many encores? They love him!"

Terezka's expression softened. "*You* love him, Mariana. You are blind with love. But the boys in the band do not love Carlos."

"Then they are stupid. They only work because Carlos is loved so much."

"Carlos can't play the guitar or the drums or the keyboard. He can't play music at all. Without those players, he is nothing. He needs to treat them better, or they will leave him. You tell him that!"

"I will tell him nothing. What do *you* know?"

"I know that you, my lovely little friend, are crazy in love with a man who loves no one but himself."

"Carlos loves me. He adores me. He says I am his angel."

"How many other girls does he say that to?"

"You don't understand!" snapped Mariana angrily. "He wants to marry me."

"Then why hasn't he put a ring on your finger?"

"It is too early. The time is not good. He will do it when he has money, when he's famous, when the world knows how big a star he is—"

"Tomorrow, next week, some time, never?" intoned Terezka. "Wake up, Mariana! Carlos likes girls around him. He puts his arms around them. He whispers things in their ears. They are probably believing him too."

Mariana stood up and grabbed her shoulder bag. "I won't listen no more. I'm finished with you. You are not my friend!"

"Oh, but I *am*, Mariana. I really am. I am your best friend, who must tell you the truth."

"I'm leaving!" The Spanish girl's eyes had filled with tears as she headed for the door.

"And when you need your best friend, I'll be here," Terezka shouted after her, but Mariana had run away so quickly that she missed it.

Mili, who had been standing to one side throughout the whole exchange, looked at Terezka in shock and concern. "I follow her?"

"Leave her. She's upset now. She will calm down."

"You said cruel things."

"Did I lie?"

Mili shook her head thoughtfully. "No, but is good *we* tell her?"

"If not us, then who?"

"Well, you are right, the boys had enough with Carlos. They don't want to work with him."

"Andy told you that?"

"Andy is very angry, but he is a quiet man, so he don't like arguments."

"What will they do?"

Mili shrugged her shoulders, her face full of concern. "Andy, Jake and Graham speaking in café yesterday. They don't know what can they do."

"They will find a way."

"Is possible," agreed Mili. "I hope it. Most I hope Mariana is not hurt."

As Kath arrived at Hope Hall on that first Monday morning in July, she spotted Brian Mack's van immediately. The builder stopped to give his two workmen instructions on what equipment was needed from the vehicle before coming across to join her. Kath stood to one side of the main hall entrance, staring at the wording on the old foundation stone:

TO THE GLORY OF GOD

AND IN MEMORY OF THE MEN FROM

THIS DISTRICT WHO GAVE THEIR LIVES

IN THE GREAT WAR 1914–1918.

THIS FOUNDATION STONE WAS LAID BY

THE RT REVD ALFRED WALTER, BISHOP,

28TH AUGUST 1920

"This is quite a moment, isn't it?" she said, unable to take her eyes off the plaque. "Do you know, I've walked past these words most days for the past two years, and I've never really thought about what they must have meant to the people who placed this foundation stone a hundred years ago. Those young men marched away, didn't they, and didn't come back?"

"That's right." Brian was a man of few words.

"Have you removed any foundation stones like this in the past?"

"No."

"So you don't have any idea if there is likely to be some sort of time capsule behind the plaque?"

"Michael Sayward thinks there might be. He's the history expert."

"Well, we've tried to keep the numbers to a minimum so as not to get in your way. Those coming will all be here for eleven o'clock for the great reveal," said Kath. "Do you and your lads want anything at the moment? Tea? Coffee?"

"Stu! Den!" Brian yelled over to his builders. "Coffee?"

"Yeah!" came the reply. "Two sugars each. And they do those nice cheese scones here, don't they? Any chance of one of them this early in the morning?"

"A couple of slices of crispy bacon and some brown sauce in them scones would go down well too," shouted the other workman.

Kath smiled. "I'll see who's in the kitchen. I'm sure something can be arranged."

A full plate of bacon scones and several cups of coffee later, the builders were ready and waiting at quarter to eleven as the special guests started to arrive. Mary and Trevor had walked through the door of Hope Hall about an hour earlier, followed by Michael Sayward and his two guests from the Historical Society, Beryl Johnson and Derek Turner, who had been looking forward to this momentous occasion for years. Kath assumed Brenda from the Women's Institute had been picked up by Roger from Rotary, as they drove up in the same car. Then, almost at the last minute, Peter Radcliffe, the council press officer, turned up with Tim, the official town hall photographer, who came with an impressive collection of cameras to record this auspicious event for the next one hundred years.

At eleven o'clock exactly, silence fell on the group as each one of them recognized the significance of what they were about to witness. One hundred years ago, another group of local people had stood on this same spot watching as the foundation stone was positioned into place. Since then, there had been a whole century of peace and war, lives and deaths, innovation and discovery. The group that had stood here so long ago could never have envisaged the technological developments that allowed the present generation to live with comforts and conveniences that were unimaginable back in 1920. But those people were the ancestors of families who still lived in the town today, linked to those who followed them by the human condition, the hopes, fears, ills and emotions familiar to all. The image of those mothers and fathers, brothers and children watching this plaque being put in place all those years back, just after the horror and loss of the war that was supposed to end all wars, had a poignancy which stretched down from that moment to this. They had chosen the name of Hope Hall for this wonderful building. Their hope was that war would never happen again, and that the sacrifice of the young men they loved and mourned would not be in vain and would never be forgotten.

"My boys have loosened the stone, so it should come out quite cleanly." Brian's voice broke into the thoughts of the group standing around him. "Is it all right for us to pull it out now?"

With general agreement all round, everyone manoeuvred themselves into a position where they could best see what was happening. With Brian supervising from above, Stu and Den crouched down to grip the sides of the stone, and then started to pull. There was a grinding sound as the old stone reluctantly shifted from its resting place, allowing the men to draw it out inch by inch until at last they could lay it flat on the ground, revealing a dark oblong cavity within. Brian looked questioningly towards Michael, who knelt down, stretching out his hand to search for anything that might be hidden within. Time seemed to stand still as he moved his fingers from left to right before lowering himself down so that he could peer directly into the hole. Then, with infinite care, he used both hands to draw something that seemed to be either heavy or cumbersome out into the sunshine of that July morning.

"It's a box!" squealed Mary. "It looks like it's made of tin."

"You're right," agreed Michael as he laid it on the trestle table that had been brought out so they could examine any contents immediately.

"Will it open?" asked Brenda. "Does it need a key?"

Michael ran his fingers around the rim of the box before giving the lid a sharp tug. At first, it didn't move, but then as he worked his way round each of the corners, the old tin lid finally creaked open. Everyone immediately moved forward to take a look inside.

Laid across whatever was inside was a piece of black satin material, which Michael gently peeled back to reveal a pile of dusty papers. With great care, he used both hands to pick up the top sheet of paper, which clearly had writing on it. Blowing away a layer of dust, he laid it down on the table and started to read.

> *This box has been compiled by the Hope Hall Memorial Committee and placed here on 28th August 1920 on the occasion of the laying of the foundation stone. We have included some pieces that represent ourselves, our town and the times we live in, which have been both difficult and painful for us as a country and as a community. For four years between 1914 and 1918, the Great War claimed the lives and health of local men who went off to fight. Many never returned. Our families and our town mourn their loss.*
>
> *To this end, we are now starting to build this hall in their memory, so that neither we, nor any generations that follow in the future, will ever forget the futility of war. It must never happen again. We will call this building HOPE HALL, because that is our hope; a hope we share with the whole of humanity.*

*May God bless all who enter Hope Hall, and may this
building provide shelter, comfort, interest and pleasure
to this community for many years to come.*

Signed
Reginald Ainsworth
Chairman
Hope Hall Memorial Committee

"Was that Celia's grandfather?" asked Trevor.

"No, Reginald was her *great*-grandfather," said Michael. "Reginald and his wife Beatrice married soon after the turn of the century, when Beatrice was still quite young. What followed was about seventeen years without any children at all because poor Beatrice went through one miscarriage after another. They'd almost given up hope when, in 1919, just a year or so before this stone was laid, she managed to carry a baby to full term. So Reginald was in his forties before he became a father to the only child Beatrice and he ever had, their son Neville, the little boy who grew up to become Douglas and Celia's grandfather."

"I don't recall ever meeting him, but I've certainly known Celia and Douglas's parents very well over the years," said Beryl, Michael's colleague from the Historical Society. "James, Celia's father, was Neville's only son, so he inherited the mill and cereal business."

"And made a very good job of it too," agreed Michael. "Celia was the oldest of James's children, but she suffered from being a girl, because even though from a young age she'd loved learning about the business of the mill from her father, tradition was more important. As tradition dictated, the mill was passed down to Douglas, the eldest son in the family. Hence, Douglas is now the chief executive, and in time his son Matthew will take over the reins."

Roger, who had only volunteered to become Chairman of the local Rotary Club once he'd retired as a teacher in the town, huffed a little. "Let's hope Matthew matures a great deal more than his recent behaviour suggests he might."

"How old is he?" asked Beryl.

Roger thought for a few seconds. "Probably about sixteen now."

"So, there's time for improvement."

"Time, yes," agreed Roger. "Inclination? Well, I'm not so sure about that…"

"Look at this next sheet of paper," said Michael, once again blowing off a layer of dust before spreading the document out on the table. "This shows the accounts for the planning of the hall. Here, look, it explains that Reginald Ainsworth donated the land on which it was built and that he committed to paying half of whatever costs were involved. The local community was charged with raising the other half themselves."

As Michael spoke, Beryl reached out to pick up the next item in the box, which she held out for all to see. "My goodness, how about this! It looks like the whole committee got together to line up just where we're standing now so they could include a picture of themselves in this tin. It must have been a real family affair. The men are here, and their wives and children are included, too."

"Are there any names?" asked Derek, the other historian. "On the back, perhaps?"

Sure enough, in neat handwriting in blue ink, was a chart giving the names of everyone in the picture.

"There are lots of Jessops, a couple of Wainwrights, and the group over on this side of the picture mostly seem to be Brownlows. Well, I certainly recognize those surnames as still being here in the town," concluded Beryl.

While they chatted, Michael had continued sifting through

the rest of the contents of the box, carefully drawing out one piece after another.

"Here are some other photos," he said, staring at the top one in detail. 'My goodness, I think this is the road running alongside the hall here, and all you can see in this picture are fields and trees. It's a bit different now!"

As that photo was passed around, others followed, showing scenes of the High Street and the old pub, several featuring men with farming implements or standing alongside huge horses, and then a photo of what was clearly Ainsworth Mill, as it had looked in 1920.

"I bet Douglas would like that," commented Trevor as he studied the picture. "They could display this at the mill. It's living history really, isn't it?"

"Oh, and the children have contributed too," exclaimed Brenda. "They've written about their school, their town and what goes on here. You know, that's more or less what the children at the school here are planning to put into our time capsule at the ceremony next month. History is repeating itself, a century later."

"That's *our* old school, which is now part of the hall," added Kath, studying the photo closely. "Of course, they built Hope Hall right next door to the local school so that all the activities and amenities could be shared. And we're still putting both buildings into constant use today. We're using it in exactly the way the pioneers in that group photo envisaged a century ago. That's a very heartening thought."

"What's this?" Michael pulled out a thick, faded envelope from the bottom of the tin. Turning the envelope over, he once again brushed off a layer of dust as he pulled out a single sheet of paper that had been folded in half, and half again. Stretching it out on the table in front of him, Michael began to read the message out loud:

Mrs Carmichael and I would like these letters to be placed in the wall of our memorial hall. Our eldest son Gerald Carmichael was conscripted into the army in 1916. He was twenty-two years old. Three weeks before he left, he married his sweetheart, Edith. They had been engaged for a year, and could wait no longer.

Edith wrote to him often and treasured the few letters he managed to write in return. I enclose his last letter written in the trenches at Passchendaele in October 1917, in what they called the Third Battle of Ypres.

Edith heard no news at all of Gerry for many months. Then just before Christmas she received this letter and a photograph of herself, which had been forwarded to her by the Soldiers' Christian Association. It read, "Dear Madam, I am sending you this letter and photo found in a wood here in the battlefield. I am very sorry to say that I could not find the owner of the photo. I cannot say whether he has been wounded or killed." That photo was the one of Edith that Gerry loved best, taken on their wedding day. He must have carried it with him right to the end.

I am the chief builder of this new memorial hall. This will be a labour of love because it is dedicated to the memory of our boys who didn't come back; to my boy who didn't come back. I have no idea if anyone in the future will discover the box we are burying today in the foundations of this new building. If they do, I hope they will get some measure of the pain, fear and despair we parents feel as we lose our sons. There wasn't even a body to bring home to his mother so she could bury our beloved boy.

Signed

Leonard Carmichael

Senior Builder

No one said a word as Michael slipped his fingers into the package and pulled out a smaller envelope addressed to Mrs Edith Carmichael.

Michael cleared his throat as he started to read:

"Dearest, if this should ever reach you it will be a sure sign that I am gone under. I will have died with your name on my lips. I love you deeply – how much, you will never know.

I am heartened that I am leaving you with a son. I have not met him but already I love our boy with all my heart. In the future, when your grief has worn a bit, speak to him sometimes of me.

Please tell Mother and Father that I think of them often, and brother George. I pray that this war will end before he too is called up. How could Mother bear that?

So, dear heart, I will bid you farewell, hoping to meet you in a time to come if there is a hereafter. Know that my last thoughts were of you in the dugout or on the fire step. My thoughts are always for you, the only one I ever loved.

Gerry"

A stunned silence descended on them all, broken at last when Michael spoke.

"Gerry Carmichael. My goodness, the grief is raw in this letter – as it must have been for so many families here at that time. I don't know about you, but I'm longing to know more about what happened to the Carmichael family. Is it okay with everyone if I delve into the records to see if happier times lay ahead for them?"

And as everyone mumbled their agreement, Kath realized that after today she would never be able to think of Hope Hall in the same way again – not now she fully understood how it was born out of pain and sorrow as a symbol of community, strength and fellowship. Whatever her role in Hope Hall, she must never lose sight of what it meant to the families who toiled to build it. As its present-day custodian, she must strive to cherish the vision of a better future, of peaceful family life and of opportunity that had inspired Mr Carmichael and his team to lay the foundation stone of the building a hundred years ago.

And there it was! As soon as she'd opened her laptop that afternoon and gone to check her emails, his name jumped out at her from the list. Phil Coleman. The name that had thrilled her when she was a teenager caused a shiver down her spine as she saw it now.

Maggie sat back in her seat staring at the screen. Well, she had a clear choice. She could open up his email, read its contents and then decide whether to reply, or she could pretend it had never actually arrived. She could just ignore it. She didn't want to be in touch with him. She didn't want to be reminded of her unrequited love for someone who never really gave her a second thought. And she certainly didn't want him, of all people, seeing her as she looked now: overweight and overwrought. She had that much pride at least.

So she shut the laptop with a snap and went off to do other things. She got out the sewing box to reattach a couple of buttons that had come adrift. She opened up the A4-sized notepad she liked to use for work, and spent half an hour happily planning menus for the coming month. She rang Steph and caught up on the family news. She even considered ringing her old friend Sylvie, to let her know that Phil had actually sent her an email.

But given that it was Sylvie who had put her in this awkward spot in the first place, she realized her old friend might try to badger her into responding, and she really wasn't in the mood for that. So she ran a bath and listened to a chapter of her audiobook while luxuriating with her shoulders under the bubbles. She dried her flyaway, biscuit-coloured hair, which never did what it was told, no matter what she tried. She watered her pot plants and rearranged the bits and pieces on her dressing table.

It was nearly eleven by then. Surely, she must be tired enough now to drop off to sleep immediately! So she made a cup of Horlicks, grabbed a packet of her favourite biscuits and headed for the bedroom. Except she never got there. Instead, without knowing quite how it happened, she found herself sitting in front of her laptop again, clicking to open his email until it filled the screen.

"Dear Megs," it started.

Maggie couldn't stop a small smile from creeping across her face at his greeting. She had almost forgotten that he used to call her that. Everyone else had called her Mags, but for some reason Phil had misheard the pronunciation of her name. When Sylvie and her brother Joe had tried to correct him, Phil had grinned across at her with a warm twinkle in his eye, and said that he thought Megs sounded prettier, and the name suited her. He was wrong, of course. No one else at school had ever described her as pretty, so she had always hugged the memory of how he'd looked at her in that moment as her very own private treasure. He would never have guessed, of course, because she was too shy to speak to him. Occasionally, as they all walked to school, she'd steal a glance in his direction when she was sure no one was looking. She would have been mortified if anyone had realized how she felt – the gauche, rotund girl dreaming about the older, good-looking, popular boy! Everyone at school would have laughed their socks off if they'd known.

I do hope you don't mind me dropping you this email, but Sylvie was kind enough to pass your email address on to me through Joe. I'm not even sure if you'll remember me after all this time. It's more than thirty years since I left school, and there's been a lot of water under the bridge for both of us since then. In case you've forgotten, I lived just a bit further away from school than you did, and you used to join the group when we walked past the end of your road. I wonder if you remember...

I didn't manage to get to that school reunion the other week. Did you? I'm living in Chichester now, and it was a bit too far to come. Actually, that's really just an excuse because of course I could have come. I enjoyed my schooldays, but I really wasn't sure about meeting up again after such a long time. Was that mixed feelings or just cold feet? Anyway, in the end, I decided to give it a miss. Joe filled me in afterwards, and it seems that a great time was had by everyone. Perhaps I didn't make the right choice after all!

Anyway, chatting to Joe, I was pleased to hear that you and Sylvie are still in touch. That's nice. You two were always great friends. It made me wonder how life has treated you over all those years since we last saw each other. It would be lovely to catch up a bit. If you are able to drop me a line, I'd be pleased to hear from you.

No pressure. I'll understand if you'd rather not; in which case, I wish you and your family all the very best.
Regards
Phil Coleman

Maggie must have read the words half a dozen times before she finally slumped back in the chair staring at the screen. He didn't go to the reunion because he had cold feet and wondered if it was wise to try and meet up again after all these years! She had felt exactly the same way. After all this time, nothing had changed. Her feet weren't just cold, they were blocks of ice!

She sighed. Even if Phil's words did suggest he shared some of the same feelings, he'd still be the same person. He would still be good-looking and popular. That was just the way he was. And she was still too small, too round and, frankly, too battered by recent events to be of interest to anyone. He would be disappointed if he could see her now, and his disappointment would be more than she could bear.

So of course she wouldn't answer. She would pretend his email had never reached her. Oh dear, what a shame. Ah well, never mind.

She shut the lid of the laptop with a determined thump so that his words were no longer on the screen challenging her. Then she did what she always did when she had something unpleasant on her mind. Even though it was gone eleven o'clock, she went out to the kitchen, turned on the oven and started baking.

Kath had trouble deciding what to wear to Celia's garden party. She wanted to look summery and fashionable, but her practical nature also made her check the weather forecast in case what she really needed was a sou'wester and galoshes. As it happened, that Saturday dawned with blue skies and warm July sunshine. Apparently even the weather obeyed Celia Ainsworth, Kath thought wryly.

Finally, she stepped out of the apartment and into Trevor and Mary's waiting car wearing a pale yellow dress topped by a flowing chiffon jacket in a range of golden shades which she hoped looked well with her trim figure and smartly cut dark hair.

"You've worn a dress!" accused Mary. "I told you I should have worn a dress, Trevor. Why did you persuade me to wear this trouser suit instead?"

"Because, my dear Mary, if you're going to be standing on grass for much of the afternoon, I thought you would prefer flat shoes, and you said you couldn't wear flat shoes with a dress!"

"But Kath's wearing pretty sandals with a high wedge heel and she looks great. I could have done that. Why didn't I do that?"

Kath smiled from the back seat. "You sound worried about this event today, Mary. Should I be too?"

"Oh, you always get things just right, Kath. But apparently there will be lots of celebrities there, and some very well-heeled people from high-class families. And there I'll be in a trouser suit, probably the only person to get the dress code completely wrong!"

"Oh, for heaven's sake, Mary, do you want me to turn around and go home so you can change for the umpteenth time today?" snapped Trevor.

"It didn't mention a dress code on the invitation," soothed Kath. "And that is a lovely summer outfit you're wearing, with those soft trousers and the colour that looks so pretty on you. I think you've chosen well."

"Really?"

"Really!"

"So, can we go now, before you make all of us late?" muttered Trevor.

"You're sure, Kath? Do I really look okay?"

"You look just lovely, and I shall be extremely pleased to walk in with both of you. I don't really know Celia at all, but I think you two have spent quite a bit of time with her in the past, haven't you?"

"Well, Trevor has. I'm not usually invited to the occasions where he meets her."

"Because they're committee meetings, Mary, and you're not on the committee. And what's more, you'd be bored to tears if you were!"

"You always put me down, Trevor, as if I'm some airhead without a sensible thought in her head. We have a guest in the car. Please don't embarrass me."

Trevor pursed his lips in indignation. Kath settled down in the back seat so she could gaze out of the window as the three of them travelled in stony silence.

The journey took little more than fifteen minutes before Trevor was turning the car in through an impressive pair of wrought-iron gates and down a long driveway towards an elegant grey-stone house with wide bay windows on both sides of the central doorway. Kath immediately saw what Trevor had meant when he said that calling this a cottage was an understatement.

It seemed the party was being held at the back of the house, and their car was duly directed by a uniformed steward towards a parking area to one side. Strains of jazz music drifted across the lawns as Kath got out of the car, noticing the slight trepidation that flashed across Mary's face as the three of them started to walk over to the gathering crowd.

"You look just fine," Kath whispered as she linked her arm through Mary's, and together they made their way towards yet another suited steward, who was greeting each guest and ticking their names off his list. There were many "madams" and "sirs" from the steward during their short conversation before they were shown to their table, where a wine waiter immediately appeared proffering glasses of champagne. Mary perked up considerably once she had a glass of champagne in her hand, and clearly decided that she might enjoy this afternoon after all. She settled herself down in a chair before turning to have a good look all around, hoping she might spot a celebrity or two from the glossy magazines she liked to read whenever she went to the hairdresser's.

Rather than sitting down, Kath thought she should probably circulate and try talking to the groups of people who were chatting very enthusiastically around her. After all, the event was to raise money for their Good Neighbours scheme, and she was the administrator of that. Perhaps these supporters would like to know more about their work? She tried standing alongside a couple of the groups, but they seemed to move even closer together to make it clear that a stranger was not welcome to join in with the conversation. Feeling rather awkward, she looked around to see if there were familiar faces she knew through her work at Hope Hall, but could see none.

Suddenly, an arm gripped hers and spun her around. Kath was surprised to find it belonged to Celia, who didn't bother with niceties as she spat out instructions.

"There you are! I could do with you keeping an eye on the donations table, just in case there are any problems with bank cards and transfers, anything like that."

"Well yes, of course. I'll help however I can," Kath replied. "I wondered if you needed me to say a few words about the Good Neighbours scheme, so your guests understand just how valuable their donations will be to the local community here."

"No need," smiled Celia imperiously. "We have a professional master of ceremonies; the best in the South East of England. He will cover all the relevant material beautifully."

"But has he ever been to Hope Hall or seen the project in action?"

Celia gave Kath a withering look. "He really doesn't need to. He's got the picture. His particular skill is in working an audience, making sure that they respond emotionally as well as financially to his appeal. If you want us to make a lot of money for your little project today, it's best to let him get on with his job. As I said, I would appreciate your help over on the finance table, making sure all the payments go through smoothly." And with that, Celia turned on her heels, leaving behind a cloud of expensive fragrance and Kath bristling with shock at the way in which she'd just been spectacularly dismissed.

"Hello," said a familiar voice behind her. Richard Carlisle came up to greet her, a welcoming smile on his face.

"Oh, my goodness, I'm glad to see you!" sighed Kath. "I really don't know anyone here, and Celia's just explained to me that I have no significant role to play today, which feels a bit strange when the whole event is in aid of the Good Neighbours scheme, which I organize!"

Richard laughed. "Oh, don't mind Celia. She gets on her high horse on days like this when she wants everything to go smoothly."

"Of course, and we really are so grateful to her for opening her home up in this way. It's extremely kind of her."

"Our dear girl is not as relaxed with all these high-class guests as you might think. It's Douglas who's done the inviting."

"But he knows nothing about the scheme he's raising money for today!"

"That's of no consequence at all. He doesn't care what the occasion is. He just loves having an excuse to invite the great and the good of both county and country to an Ainsworth residence for tea! The Lord of the Manor role suits him very comfortably indeed."

Kath couldn't hide a wry grin. "I think I move in rather different circles."

"I think you would be an asset in whatever circle you chose."

She looked at him quizzically. "But isn't this *your* circle of friends too? You must be used to this."

"These are Celia and Douglas's business and social acquaintances mainly. I'm in agricultural machinery. That's a bit too down-to-earth for most of the people here! Now, do I see that your glass is empty? So's mine. Shall we walk over to the bar to see what's on offer?"

"Good idea," she laughed. "I'm really not that used to champagne. I think I might need a soft drink after this!"

"Will home-made elderflower cordial do? The cook here is renowned for her brew."

"That sounds delicious."

As Richard guided her over towards the drinks tent, she asked, "Isn't William here today? I thought he might be."

"You remember he was going off on that training course with the Sea Cadets in Portsmouth when we last met? Well, he's staying down in the area for a couple of weeks with old family friends of ours who've got their own boat. He goes there every summer holiday because he's grown up with their kids. In fact, their boy Stephen is probably William's best friend."

"How lovely for him! He'll certainly enjoy that. So you're rattling around at home with no teenager to look after at the moment, then."

He grinned widely. "It's bliss. No thumping music bouncing off the walls! I'm really enjoying the peace and quiet."

"Richard, darling, I need you!" The voice was unmistakeably Celia's. She was completely oblivious to Kath as her eyes fixed on the man standing beside her. "Diana's driving me mad, and those two boys of theirs certainly haven't learned any manners at that posh school they send them to! Worst of all, Douglas is being a pain in the neck trying to lord it over everything. This is *my* house and *my* party! I know if I say anything it'll only start a row. You're so good at smoothing things over with him. Be a love and go and have a word, please?"

Richard shot a look of apology towards Kath, which Celia noticed immediately.

"I thought you were supposed to be helping on the banking table, Kath. Have you checked in there yet?"

"That's not fair," said Richard. "Kath is the administrator of the scheme you're raising funds for today. She has much more important work to do mingling with your guests and answering what I'm sure will be many questions. I'll find someone suitable to oversee the banking table, if that's what's needed."

"You're right. You're always right, you wonderful, irritating man! I just thought she might like to make herself useful. Anyway, I can't think about that now. Darling, I need you to go and speak to Douglas. Sort him out, will you?"

As Celia took Richard's arm and purposefully led him away, he turned to grin at Kath, mouthing the words, "I'll be back!"

Kath took a very deep breath, paused for a few moments, then smoothed down her dress and hair and headed off into the crowd. Almost immediately, she was greeted by the familiar figure of the mayor who, along with his delightful wife, was very popular in the town. Other local dignitaries came to join them, and she found herself relaxing in their enjoyable company.

Before too long, the master of ceremonies announced that lunch was about to served, so would they all make their way to their tables, where waiters would be happy to take their orders. Kath moved back to her table to find that while Trevor had obviously been circulating, Mary hadn't moved at all, and there was now a row of three empty champagne glasses in front of her. A little worried, Kath bent over to check in with Mary, who responded by throwing her arms around her neck and greeting Kath as if she hadn't seen her for several years!

Thankfully, Trevor made his way back to the table at that moment, which was just as well as Kath had been allocated a seat on the other side of the table from them. She found herself sitting between two businessmen: one with an exclusive performance car garage in Guildford, and another who lived with his wife and family in Richmond but worked as a banker in the City. The former immediately started telling her about himself, outlining with great pride all the money he'd made from cars in the past few months, obviously thinking she'd be riveted and hugely impressed by his success. In fact, as she realized from the start that this was a monologue that wouldn't require her to respond in any way, Kath largely tuned out. After more than ten minutes, just as she felt her eyes begin to glaze over, she was delighted when the gentleman on her other side tapped her on the arm to offer her a bread roll, which she took gratefully as a cue to strike up an alternative conversation.

They chatted for a while about London, and Kath found herself explaining about her former role as Senior Administrator at one of the leading London hospitals. He knew the hospital well, and could even name some of the board members. He went on to explain that he was a partner at the large City firm that organized the hospital's pension arrangements.

"Of course. That's probably how you know Celia, then," said Kath. "I believe she runs the pension scheme at Apex Finance?"

"She does indeed, and it's a very significant investment portfolio. She's an impressive expert in her field."

Kath silently considered other adjectives she might choose to describe Celia, but decided it was better to keep her thoughts to herself. Instead she said, "Well, it's certainly very kind of you to come all this way in order to support our work with the local community here."

"Oh, is that what we're doing? There's always some sort of charity appeal, but I hadn't clocked which one it was this time. It doesn't really matter, because we all just like coming. This is one of those events where it pays to be seen. There's a lot of money sitting around these tables."

Kath was both slightly shocked by his offhand attitude towards the charity and pleased that however offhand the attendees were, the vulnerable and often very lonely people who benefited from the Good Neighbours scheme wouldn't care one jot where the money came from. They'd simply be grateful for it.

Lunch was exquisite, as plate after plate arrived in front of them on which there were tasty, beautifully displayed morsels with flavours that were difficult to define and mouth-wateringly delicious. After about an hour of sampling one sumptuous flavour after another, Kath had reached the point of thinking she would never be able to eat again. At that moment, just as coffee and petits fours were presented to every table, the master of ceremonies took over the proceedings, introducing the auction items that had been donated in aid of today's charity.

Without a note in sight, the MC faultlessly repeated the exact words Kath had written to describe the Good Neighbours scheme in their latest brochure. He was good. Celia certainly wasn't wrong about that, because he went on to speak in moving terms about how much difference this money would make to people in the area who lived dangerously isolated and often very lonely lives. Even Kath felt her eyes pricking with tears as he spoke; the MC was clearly adept at tapping into people's emotions to cajole money out of them. Well, let him! If he raised the money, she could get on with her job of making sure the proceeds were used to the best possible advantage.

As the MC got underway with a seemingly endless auction of exclusive and once-in-a-lifetime opportunities that just took Kath's breath away, she found herself looking for the first time at the top table, at which Celia was seated alongside a younger man with whom she shared an obvious family likeness. *That must be Douglas*, Kath thought, as she watched him cheering loudly, encouraging potential buyers, and noisily tapping a knife against his wine glass whenever a sale was made. Next to him was a strikingly beautiful woman who she figured must be his wife, Diana. The daughter of a wealthy landowner, she had been a debutante, Kath knew, and there was no denying the loveliness of her bone structure and her casually elegant style. Their two sons were not beside their parents, so were probably sitting among the crowd somewhere. In fact, the only other person at the top table was Richard Carlisle, sitting right next to Celia. Well, where else would he be but alongside his "other half"?

The auction was a very relaxed affair that went on for almost an hour, during which time Trevor was obviously becoming very worried about Mary's increasingly erratic behaviour. She rarely drank alcohol, but she'd certainly had her fill that afternoon!

"We'd better go," Trevor mouthed to Kath across the table.

Kath immediately got up, said her goodbyes to her nearest lunch companions, and went over to put her arm around Mary in a way that she hoped would make her inebriated state less obvious.

"Are you leaving already, Kath?" It was Richard speedily making his way over to her. "There's plenty more to come this afternoon. There's a great band on next."

Taking his cue, Trevor gently extricated Mary from Kath's arms and continued to lead his wife towards their car.

"Trevor and Mary were kind enough to give me a lift today. Unfortunately, Mary's feeling a bit unwell."

"The heat, I expect," said Richard.

"Well, it is a very warm afternoon," Kath tactfully replied.

"So, I'm not going to get a dance with you, then."

"I'm afraid not."

"We'll save that for another time. Take care, Kath. Oh, and you look lovely today, by the way."

Caught off guard for a moment, Kath almost forgot to answer. Finally, she said a brief goodbye and quickly turned away in the direction of the parked car.

Chapter 9

Ray and Shirley both arrived at Hope Hall early the following morning, Sunday, to clear up after a wedding party the day before. The guests had obviously done their best at the end of the evening, but it had clearly been a tired and rather disorganized affair.

Ray glanced at Shirley as she immediately headed for the cupboard to pull out all the equipment they needed to get the place sparkling again. "Most people would look at this mess and groan. You look at it with a great big grin on your face!"

Shirley stopped to look over at him. "Mad, isn't it? The sight of mess like this makes my fingers itch. I can't *wait* to clear it up. I just want everything to be shiny and clean, as it should be."

"That's my girl!" laughed Ray, grabbing a huge roll of heavy-duty black bags. "Oh, and by the way, your *boy* is doing okay too."

Shirley snapped upright. "Tyler? What do you mean by *okay*?"

"He's proving to be very useful. He's got a real talent for computers and he's brilliant at fixing things that go wrong, sorting out bits I can't fathom, and setting up easy ways for me to organize my work. He's helped Trevor out a lot too, and even Kath was impressed by the new booking system he suggested. You should be very proud of him."

"I'm his mother. I know him too well. Of course I'm proud if he's helping people, but I've also got a long memory."

"You're just waiting for him to get something wrong, you mean."

"Precisely. He's mucked up a lot of good opportunities in the past. Hope Hall is where I work. I won't tolerate him mucking up things here."

Ray's expression was affectionate as he gazed at her. "So far, so good, Shirley. What he's responded to most is recognition when he's done something really efficiently. I've found that the more I encourage him, the more confident and helpful he becomes."

"I nag him too much. That's what you're saying."

Ray laughed. "You? Nag?"

"Look, I know I'm tough on him. I have been with all my kids. But life's hard, and they need to understand that they're not always going to have Mum and Dad picking up the pieces after them. They've got to grow up and get on with being adults. No one can do that for them. We can't give them a rosy future. Nothing but hard work will get them that – and hard work has never really been on the agenda for Tyler."

"But it's horses for courses, isn't it?" Ray suggested. "Some of us are built to work physically hard. You and I are like that. We actually enjoy it. But I struggle with figures and paperwork, and those bloomin' computers drive me to distraction! Tyler is the other way round. He's got a good head for all those office procedures and technology, and surely that *is* the future for his generation. I think you should encourage him to get some proper qualifications in that whole area."

Shirley nodded, looking thoughtful. "He said something about college the other evening, but his dad wanted to watch a football match that was just starting, so Tyler gave up. They both ended up on the sofa in front of the TV instead."

"He's been reading up about the courses he could take, and what qualifications he needs to get a place."

"He's passed his GCSEs. He did quite well, really, but he just wanted to get out of school as quickly as possible, so Mick organized for him to get a labouring job at the place where he

176

works. He did all right for a couple of months, but then he started missing his shifts. They got rid of him pretty soon after that."

"Yes, he told me he's tried a few jobs."

"He did deliveries for a friend of ours who has a distribution business, then worked at the garage on the ring road for a while. He even tried doing night shifts in one of those warehouses on the industrial estate, but that didn't last long. Our Tyler definitely likes his sleep."

"I think that was just the wrong type of work for him. Those were the jobs he could *get*, rather than ones he could actually *enjoy*."

"And you think going to college might be the answer?"

"It might be an idea for you and Mick to talk it over with him. Tyler's done a lot of research, but he's not sure of what your reaction will be, so he's nervous about bringing it up."

Shirley pulled a face.

"Oh, come on, Shirl. You're terrifying! You even scare me."

"He knows he can always talk to me, though."

"What he doesn't know is whether you'll listen – *really* listen."

Shirley fell silent while she considered this.

"Anyway," continued Ray, "changing the subject completely, Kath's asked me to organize someone to put up a few posters around the town about the centenary of Hope Hall. After the official ceremony, we'll have the display here throughout the following week and there'll be some really great events and activities going on to reflect the history of this place.

"Peter at the council has organized a few public marketing spaces where we have permission to put up our posters, and he's even agreed that we can erect a really long banner on our own display stand in that lay-by – you know, the one on the bypass that lots of cars pull into because the coffee and bacon butty van is usually there? The traffic's always slow along that stretch of road in rush hour, so drivers will have time to take a good look at our poster while they're queuing. It's a fantastic opportunity for us."

"You can say that again!"

"But I need someone to put the posters up. I've asked Tyler."

"Tyler who doesn't like hard work – *that* Tyler?"

"He seemed quite keen. He got on to the computer straight away to look up the best design for the display stand."

"What, you mean he's got to build it?"

"He seems to think he can. Can he?"

"Actually, he probably could. Mick's great at carpentry, and Tyler's always taken an interest in learning about the right tools and techniques since he was a youngster."

"Apart from that one huge poster on the bypass, all the rest are just the usual size and can be slipped into the display frames that are already there."

"When's all this happening?"

"The posters are due to be delivered here today, so perhaps tomorrow."

"Well, now I know, I'll have a word with Mick. He could talk through Tyler's design for the lay-by display stand with him, just to make sure it'll all work."

"That's what I was hoping you'd say."

"Right," said Shirley, gazing around the messy hall and grabbing the biggest brush from the cupboard. "I'm off to have fun!"

Maggie avoided opening her laptop all weekend. Steph, Dale and little Bobbie came over on Sunday morning for one of her wonderful roast dinners. It became a leisurely family day, with Bobbie helping his dad mow his nanny's small patch of grass at the end of the garden. When Maggie bought the apartment, she had been relieved to hear that her responsibility regarding the large garden at the back of the house was conveniently limited, as the majority of it nearer the house was owned by the couple below, who were keen gardeners, leaving her a strip of grass at the bottom that was just big enough for a garden shed and a rotating washing line.

During the afternoon, Steph gave her a hand sorting through a couple of cardboard boxes that still remained unopened after the move, and putting a few more "wanted but not needed" items out of the way up in the attic space. After tea, when everyone had tucked into thick honey roast ham sandwiches and a Victoria sponge cake with fresh cream and real strawberries, it was nearing Bobbie's bedtime. As Maggie scooped the little boy up on to her lap to give him a goodbye hug, she noticed his trouser pocket seemed unnaturally bulky. Gingerly, she slid her fingers inside to pull out what looked like a half-eaten piece of cucumber, soggy chunks of Victoria sponge cake, several raisins and the remains of a small white chocolate lollipop.

"Bobbie, what's all this?" asked Maggie, pointing at his pocket.

He looked down at the pocket as if he didn't understand the question. "My snack hole, where I keep my snacks."

Smothering her giggles, Steph knelt down to investigate the other pocket, which was obviously another of Bobbie's "snack holes". Much to Bobbie's alarm, Maggie gathered up the sticky mess to throw it away, while Steph tried to explain to him that trouser pockets were really not made for sweets.

"What are they for, then?" Bobbie demanded to know.

About to answer that they were for handkerchiefs, keys and wallets, Steph looked down at the tiny pockets on her little boy's trousers and realized she couldn't think of one thing that could sensibly go in them. Instead, she smiled with relief as Dale stepped in to pull his son up for a piggyback ride, making sure his small arms were tightly clasped around Daddy's neck.

"Blow a kiss to Nanny!" said Dale.

"Night night, Nanny!" Bobby called as he and his dad disappeared through Maggie's front door, Bobbie squealing with delight as he rode downstairs on his father's back. Steph and her mum laughed and hugged before the family were finally all in the car and on their way.

The following morning, when she reflected on the rest of her evening, Maggie found herself recalling a phrase she'd come out with years earlier that had gone down in family history. It had been during one of those countless periods when she'd been on "yet another" diet, and Dave and the kids had caught her red-handed, tucking into a box of chocolate eclairs. Much to their mirth, she had defended herself by explaining, "I went into the cake shop, and I can't remember what happened next!"

Well, that more or less described the events that unfolded once Steph and family had gone home. Maggie knew she had pottered around the apartment for a while, clearing up the kitchen after the family visit, tackling a pile of ironing, which included a blouse she wanted to wear to work the following day, and poring over her favourite cookery books to dig out an old recipe she fancied trying again. She remembered thinking it was time to change the sheets on her bed, which was a job she hated, because years of experience had proved that her legs and arms were just too short to tackle the huge expanse of a king-sized duvet cover. Nevertheless, she knuckled down to the battle of the bedclothes with gusto, sighing with triumph as she gazed over the fresh new linen on the bed, thinking how nice it would be to slip into sheets that smelt of the hours they'd been blowing in the summer breeze in her garden. She had a shower. She tidied up the bathroom cabinet, which had been irritating her with its clutter, and then, glancing out of the window, she realized it had grown dark outside and it was time to draw the curtains in the front room.

And that was it! Sitting on the coffee table in the middle of that room was her laptop, and she couldn't quite remember what happened next. All she knew was that somehow, somewhere along the line, she ended up replying to Phil's email. She had been mulling over various possible responses in her mind for nearly two days by then, but had always ended up thinking it would simply be better not to reply. But that night, in a moment of complete madness after a cup of drinking chocolate and a coconut macaroon, she must have opened the laptop, found the email and started typing.

> Hi Phil
>
> What a surprise to hear from you after so long. I'm glad to hear you're doing well.
>
> I've thought about our walks to school each morning quite often lately because I recently moved to Linden Avenue. Do you remember Susan from my year who used to join us as we walked along this road? Well, her house has now been divided into apartments, and I've just bought the top one. I'm loving it here, and it's certainly brought back memories from our schooldays.
>
> I've lost touch with Susan now, but Sylvie and I are still good friends. Because she lives a good few miles away, she didn't get to the reunion, and I didn't either. Honestly, I didn't fancy it – a bit like you, I suppose.
>
> Anyway, I wish you well.

She didn't sign her name at the end. He had called her Megs, which sounded dainty and delicate. In reality, Maggie suited her better: down-to-earth and practical. The no-nonsense side of her nature had her finger hovering over the Send button for several seconds.

Then she gave it a push, shut the laptop and headed off to bed.

"You'll never believe how much Celia's garden party raised on Saturday!" exclaimed Trevor as he burst through Kath's office door on Monday morning. "£32,300!"

"What?" Kath sat back in her chair in amazement. "We can run our present service for a whole year on £32,300! That's a nice round figure, I must say. No loose change, then?"

Trevor grinned. "I don't think any of those auction bids were made in units of less than £100. They live in a different world, my dear Kath."

"They certainly do."

"Who cares, though, if it benefits our Good Neighbours scheme? Speaking of which, Celia asked if we would consider spending a significant portion of that money on a really specific item – something we might never be able to afford ourselves, like a minibus. If that seemed like a good idea, she has a contact who could get us a brand new minibus, purpose-built for the elderly or disabled, at a hugely discounted rate."

"Well, that would be wonderful. We've needed a decent minibus for ages, and to have one that caters for all sorts of disabilities would be just perfect. Are there any strings attached to that offer?"

"Two. Would we be okay with having an Apex Finance logo somewhere on the bodywork?"

"Of course. Provided that there's also a huge sign on the side that says HOPE HALL GOOD NEIGHBOURS SCHEME. What's the other condition?"

"Well, this one comes from Douglas, I reckon. Have we got, and I quote, 'a bunch of old ladies and gents who'd like to be photographed demonstrating the benefits of the new minibus, and would they mind having their picture in *Hello!* magazine'?"

Kath threw her head back and laughed out loud. "I think we'd have enough volunteers to fill a double-decker bus!" she spluttered when she could finally find her voice. "Say yes, Trevor! YES PLEASE!"

Just before the Food Bank opened for business that afternoon, Sheelagh had a phone call from Jackie at the Salvation Army. She'd just checked with her contact at the Family Tracing Service, but there was still no news that might help them identify and hopefully support the elusive Michael. They'd been making enquiries with the head offices of the supermarket chains that had branches in Basingstoke to see whether they could throw any light on a past employee who might fit Michael's description, but it was a slow business, complicated by data protection issues and other employee safeguards.

"Apparently," explained Jackie, "the HR managers they've been talking to at the supermarkets are all very understanding about the delicacy and urgency of the situation, but all the data protection rules might mean they're not able to help as much as they'd like. My contact at Family Tracing says it's just a matter of waiting now, in the hope that they may be able to unearth something that could be useful."

"I'm hoping Michael will put in an appearance this afternoon," replied Sheelagh. "Perhaps I can get him to say a bit more about himself. I really do hope so."

"Give me a ring later to let me know what happens. Bye, Sheelagh."

It turned out to be a particularly busy day at the Food Bank as a steady stream of regulars called in to collect the rations they needed for themselves and their families. Sheelagh found herself engrossed in an emotional and complex conversation with a single mother of three children who was having problems on every level: with a bullying ex-husband, credit and loan companies, the Council Tax department at the town hall, and a private landlord who had started eviction proceedings against her after several months of her not paying rent.

It was only as the woman stood up to take her family over to help themselves to the buffet, which offered hot pies and sausage rolls that day, as well as baked potatoes, beans, cheese, tuna, and a variety of fruits and salads, that Sheelagh suddenly caught a glimpse of Michael hovering around the door. Quickly gathering up the plastic bag of food she had already prepared for him, she poured out two cups of sugared tea and walked out of the main door as casually as she could manage. For a moment she peered around in search of him, worried he might have slipped away, but suddenly, almost as if he'd been watching out for her, he pulled out a little from behind a large tree that lined the pavement some distance down from the main entrance to Hope Hall. Giving him an encouraging smile, she went to sit on the low wall nearest that tree and put the two cups of tea down. She then delved into the carrier bag, pulling out a couple of packs of sandwiches, which she also laid out on the wall where he could easily reach them.

"How about sitting here, Michael?" she suggested. "Then you'll be able to see if there's anything here you fancy. There's plenty more in the hall, if you tell me what you'd like."

She didn't look at him directly, but instead busied herself pulling out some biscuits, cakes and other savouries from the plastic bag. She didn't really expect him to join her, so it was with surprise and some relief that she sensed him inching closer, finally sinking down on to the wall, where he grabbed a tea, took several large gulps, then reached out to tear apart the packaging of the nearest box of sandwiches.

Sheelagh said nothing, just let him get on with the urgent

business of eating.

"Do you need more tea?" she asked at last. "We've got some hot meat pies inside too, chicken or beef and onion. Choose your favourite, or I'll bring you one of each if you can't decide."

He looked at her with instant interest. "Both," he grunted.

"We've got some beans to go with them. Any sauce needed? Red or brown?"

From his nod, she got the message that he'd like anything that was going, so this time as Sheelagh made her way over to the hall she felt reassured that Michael would be waiting for her when she got back. She loaded two meat pies and a huge spoonful of baked beans on to a plate, grabbed a knife and fork, and walked back to join him. He was just finishing his second cup of tea as she placed the plate on the wall beside him.

Again, she allowed him to eat in silence until she sensed he was feeling replete enough to suggest conversation might be possible.

"I've been looking out for you since we last met. It's good to see you today. How have you been?"

He shrugged, and kept on eating.

"I can see how much you're enjoying that meal. Do you manage to find something to eat every day?"

He shrugged again. "Sometimes."

"Do you mean that you sometimes have nothing to eat all day long?"

"I've got a few bits stashed away. It depends what I'm doing. I'm not always in town."

"Oh? I thought you were probably living nearby."

He snorted. "I don't like towns. Too many people."

"People who might be able to give you a hand, though. People who hate the thought that you haven't got enough to eat. People who'd like to help – like me."

He looked up at her, as if he was considering what she'd

just said, then abruptly turned back to concentrate on what he wanted to eat next.

"Why should you worry?" he said eventually. "I'm nothing to you."

"Well," she said slowly, choosing her words carefully, "you're right. You and I have only just met. But I wonder who might *really* be worried about you – your family perhaps? If you were part of *my* family I'd like to think that someone was looking out for you, caring how you are, and thinking about what you might need, even if you had your reasons for staying distant from us."

He stiffened, keeping his eyes resolutely on the food on his plate.

"Are you married, Michael?"

"Not any more."

"Children?"

"None that need me."

"And what do *you* need?"

His eyes flashed with anger. "I don't need some do-gooder busybody trying to stick her nose into my business."

Sheelagh immediately backed off, changing the subject when she spoke again. "We've got some new men's clothes in this week. Do you need anything? Shoes? Underwear? Trousers and tops? We had pillows and bedding in too. Any good to you?"

"Shoes."

"What size?"

"Ten."

"There are quite a few pairs there. Do you want to come and take a look yourself?"

"No."

"Okay. I'll bring a few bits out. Would you like another food box, like last time? Anything in particular that would be useful?"

"Some razors."

"What about other toiletries? Shampoo, deodorant?"

She looked up to see that he was smiling a little as he replied, "Some of that body spray that makes you smell better."

She smiled in return. "I'll see what I can do. But we do have a shower here, if you'd like to use it any time. Or there's one at the Salvation Army hostel, of course. Do you ever go there?"

"I have been. Not now it's summer though."

"Why? Isn't a comfy bed a good idea whatever time of the year it is?"

"I don't mind the summer nights."

"Are you sleeping somewhere dry and warm?"

"Well, it's got a lot of unintentional ventilation, shall we say?"

"Not weatherproof, then?"

"It used to be. It was a good place then. It's pretty old now."

"Is it a building?"

He shook his head.

"A shed perhaps?"

"Stop asking. I've said all I'm going to say."

"Then I'll just say this," replied Sheelagh. "My name is Sheelagh Hallam, and if you need anything, I want you to let me know." She pushed a piece of paper along the wall towards him. "That's my number. Get someone to ring me. Or you could just ring my number twice and put the phone down straight away. I'll know it's you and call you back straight away. I won't mind. Any time, about anything at all. I'll worry a lot less if I know you're staying somewhere safe and secure. And if, one day, you feel you'd like to share some of the things you're facing with a friend who will respect your need for privacy, then I'm here."

She thought he might just get up and go. Instead, he stared at the piece of paper for a short while before reaching out and stuffing it into his pocket.

"Do you fancy coming in to take a look at what clothes are there?" she suggested again.

He shook his head. "Just grab me anything. And a pillow would be nice. A duvet too, if you have one."

She smiled at him. "I'll go and see what I can find. Will you do me a favour?"

He shrugged indifferently.

"Don't sleep rough if you can have a bed. Go to the Salvation Army. Have a good meal. Take care of yourself, Michael – please?"

He said nothing and the silence stretched out between them.

"Size ten. You remember what I said?"

She smiled. "I remember. And *you* remember what I said too!"

When she turned on her laptop the following evening, Maggie's stomach did a flip as she scanned the list of emails waiting for her. He'd answered! Sitting back for a few moments and taking a big breath to calm her nerves, she finally found the courage to open the message and start to read.

Hi Megs

It's good to hear from you! You're right, school was a long time ago and I'm aware I've done a very poor job of keeping in touch with old friends. Ever since I wrote that first email, I've been wondering why on earth I ever imagined you'd have any recollection of me at all. I can't tell you what a relief it was to hear from you after that, just to know that I hadn't made a complete fool of myself!

Perhaps you'll think me odd for saying that I felt a bit nervous about digging up the past. It's not that I haven't got many happy memories of my schooldays and living at home with the family. It just seems like another life. So much has happened since that I hardly recognize the young lad I was then.

Fancy you living in Linden Avenue now! Those houses always seemed so roomy and stylish to me, because they were built in such a different way from the Victorian terraced houses on our estate. I always loved looking at buildings when we were at school, trying to work out why they chose that particular design, or what the problems might have been when they were in the process of building. You won't be surprised to hear, then, that I've been an architect all these years, and I've loved every minute of it. I'm a partner in a practice in Chichester now, but I worked for a big design firm in London for quite a while, which gave me some wonderful international experience. I've designed and supervised projects in the Arab States, across Europe, India and South America. I was abroad more than I was ever at home. Then I met my wife Sandra and we got married in 1997, and when, after a couple of years, our first son was on the way, I realized it was time to clip my wings and settle down to family life.

We had three children, David and our two younger girls, Melanie and Sarah. They're all grown up now. David's a bright lad. He did a joint degree in computer science and Japanese, would you believe? It was a great idea, though, because he's now based in Tokyo working for a British company that designs electronic components for manufacturing machinery. He's going out with a Japanese research scientist who's really lovely. He's blissfully happy and earns an absolute fortune – so he's okay! Melanie's next. She's just 22 and married her childhood sweetheart, Simon, earlier this year. Simon's working in an estate agent's in Bromsgrove up near Birmingham, so I don't see them as often as I'd like to these days.

There's so much more to say, but I'm probably boring you already. It would be much more interesting for me to hear about you and your family. Joe tells me you're the most marvellous baker, and that your cakes are out of this world. I've always had a sweet tooth, so that sounds like heaven to me!

I'd love to hear from you again if you'd like to keep in touch. I'll look forward to hearing your news.

All the very best
Phil

Maggie read through the email a couple of times before sitting back and gazing at the screen.

He sounded lovely. He was friendly, successful and a devoted family man. But what was he doing writing to her? Did his wife know? She didn't get much of a mention. Perhaps she was just really easy-going about his friendships, but how would she feel if this developed into a regular exchange of emails, even if it were only once in a while? Maggie doubted she'd be so happy about that.

And when he said how much more interesting it would be to hear about her, he had no idea how wrong he was! The "Megs" he imagined didn't actually exist. Instead, there was just plain old Maggie, recently dumped and divorced, with self-esteem issues and a very sweet tooth that had created quite enough problems already, thank you!

No, this contact wouldn't be going any further. She pushed the laptop away and switched on the TV in time for the main evening news. The newscaster was speaking in urgent tones about the events of the day, which were dramatic and challenging.

Maggie didn't hear a word of it.

"He's bailed on us again!"

There was an uncharacteristic hardness in Andy's voice as he and the other members of Friction waited in the back room of the King's Head for their lead singer to arrive.

"We've wasted half an hour hanging around for him already." Drummer Nigel's irritable comment was at odds with his usually relaxed and easy-going nature. "I promised I'd meet up with my brother after this, so why don't we just get started without him?"

"I don't think we should bother with Carlos any more," grumbled Jake, picking up his rhythm guitar and fastening it on to his shoulder. "We can all sing reasonably well; enough to belt out some really strong harmonies at any rate. We've got Graham too, and honestly I'd choose your vocals over Carlos's any time, mate."

"But we need him, don't we?" asked Andy. "I mean, as much as I hate to admit it, the girls do seem to like him."

"I think the girls like *all* of us," retorted Jake. "In fact, I think audiences in general like us because we're just a group of guys who want to play decent music that entertains the people who come to hear us. I know Carlos likes to think it's all about him being a babe magnet, but we're actually a *great* band. That's why I like playing in Friction, because of you guys. We all love music and we're good at what we do. The only one without any training or talent is Carlos."

"So, what are we going to do about it?" Nigel's question hung in the air as they all considered the possibilities.

"I think we should get rid of him," Jake said with a determined gleam in his eye.

"How?" asked Graham. "He loves being the centre of attention. He's not going to give up singing with Friction voluntarily."

"We'll have to make him want to leave then," said Andy thoughtfully.

191

"He's got a terrifying temper," said Graham. "It'll be World War Three if we get this wrong."

"Then we'll have to be really subtle about it." A slow smile spread across Andy's face.

"Have you thought of something?" asked Graham.

"You know what? I think I have!"

The posters for the centenary celebrations had arrived safely. Twenty of them were to go in display cabinets at bus stops around the High Street and in the shopping centre, and the large banner needed to be erected in the lay-by on the ring road.

True to her word after the conversation with Ray, Shirley made a point of telling Tyler how pleased she was to hear how his work with the Hope Hall computers was proving helpful. She also said that she'd heard about the centenary posters he was going to circulate, and how he was planning to create his own wooden display structure for the banner. Anxious to impress her, Tyler rushed to show her and his dad the plans he'd come up with to build something large enough to show the banner off to its best advantage, while also being sturdy enough to withstand the worst of the British summertime weather. He'd already built most of it in Ray's workshop at Hope Hall, so Mick went down with him to see how the project was coming along.

As father and son arrived home two hours later, Mick gave Shirley a cheery thumbs-up and a big smile to reassure her that Tyler really was working along the right lines.

On Friday morning, Mick added Tyler to his van insurance so he could transport the structure to the lay-by. Tyler was used to driving his old Ford Fiesta, but this van was a much bigger challenge, and his heart thumped as he backed out of the drive under the eagle eyes of his parents. A mile or so down the road, though, he felt as if he was really getting the measure of the van. It was larger and wider, but it was also newer and more manoeuvrable. In fact, in some ways it was a good deal easier to drive than his shaky old banger.

His optimism sank a little as he approached the lay-by. The butty van wasn't there, but there was a truck parked towards the far end of the pull-in, leaving space for perhaps three or four other vehicles behind it at most. Tyler had thought very carefully about the positioning of the banner, and had decided it would be most visible if it were right at the start of the lay-by, closest to the road. So he gingerly pulled the van into the middle of the available space, leaving the area where he planned to erect the banner frame clear so he could get a good view of its position as he worked. He shunted backwards and forwards a few times, but it was soon clear that reversing a van was quite a different experience from parking his small car, and after three attempts he gave up trying to park in a straight line, and leapt out. The van was sticking out at an awkward angle, but he'd only be there for a few minutes.

He opened up the back doors of the van and pulled out the various components of the display board, which were all ready to be fixed together on site. Then he climbed up inside the van to collect the tools he needed, completely oblivious to the fact that a Volvo estate with a middle-aged lady at the wheel had just driven into the lay-by looking for a space to park. Because the poster frame was now in the space at the beginning of the lay-by, and Tyler's clumsy parking was taking up nearly two spaces in the middle, she had to try back into the small space between Tyler's van and the truck. Eventually, red-faced with frustration, she pulled out again and slid on to a piece of wasteland at the very far end. Then, after several loud blasts on her car horn, she got out and started marching back down the lay-by to have a word with the inconsiderate driver who had abandoned his van in a terrible position and prevented anyone else from parking there.

Tyler heard her car horn and peered around the back door, immediately realizing what he'd done. Anxious to explain and apologize, he jumped straight out of the back of the van and started running to meet her.

But all the unfortunate woman saw was a strange young man storming towards her wielding a sledgehammer and a wooden stake. Screaming hysterically, she turned tail, ran as if her life depended on it, and drove off in a cloud of dust.

Chapter 10

"Didn't We have a lov-er-ly time. the day We Went to Southsea!"

The singalong was in full swing as the coach wound its way through the outskirts of Portsmouth towards the popular old seaside resort of Southsea. The thirty Grown-ups' Lunch Club members, plus Shirley, Liz and a group of volunteer family members who'd come along to help, had chattered and sung old favourites all the way down, occasionally knowing the words, but mostly filling in the gaps with a lot of la-la-las.

"Would you like me to take you on the pretty route to Southsea?" asked Reg, the coach driver, over the tannoy. "Do you fancy taking a look at some of the sights of this old naval town of Pompey on the way?"

"Yes!" came the general reply.

"Make it quick," hissed Vera. "I need a wee!"

Ida gave Vera a disapproving stare from across the aisle. "You're not being very ladylike, Vera. There are gentlemen present."

"On this bus?" chuckled Percy from the seat in front of her. "No chance of that!"

"Anyone here been in the navy?" continued Reg.

There were several men's voices throughout the coach who acknowledged they'd been naval men.

"My first hubby was a naval rating," another lady said. "The blighter ran off with a wren! Never trust a sailor – that's what I say!"

"Were any of you based at HMS *Vernon* in the old days?" asked Reg.

"It was the torpedo base," came a comment from the back. "I had two tours of duty there."

"Well, you can do your shopping there now. Look, it's become the Gunwharf Quays retail park."

"Are we going shopping?" asked one lady at the front hopefully.

"Have they got a loo there?" asked Vera.

"Vera!" hissed Ida.

"And who remembers the dockyard?"

Several men answered together about their time there.

"Well," said Reg, "a bit like all of us, our old dockyard has become historic. Portsmouth Dockyard is now a place the kiddies can visit to find out about our maritime past."

"I worked there for about ten years," said Robert, who was sitting next to his old friend John. "I'm not sure I like being thought of as a piece of history!"

"Inside the gates you can visit King Henry VIII's flagship, the *Mary Rose*, which they raised from the floor of the Solent nearly forty years ago now. It had been down there since 1545, when King Henry VIII watched from Southsea as it sailed out with hundreds of men on board to face a huge French fleet waiting alongside the Isle of Wight, ready to attack. Who knows what happened? Was it hit by a French cannon? Did it just topple over because it was overloaded and top-heavy? Or was it just human error?"

"It must have been a man driving," cackled a woman's voice from the middle of the coach.

"Well, the part of the ship they managed to bring up more than four centuries later is on display inside the dockyard now," continued Reg. "But we've not got time to go in, so give it a wave and we'll keep moving!"

"Is there a ladies' around here somewhere?" Vera was pleading now.

Ida rolled her eyes and deliberately looked out of the window.

"See that archway over there?" shouted one man on the right. "The best tattoo artist in Pompey used to work in that tunnel. It was called the Hole in the Wall, and I've still got his handiwork on my arm. Look! He engraved the name of my ship alongside the name of my lovely wife, Brenda. It brings tears to my eyes even now whenever I look at it."

"Yeah, I cried when a tattoo artist got to work on my arm with his needle too," said Robert. "It bloomin' well hurt!"

"So now, ladies and gents, we're heading in the direction of the Old Town of Portsmouth. Back in medieval times, these old cobbled streets used to be a hive of vice and debauchery. Nowadays, it's a great place for traditional pubs and quaint tearooms."

"I could do with a cuppa!" called Flora.

"Me too," agreed Betty. "Are we nearly there yet?"

"Will there be facilities where we're going?" Vera pleaded. "I'm really desperate…"

Ida turned to glare at Vera again with a look that said it all.

"Hold on," instructed Reg, "we're not far off now. Take a look to the right to see the traditional funfair, which has been a familiar sight here on Clarence Pier since the 1960s, when the old Victorian pier was refurbished after it was damaged in the air raids during the war."

"My Eric kissed me for the very first time on that big wheel," sighed Connie.

"That's a coincidence," quipped Percy. "I was slapped round the face for the first time on that big wheel!"

"*So* common," huffed Ida, turning away from Percy as if he were a bad smell under her nose.

"Keep looking," said Reg, "because Southsea Castle's coming up on the right. That's where King Henry was standing when the *Mary Rose* sank right in front of him. But this other building coming up on the right-hand side might be of greater interest to some of you. It's called The D-Day Story. As you know, this area of coastline was right at the heart of the action on D-Day, and it's all brought to life in there. So, if you've got time this afternoon after you've hit the big wheel, I reckon a few of you might enjoy paying that exhibition a visit."

"I'm going to embarrass myself, I really am!" wailed Vera.

"Sit tight, Vera!" boomed Shirley's voice from her seat at the front next to the driver. "We're heading for the Queen's Hotel, which is just on the other side of the common there. That's where the loos are. That's where we're going now to sit in the garden with a cup of tea and one of Maggie's wonderful packed lunches. While we're all eating, we can work out who wants to go where in Southsea; who wants to do their own thing and who might need reminding that they've got to get back to this same hotel at four o'clock for our magnificent high tea. If you don't remember that, we might just end up going home without you! So, wait until the coach has come to a complete standstill, then gather up any bits and pieces you might need this afternoon. Reg says you're welcome to leave anything you don't need on the coach. And while we're at it, can we have a big thank you to Reg please, for his unscheduled detour around Portsmouth and the fascinating commentary?"

A cheer and a chorus of "Thank you, Reg!" went up around the coach.

Fifteen minutes later, the Hope Hall visitors were all sitting in the hotel's lovely enclosed garden happily munching their way through their packed lunches.

"It's like taking out a class full of infants!" muttered Shirley, sinking her teeth into one of Maggie's home-made pasties.

Liz, Maggie's assistant, grinned. "Ah, I don't mind. It's a nice day out for me, and I like this lot. Most of them have a great sense of humour—"

"Some of them can be a bit *too* cheeky, like Percy," interrupted Shirley.

"And then there's Ida, who doesn't seem to have a funny bone in her whole body."

"Oh, Ida's scary – and that's really saying something coming from me!"

"But they've been through a lot, haven't they, this generation?" mused Liz. "Any of them over the age of seventy-five would have been born during the war years. Their childhoods must have been pretty tough as life got started again. Just think how many families must have been without a husband or father. And imagine what it was like for couples who'd been apart for years, leading very different lives. Would they still feel the same way about each other once they had to settle back into married life again? There wasn't much money, jobs were hard to get, and they were still rationed for food and groceries for years, weren't they? It's all so different nowadays, especially for young people with all the technology they constantly have at their fingertips. Everything's available at the press of a button on their mobiles. Just think of all those things they already know that we never will."

Shirley grunted. "Oh yes, the generation that thinks they know everything. Look at Tyler! He won't listen to a word I say. We've *lived* and learned a lot along the way. Experience is a great

199

teacher. So why don't kids ever listen and learn from an older, wiser generation?"

Liz laughed. "I bet every parent from every age has said that at some time or other."

Shirley glanced at her wristwatch. "Time to get going!" she announced, standing up and putting two fingers in her mouth to give a piercing whistle. After an initial squeal of shock, everyone in the party looked at her in surprise.

"Now I've got your attention, let me just talk you through the options for this afternoon. There are several groups going in different directions. If you'd like to go to The D-Day Story, Liz is in charge of that. Anyone wanting to walk along the prom and through the gardens, Donna – who's waving her arm over there in the corner – is leading that group. There's another group making for South Parade Pier, where you can sit in the sunshine, watch the waves and try to stop the seagulls munching your cup of fresh cockles! Now, I gather some of you ladies would like to look around the shops, in which case follow Brenda. I'm going to be in charge of the bunch of rascals who've opted to go to the funfair, because knowing who's shown an interest in that – and Percy, I'm looking directly at you here – I think that group is most likely to get into trouble! Any questions?"

"Which one of those has the most loos?" asked Vera.

"This one, I reckon. Why don't you just make yourself comfortable on the front veranda of the hotel, order a pot of tea and watch the world go by? Then you'll be first in the queue not just for the ladies', but for our high tea as well."

Vera beamed with pleasure at the suggestion.

"Right, find your groups, and don't forget to be back here by four o'clock at the latest. We won't be saving you any pastries or cream cakes if you're late!"

Organized chaos ensued as everyone found the group they

wanted to join, but ten minutes later, with the exception of Vera who was sitting on the veranda humming to herself as she basked in the July sunshine, everyone else had headed off in whichever direction they had chosen.

One other person failed to join a group. Ida had deliberately taken herself off to the ladies' as the various parties gathered, and only reappeared once she was sure everyone else had gone their separate ways. Tidying her jacket and placing her handbag neatly over her arm, she stepped out of the hotel and turned slightly to the left as she walked across the common, which stretched out in front of the hotel towards the sea.

A few minutes later she had reached her goal: an area of green several hundred yards further on from the war memorial, which stood proudly on the edge of the grass as it lined the shore, looking out across the Channel. Finding a rather battered old park bench that stood off to one side, she took a seat, laid her bag flat on her lap and gazed out to sea. Lost in her thoughts, she had no idea how long she'd been sitting there before she became aware of someone taking a seat at the other end of her bench. She looked up in alarm, annoyed that her peace and quiet had been shattered. Her alarm turned to frustrated fury when she identified the intruder.

"Percy Wilson!" she spluttered angrily. "Will you *please* leave me alone?"

"You're on my bench," he replied. "*I'd* like to be alone."

"It's not your bench. I was here first."

"No, you weren't, my dear lady. I've been coming to sit on this bench for years."

Ida stared at him. "So have I."

They looked at each other, the anger draining away from them both.

"You lost someone, did you?" Percy asked softly.

"My mother did. Her brother Jack. I never knew him. I was only a baby when D-Day happened, but when the news came through that Uncle Jack never even made it off the beaches it hit the family hard. For as long as I can remember, my mother was deeply affected by the loss of her brother. More than that, Grandma was never the same after she lost Jack. He was her only son, and she had no one else to share her grief with but the child she had left, my mother."

"What about your grandfather? Losing his son must have hit him hard too."

"Oh, I only ever remember Gramps as very remote and uncaring. I suppose you could say he was there in body, but in a world of his own."

"In the trenches, was he, during the Great War?"

"He was."

"My gramps was just the same. Those men went through hell. It changed them. They weren't the same husbands when they got back home."

Ida nodded with understanding. "You're right. In some ways, I don't think Grandpa ever really left the trenches. He saw enemies everywhere and that included us. From the time I was small, I can remember him flying into a terrible temper for no reason I could tell."

"Was he violent?"

"He didn't use his fists, but he glared as if he hated us, and his words were like daggers. There were so many times over the years when I'd find Mother working away in the kitchen with tears rolling down her cheeks at something Gramps had said or done."

"Did they live with you?"

"In the house next door. It *felt* as if they lived with us. My own dad hated that, although he was too nice to say anything. He was a lovely man, soft as sugar, but clever too. He was an accountant, you know. So when they started building that new estate on the other side of the park after the war, he finally put his foot down and made the decision to buy a house there. We were all much happier then, and it gave Grandma somewhere to come and spend several hours each day, away from Gramps' constant outbursts and bad temper."

"And this bench? Why are you here?"

"Jack left on those D-Day landing crafts from this bit of coastline, so it was Grandma who first started coming here as near to June 6th as she could manage every year. And my mother would come with her, so that meant bringing my little brother Jimmy and me along as well. We loved it. For us it was a great day out, all this grass and the sea to paddle in too. This huge memorial was already here then. They built it after the First World War as a tribute to all that was lost. 'A Memorial to the Missing', they called it. Well, my gramps lost his mind, and Uncle Jack lost his life – and our family never stopped missing them both."

"And you still come?"

"Not so much now. I don't travel well on my own these days, so this outing was a godsend. I was determined to slip away and spend some time here if I could."

"It's a good place to sit and remember."

Ida nodded and the two of them sat together in silence for several minutes before Ida spoke again. "And you?"

"I come and talk to my Margaret here."

"I remember Margaret. We were in the same class at school. I was jealous of her ginger curls."

He sighed. "She was always a real beauty. Far too good for the likes of me."

Ida smiled. "That's my line, isn't it? Margaret was definitely far too good for you! She had a queue of young men hoping she'd look their way, but she chose you, Percy Wilson, the biggest flirt of all!"

He chuckled. "Well, I wasn't so bad, was I, Miss Hoity Toity? I seem to recall that you and I even had a dalliance at one time."

"We did. A very *short* dalliance. I really wasn't interested."

His smile softened as he looked at her. "Neither was I, so that worked out just right then."

Her eyes held his gaze for a few moments before she took up the conversation again. "Did you and Margaret come here a lot?"

"She loved the seaside. This was her special place. She always said she wished we'd had children to come here with us."

"No youngsters for you two, then?"

"It just didn't happen. There were no miscarriages, no near misses at all. It just never happened."

"And the doctors couldn't help?"

"It was one of those things, they said, and that's how we looked at it. Margaret was a wonderful wife and we had a good life together. I still miss her every minute of every day. Coming here without her, well, it's…"

To Ida's alarm, his eyes filled with rheumy tears. She fumbled in her handbag to draw out a neatly ironed linen handkerchief, but by the time she produced it, he'd wiped his eyes with the back of his shirt cuff in hasty embarrassment.

"If you tell anyone you've seen me crying, I'll tell them how enthusiastic you were about kissing me all those years ago!"

A smile twitched at the corners of Ida's lips. "It's a deal."

The two of them sat together, each alone with their thoughts as the seagulls circled the skies above them.

"Sheelagh, it's Jackie. I've had some news from my contact at the Family Tracing Service."

"I'm all ears!"

"Well, as I said, the supermarkets have to toe the data protection line, but it was quite clear that the area manager from one of the biggest chains was very sympathetic to my reason for calling. She thinks it's very likely that Michael was based at their superstore on the outskirts of Basingstoke."

"How do we know that?"

"Well, she rang me back yesterday afternoon to say she couldn't tell me anything herself, but that she'd passed my phone number on to a colleague of hers in the town. If that colleague chose to ring me privately of her own accord, that was nothing at all to do with the company."

"And did that colleague ring?"

"I got a call last night from a lady who preferred not to give her name. Unofficially, though, she told me in confidence that, since the store opened, she has held the position of Personal Assistant to the manager of the huge twenty-four-hour retail unit they've recently opened on the outskirts of Basingstoke."

"There's only one place I can think of like that," commented Sheelagh. "Bob and I called in there when we were coming back from visiting my sister-in-law who lives not far from that store. It's absolutely enormous."

"It certainly is, and these new superstores are still breaking ground in terms of deciding what retail techniques work best in an outlet of such capacity. So when that one opened with a great fanfare just under a year ago, a bright new manager was brought in to oversee the operation."

"Michael?"

"Well, that manager *was* called Michael, and he's no longer there now. He left under a cloud about six months back."

"What happened?"

"There were a lot of local problems apparently. The building itself wasn't finished on time, and they were still trying to rectify some structural, wiring and plumbing problems on the day the store actually opened. Then the agency they'd called in to recruit local staff were very slow at the job, and that meant they were short of personnel at all levels from the very beginning. And I gather the council weren't as helpful as they might have been, so some of the decisions they needed to make about flow of traffic, parking arrangements, refuse collection and security of the site took much longer to come through than had been expected."

"And all of that responsibility fell on to the shoulders of the new store manager?"

"Who apparently was extremely experienced and excellent at his job. But then, on the day of the big opening, everything started to fall apart. When the bakery department switched on their ovens in the early hours of the morning, it fused the whole electrical system, and they had no power at all until halfway through the day. There weren't enough overnight staff to get the shelves properly stocked, so there were glaring gaps along every aisle. The ladies' toilets were declared out of order; the new cashiers hadn't got to grips with the intricacies of the tills, so there were long queues at every aisle – and a couple of customers had a proper punch-up outside the front door because of a disabled parking bay that should have been properly labelled, but wasn't. That gave the local press a great photo for the front page at the top of their lead article, which declared the store was too big, badly planned, inefficiently organized and not needed or wanted by local people because it threatened the future of all their High Street shops."

"Oh dear. Well, if it was our Michael trying to cope with all that lot, no wonder it was too much for him."

"Absolutely right. He worked round the clock for months in an effort to get everything running smoothly, and for the most part he was successful. But then head office started having a go at him because the sales revenues were down on their corporate projections. They needed the store to show high sales figures right from the start, and it was Michael's job to push up the income. And he really tried. He came up with all sorts of special promotions and incentives, but it was a bit like climbing uphill through treacle because, for that local community, a lot of damage had already been done. They hadn't enjoyed their initial visits. Improvements were too slow, explanations were unsatisfactory, and the huge complexity of the place made them complain that they couldn't find anything they'd actually come in to buy."

"An impossible situation for any manager."

"And in the end it was too much for him. He wasn't sleeping. He never seemed to find time to eat properly. He became tetchy, and handled some personnel situations in a way that created more problems than it solved. There was a lot of grumbling about him from staff at all levels and that obviously affected his confidence because he sensed people thought he wasn't up to the job."

"Do we know anything about his home life?"

"Apparently, he has a wife. I'm not sure if there are any children. The lady who rang me couldn't really say, because work was so constantly busy that she didn't meet the family or get to know them at all. But as his personal assistant, she certainly recognized the immense pressure her boss was under. He seemed to be at work morning, noon and night, rarely going home unless she actually pushed him out of the door. That can't have been easy for his wife."

"What was the final breaking point?"

"Without warning, one of the big bosses came down from head office, and he didn't come alone. He brought with him a new troubleshooter manager to take over the running of the store. The boss then told Michael he was immediately relieved of his duties. He was to take garden leave for the next two months, after which time the company would consider whether they had any further need for his services."

"Oh, what a stab in the back!"

"Michael was destroyed by that news. He said very little. He didn't even go back to his office to collect his personal things. He just walked out, left his company car in the car park and disappeared."

"You mean, he didn't go home?"

"From that day to this, no one's seen or heard anything of him. The lady on the phone was terribly upset when she told me that. I could hear she was choking back the tears. She blames herself for not realizing how badly depressed he was. She felt she should have supported him more. That's why she offered to break company protocol and speak privately to me, in the hope that we might have news of him at last."

"And have we? Are we absolutely sure he's our man?"

"She sent me a photo. Take a look. I've just forwarded it to you."

Sheelagh took the phone away from her ear so she could check her messages. The one from Jackie was at the top. She opened it immediately. It showed the image of a smart-suited, middle-aged executive with a confident air and a warm smile. It didn't look a bit like the shuffling, scruffy, filthy Michael she knew.

But without a doubt it was definitely him.

Four days after his last email, Phil Coleman wrote again.

He's insistent, thought Maggie, *but whatever he says I won't reply.* She didn't like the idea of a married man getting friendly with another woman without his wife being involved in the conversation too. That was how these things started. All very innocent at the beginning, but she knew from bitter experience where these innocent encounters could lead. She deleted the message and tried not to think about it again.

The following morning, she checked her emails as usual before leaving for work. Half a dozen items had come in overnight, mostly adverts that arrived in her inbox every day, except for the one at the very top. It was from her ex-husband, Dave. With shaking fingers, she clicked to open the message.

> Hi Maggie
>
> I hope you're okay. Darren tells me your new flat is great. I'm pleased that you are now happy and settled. I'd like to say I'm happy and settled too, but that wouldn't be quite true. We found a house Mandy really likes, but we're a bit short of what we need to buy it, even after I put in all the money I got from my share of our house sale. But I'm applying for an extra loan now, so fingers crossed that goes through. The repayments will be crippling, especially with a big mortgage to cover for the next twenty years. I'd forgotten how much mortgages cost every month, especially as you and I had finished paying ours off – a couple of years ago, wasn't it? You always dealt with our bills, so I can't quite remember when we were finally mortgage free.
>
> I'm trying to get a few delivery jobs in the evenings to boost our income a bit, but I just find I'm tired all the time. The kids are really noisy, so it's difficult to sleep whenever I can find an hour during the day. They seem to be constantly arguing too. I don't remember Steph and Darren being like that. Were they? And, of course, there's a new baby now. Aurora is really sweet. I think she looks a bit like Steph when she was little, although Mandy didn't like it when I said so. I know how you

209

like babies, so I'll send over a picture so that you can see what you think. Mandy's still feeling exhausted from the birth. She says it always takes her months before she feels anywhere near normal again. She needs a lot of support and rest right now.

I probably shouldn't say this, but I do miss you, Mags. In spite of everything, we were always good friends, weren't we? I could do with a chat with my good friend now. Anyway, I'd love to see your new flat. Well, more than that, I'd love to see you. Perhaps I could pop over for a cuppa one day soon. What do you think?

That's all I need to say really. Hope you're well.

Keep smiling; it confuses your enemies!

Dave xxxx

It wasn't until she'd finished reading that Maggie realized she had been holding her breath from the start. So young love wasn't quite so exciting after all! Of course, Dave wasn't prepared for the noisy messiness of life with young children, not to mention the constant demands of a new baby. That was because, when their children were growing up, she had loved being a mum so much that she had happily coped with all the work, washing, refereeing and total exhaustion of bringing up a family. Dave had gone off to work all day, and when he came home in the evening the kids were in bed, dinner was on the table and the TV remote control was right next to his reclining armchair. No wonder this had all come as a huge shock to him.

And now he wanted to come and see her because he needed a chat with a good friend! Well, it didn't feel as if he'd been much of a friend to her lately. And even if there was just a remnant of affection for this man with whom she had shared so much over the years, the pain of their break-up was still too raw. She'd managed to get this far, and was now feeling quite settled in her lovely new home – but her confidence was fragile. She couldn't run the risk of seeing him again just yet. And most of all, she couldn't bear listening to him moan about how unhappy he was with the woman he had chosen over their own family.

No, she had nothing to say to him in reply to this email. Without a moment's hesitation, she pressed the Delete button. Then she stopped for a moment as it crossed her mind that within twelve hours she had deleted two messages that had both been sent to her by men. She definitely wanted to be rid of this message, but what about the other? She hadn't even opened Phil's email to see what it said. Perhaps that was the very least she should do before she condemned it to Trash for ever? She quickly retrieved the email and started to read:

Dear Megs

I had been hoping I might hear from you again after my last message, but now several days have passed I realize that I omitted to tell you one very important thing that perhaps you need to know before you decide whether you should answer or not.

I mentioned my children and my wife Sandra. What I didn't say is that Sandra and I are no longer together. We parted very amicably nearly two years ago, after the children had left home. There's an old saying about marrying in haste, regretting at leisure. When I met Sandra, I was working overseas most of the time, so we hardly had the chance to see each other. It all felt very dramatic and exciting when we decided to get married. But then, as time went on, we both looked back to realize, too late unfortunately, that we actually had very little in common. I have nothing but admiration for Sandra, who is a lovely person and a wonderful mother. That said, it became very clear over the years that we had totally different personalities and interests, which meant that we shared very little, apart from the children. I liked travelling, DIY, gardening and playing a bit of sport every now and then. She was a home bird, very close to her sister and not wanting to go away even for summer holidays with the children. And she never enjoyed going out in the evenings because it would mean missing an episode of her favourite soaps!

It wasn't that we were unhappy. We were just two people living parallel lives that never really touched. It was actually quite lonely for us both – and finally, when the children were safely on their way, we employed one solicitor between us, told him how we wanted to divide things so that we could each get on with our own lives, then we organized our parting of the ways by helping each other however we could. The fact is that neither of us wanted our marriage to fail. It was the very last thing we intended when we got hitched, but having made our joint decision to part, we're both so much happier these days. We keep in touch about the family. We're friends. We were saying only the other day that neither of us has ever broken our promise to love each other until "death do us part". We will always love each other, but not in the way married couples should. We're both just getting on with our own lives, and feeling much better for it. The kids are okay about it too. Our daughter said we should have separated long ago!

Anyway, that's probably far too much information and I may have scared the living daylights out of you, *but I want to be honest. It's only fair.*

Forgive me for mentioning this if it's inappropriate, but Joe said that you'd been through a divorce in recent times. I can only guess how much upheaval and emotional challenge that has meant for you lately.

In view of that, the very last thing you may need is a long-lost acquaintance taking up any of your precious time when you have enough to think about already. However, if a bit of entertaining email banter with an old friend every now and then might find a place in whatever shape your life has now taken on, I'd love to hear from you.

And if you prefer not to reply, I'll understand completely. I wish you well always.

Yours

Phil

Maggie stared at the screen, her thoughts in a jumble. Then she clicked Reply and started to type.

Chapter 11

"Good morning, Kath."

To Kath's surprise, it was Richard Carlisle who had popped his head around her door.

"Hello. What brings you to Hope Hall?"

"Trevor's prepared a report I need to see, and I decided to collect it myself as I was passing. How are you?"

Her expression was wry as she looked at the stacks of boxes and papers of various shapes and sizes lying over and around her desk. "The centenary event is making me slightly cross-eyed, but I'm getting there. There are so many different groups involved, each of which needs this bit of paperwork or that set of posters, and they all have their own ever-changing list of requirements. I guess my desk will *have* to look like this for the next few weeks, but I have to admit, I find it hard to work properly when there's clutter all over the place."

"I'm just the same," he agreed, pulling up a chair on the other side of her desk. "It's a necessary evil of being involved in a complex business, but it does drive me crackers!"

"At least I go home to an apartment that has the right sort of clutter; you know, mostly tidy but homely too."

He grimaced. "I live with a teenager. Need I say more?"

"How is William? Is he back from Portsmouth now?"

"He is. He took two nautical navigation courses while he was there and passed them both with flying colours. He's going to need longer sleeves on his Sea Cadet uniform if he gets many more!"

"Well, I gather from Muriel Baker that the asbestos repairs on the Sea Cadet hut are going well, and that the corps may be moving back to their own premises again in a few weeks' time."

"Yes, that's good news. I do think their stay at Hope Hall has worked out really well for them, though. They'll be quite sad to say goodbye."

"And we feel exactly the same way. It's been a pleasure having them here. And did you know that they've offered to take part in the centenary service, providing a guard of honour at the church? We're absolutely delighted to accept."

"Speaking of offers that might be good to accept, could you spare an hour or so this morning? It just so happens that the engineer who is most knowledgeable about the disability modifications for the new minibus is going to be at the dealership in Portsmouth this morning, with a vehicle just like the one you'll be having. Is there any chance you could come down with me to take a look? Make sure it's suitable?"

Kath's mind raced through her programme for the morning. "I've got a quick meeting here in ten minutes, and a couple of phone calls I really ought to make, but if you could give me half an hour or so, that would be lovely."

"I'll need some time with Trevor to talk over the report, so that should be perfect timing."

"Should Trevor come too?"

"Yes, that would be helpful, if he's able to. I'll ask him."

But forty minutes later when Richard came back into Kath's office, he was alone.

"Trevor can't join us. Something about 'she who must be obeyed'! Apparently, Mary has a chiropractic appointment and needs him to drive her home after her treatment. So you're lumbered with just me, I'm afraid."

Kath laughed. "Lead on, then!"

Richard's Range Rover made short work of the drive to the centre of Portsmouth, where he turned into a large garage complex belonging to a well-known international car manufacturer. Standing in the middle of the forecourt was a sparkling new minibus that quite simply took Kath's breath away. Within minutes, Richard was introducing her to Adrian Morgan, the engineer, who was able to answer all her questions with enthusiastic explanations about the range of modifications and additions that could be made to create a minibus especially for Hope Hall. The new vehicle would be capable of catering for a wide range of passenger disabilities and physical limitations.

Kath was thrilled. "This will make such a difference to the service we can provide. I can't tell you how much the gift of this minibus means to us."

"Well," beamed the engineer, "we'll get cracking on it, then. And Richard, if you could ask Celia to confirm the image and wording needed on the side of the bus, I can organize that too."

"That's something we can talk about over lunch if you've got time, Kath?"

Perhaps it was her excitement over the minibus, or maybe it was just that breakfast had been a long time ago, but Kath realized she was actually quite hungry. And so it was that the two of them found themselves in a quaint little pub in Old Portsmouth, looking out across the busy harbour as huge plates of fish, chips and mushy peas were placed before them. Conversation flowed easily between them, as it had during their previous meal together.

One minute they were talking as two business executives, discussing the issues and challenges they faced in their different areas of work, and the next they were laughing about a shared joke that amused them both. Somehow, they got on to recalling the first record they had each bought and sharing stories from

216

their schooldays. They discussed books they had loved and stories that moved and inspired them. Like old friends, they chatted away so comfortably that it surprised them both to find that nearly two hours had passed and they were still there.

Their conversation continued as they travelled back to Hope Hall together, where Richard drew up by the main entrance to drop Kath back at the office. He got out of the car to come around and open her door, by which time she was already standing on the pavement.

"Thank you for today," he said with real warmth in his eyes as he gazed at her.

"It's been an unexpected pleasure," she said, smiling in return.

He stretched out to take her hand, which he brought to his lips to plant the softest of kisses on it. "You, Kath Sutton, are a very, very special lady." And with a slight farewell nod, he got back in the car, giving a cheery wave as he drove off.

And you, Richard Carlisle, are Celia Ainsworth's partner. I need to remember that. And so do you.

There was a great air of excitement about Michael Sayward when he called in at Hope Hall the following day.

"I think I've traced the family of Leonard Carmichael – you know, the chief builder of Hope Hall who left that really moving set of letters behind our original foundation stone when it was laid?"

"Really?" asked Kath, catching his enthusiasm. "Tell me more!"

"Well, it's taken quite a while to dig out what we needed to know, but it's been so worthwhile. Do you remember that the last letter Gerry Carmichael wrote to his wife mentioned they had a son? Well, the baby's name was Walter, and his mother Edith never married again, so he was the only child she ever had. He was born in January 1917, and his father Gerry died on the battlefield at Passchendaele in August of the same year. So although he knew Edith was pregnant, he never actually met Walter.

"Years later in 1939, when Walter was twenty-two, he got married to Florence, a girl who apparently lived almost next door to his mum. But then, within a year of them tying the knot, Walter was sent over to France with thousands of British troops in the early months of 1940. Fortunately, he got through the war relatively unscathed, and when he came home in 1945, he went back to his old job in his grandfather's business, Carmichael Builders.

"I've managed to find some records for Walter and Flo. They had two children, although sadly I came across an article on the front page of the local paper in 1963 saying that their son, David, was killed in a motorbike accident just outside town. He was only seventeen. Their older daughter, Joyce, was born during the war years after her father Walter came home for leave in 1941. And do you remember there were a few local family names mentioned on the back of that group photograph we found behind the foundation stone? Well, one of those families was the Jessops, and Joyce ended up marrying Ken Jessop. She's a widow now, seventy-nine years old, but she and Ken had four children, seven grandchildren and even a couple of great-grandchildren – and all of them grew up in this town."

"Oh, my goodness! Do we know where she lives now? Wouldn't it be wonderful if she were able to come along on Centenary Day?"

"She is still at the same house they moved into on the day they were married. And I know that because one of their sons, Derek, sings in the same choir as me."

"You sing in a choir? Michael, you're a dark horse! I never knew that."

He chuckled. "Why would you? It's an all-male barbershop

choir. We have waxed moustaches and wear striped jackets and boaters for our performances."

"Well I never!" laughed Kath. "That sounds great. We'll have to book you to perform at Hope Hall."

"Oh, I wouldn't hold your breath. We're not that good – more enthusiastic than skilled, I would say. It's good fun, though."

"So could you have a word with Derek? Maybe he should be the one to break the news to his mother about what we found behind the stone?"

"I was hoping you'd say that. I'll give him a ring tonight."

It was the third Friday in the month of July – time for Hope Hall to host another of its popular monthly dance nights. Once again, Friction was the band booked to play, which more or less guaranteed a full house with a queue of people waiting in line the moment the doors opened at seven thirty.

On this particular evening, drummer Nigel eased his battered old van into the playground earlier than usual. Once the van was parked, guitarists Jake and Graham opened the passenger door and jumped out to start unpacking their equipment from the back. They loaded it on to a huge trolley that they then pushed through the building to where it was needed on stage.

Minutes later, Andy's smaller car arrived, and he immediately started unloading his keyboard before helping the others carry it into the hall, along with several other large items of gear. Once inside, they set to work laying out their array of amplifiers, sound boxes and pedals that controlled the exact tone and balance the band wanted to create. Having been involved in the music business for some time, Andy was acknowledged as their sound expert. From his position at the keyboard, he was able to plan and monitor all the sound and mixing requirements from the boards and controllers he kept close at hand.

Andy liked nothing more than setting up for a gig, making sure everything was wired up correctly, with mikes working, sound levels balanced to perfection and special effects programmed in so that they could be introduced at exactly the right dramatic moments throughout their programme of songs. There was only one area of frustration for Andy, and that was the fact that Carlos had worked out how to override Andy's control of the bank of foot pedals, which the lead singer insisted lay on the stage floor right in front of him. This meant that if the singer wanted his voice to boom out louder than the others, or if he wanted to create an echo or reverb to call attention to his voice, he could do so – regardless of its effect on the overall sound or on the needs of the other individual band members.

With great concentration, the group worked together as a team until finally, as the time ticked round to half past seven and the doors opened, they all looked at each other intently. A silent understanding about how they hoped the evening would unfold seemed to pass between them.

Sean, the DJ, swept into action, filling the hall with a series of tracks that he knew would get people up and dancing. Mili and Terezka made their way through the hall to their usual table at the front, which the band had reserved for them. They were quickly followed by Nigel's wife Jayne, and Graham's partner Ali. The boys came down from the stage to join the girls, hugging them and then huddling into a tight group, where they had a whispered conversation that seemed urgent and slightly furtive. All eyes were on the entrance to the hall as they waited for Carlos to arrive.

Predictably, their singer strode in only a few minutes before their first set was due to start at eight fifteen. He was far too late to help the rest of the band members set up their equipment, but just in time to be sure that his adoring fans were ready and waiting to greet him.

Five minutes later, Carlos jumped up on stage without even bothering to say hello to the other players. The last time they'd seen him, he'd marched out of their pub rehearsal room like the prima donna he loved to be. He hadn't bothered coming to their next rehearsal, and here he was striding on to the stage without even acknowledging their existence. Taking a deep breath, Andy made a slight adjustment to the set-up of the sound system, nodded to the others, and counted them in to the first number, "I've Gotta Feeling". Andy did have a feeling about what a great night this was going to be.

The band played as usual and Carlos sang as usual, but the audience appeared to be looking curiously in his direction. Carlos showed no sign of having noticed, because as far as he was concerned, it was only important that *they* were watching *him*, not the other way around. On went the music, with one favourite dance number following another: "Love Shack", "Sweet Caroline", "Mony Mony" and "Thriller". No one could deny that the band were superb. However, one by one, the dancers began to gather around the stage in front of Carlos, first looking puzzled, then trying to shout out messages to him. Not bothering to look at their expressions, because he simply thought they were standing there to get a better view of him, Carlos carried on regardless – "Don't Stop Believing", "Stayin' Alive", "It Takes Two" – until everyone in the hall was aware there was a problem. Everyone except Carlos, who seemed to have no idea at all that he was singing painfully out of tune. People actually had their fingers in their ears as they made their way back into the foyer carrying their drinks for a break from the dancing and the jarring sound. It was only as the hall emptied after about twenty-five minutes of them playing that Carlos threw both his hands up in the air and turned angrily to shout at the band.

"What have you done? You've done something! People are leaving. This is not my problem. You have made a problem. Sort this or Carlos will leave!"

The boys in the band looked at Carlos and then at each other with expressions of complete bewilderment.

"What do you mean? We've just been back here playing as we always do."

"And I sing as I always do, but people are leaving. This is your fault. People do not leave when Carlos sings."

Nigel on the drums shrugged. "Well, they are tonight. Have you got a bad throat or something?"

Carlos clutched his throat with alarm. "No, my throat is fine. My voice is fine."

Jake shook his head, his face thoughtful. "Sorry mate, but your voice is awful tonight. You're singing sharp all the time. No wonder everyone's leaving the hall."

"Why don't you try drinking a glass of port?" asked Graham, sounding really concerned. "I always find that helps me."

Carlos did not look amused at the suggestion.

"Look, Carlos, if you feel ill or want a break, just let us know," said Andy. "Graham can always stand in for you if you're not well."

"I am fine, I am great! This is *your* fault. You are in charge of sound. You do not leave this stage until you find my voice again. I am going for a drink."

"Port!" shouted Graham as Carlos stomped away. "That'll do the trick."

The group watched him march down the middle of the hall towards the bar.

"Well then, lads," said Andy quietly, "as Carlos says, we need to get to work. On to Round Two!"

DJ Sean leapt onto the stage to take over the music quite a bit earlier than he had expected. He came over to give Andy a high five.

222

"Good on you!" he smiled. "That was hilarious. I haven't enjoyed myself so much in years!"

Andy grinned. "I have no idea what you're talking about."

"Yeah, right. You'd better take a look at your pitch shifter, then. I think it must be faulty! Like him or not, you can't deny Carlos always sings in tune, and I bet his voice sounded perfectly normal to him, but that pitch shifter effect made sure the audience didn't hear it that way!"

Andy remained silent, a picture of innocence.

"Well, Carlos sure had it coming to him," chuckled Sean. "I can't wait to see what you've got up your sleeve next."

Half an hour later, as Sean got to the end of his set, Carlos made his way back to the stage with a face like thunder. "Get this right!" he hissed, before turning a smile full of charm towards the audience. "I am sorry, my friends. We had a few technical problems just then that our sound manager was not capable of solving. We are fine now. Carlos is fine now."

A half-hearted cheer rippled around the room.

"So let's dance!" he shouted as the band began the intro to a dance night favourite.

Once Carlos was certain from the attitude of the audience below him that his voice was back to sounding as glorious as ever, he decided it was time for his dulcet tones to drown out the idiots playing and singing behind him. He stamped on the floor pedal in front of him so that a resounding echo would turn everyone's attention to his voice. But there was no echo. In fact, quite the opposite. The more he kicked the pedal in angry frustration, the quieter and quieter his voice became.

He turned to glare furiously at Andy, who was looking in completely the wrong direction and didn't appear to notice him at all.

"Turn this up, you moron!" snapped Carlos.

223

"I haven't changed anything," mouthed Andy, his face puzzled.

Carlos turned to the pedals again, this time thumping his foot on the one that added an atmospheric reverb to the vocals. The pedal worked immediately, except that once Carlos had taken the pressure off, the reverb effect kept rising until his voice sounded warped and booming. Once again, the dancers below began to put their hands over their ears, and the mood in the hall became tense with irritation at the sound coming from the stage. They could see the rest of the band were playing normally, but Carlos was behaving strangely, thumping his foot on various pedals and altering the sound in the most random and petulant way. What on earth was he doing?

As that song came to an end, Carlos spun around to point his finger in Andy's direction. "Stop! Whatever you are doing, stop it!"

The band members looked at each other and out towards the audience, shrugging helplessly, seemingly as confused as everyone else in the hall by their lead singer's irrational outburst.

"Let's go into the medley," suggested Andy. "The one we've rehearsed."

"I know the medley," snapped Carlos. "No more funny business."

This medley was a dance night favourite. Many popular hit songs were based on a common four-chord pattern, which meant the band could move from one first line to another with ease, and the audience loved joining in with the words they recognized instantly as the songs changed.

Andy led Friction into the intro and Carlos began the first song, except that while he was singing "Don't Stop Believing", the rest of the band launched into "With or Without You". Confused, Carlos just managed to join in with the right words as they changed song again. This time Carlos led into "You're Beautiful", the song that usually followed "With or Without You" in their medley list, while Andy and the others were busy blasting out "Can You Feel the Love Tonight".

For five minutes of absolute audience torture, Carlos sang at odds with the band. He found himself singing "No Woman, No Cry", while the band sang "Beautiful". Finally, as the singer realized the medley was coming to an end, he led into their usual last song, "Time to Say Goodbye", just as the band started singing "Auld Lang Syne".

The whole effect was so terrible that the audience actually started laughing. They had caught on to the fact that the band was playing tricks on Carlos, but his reactions throughout the evening had been so bad-tempered and spiteful that even his staunchest fans were beginning to see him in a very different light.

As the medley came to a painful end, the audience roared with laughter and applause while Carlos shouted and swore at both them and the band members in fury. Eventually, he shrieked into the microphone, "This band is amateur! They are not worthy to support Carlos. I quit!"

And, grabbing his leather jacket from the side of the stage, he jumped down and marched through the parting crowd, heading straight out of the door at the back of the hall.

Once the furore had died down, Andy stood up to speak into the main mike.

"Sorry about that, but just so that you can judge for yourselves whether or not the remaining members of Friction are amateurs, let me introduce you to our other great singer... our lead guitarist Graham!"

As Andy moved back to take his place at the keyboard, Graham stepped up to the mike. The lights dimmed and the hall fell silent as the band led into the familiar introduction of the old

Simon and Garfunkel classic "Bridge over Troubled Water". In a voice with a unique tone that was both sweet and pure, Graham started to sing, quietly and with great feeling at first, but building in power and intensity as the song progressed, helped along by strong harmonies and expert musical interpretation from the rest of the group. As the song crescendoed to a powerful and emotional ending, the hall exploded with cheering and applause that seemed to go on and on.

"I think," said Jake, holding out his arm towards Graham in a gesture of recognition, "that from now on this band should be called Friction-less!"

And with the enthusiastic response of the audience ringing in their ears, Andy grinned as he counted them in to their next number.

To Sheelagh's great relief, Michael seemed to have decided to come along to the Hope Hall Food Bank every Monday afternoon. She always looked out for him, with a supply of food and provisions at the ready so she could slip out to sit on the wall alongside him and chat further.

This week, however, she had a lot to discuss with him. She knew she had to tread carefully, and that she would have to call on her decades of experience as a senior social worker and trained counsellor to get the tone of their conversation just right. The reason she was so anxious was that, following discreet enquiries made through the appropriate channels of the Salvation Army, initial contact had been made with the wife of Michael Ford, the manager of the Basingstoke superstore who had disappeared without trace following many unhappy months in his post there. It had been agreed that local Salvation Army officer Jackie would accompany Sheelagh when she travelled to Basingstoke to meet up with Michael's wife Anne.

It had been an intense and emotional meeting during which all three women realized there was no doubt that the scruffy, wounded man who visited the Food Bank was indeed Anne's husband.

"Why do you think he ended up in our area?" asked Jackie. "Does he have any connections there?"

"Not recently," replied Anne, her eyes red with tears, "but when he was growing up, his grandparents managed a farm just outside the town. He always spoke so fondly about the happy summer holidays he spent there as a boy."

"Are any of the family still there?"

"His grandparents both died long ago. They didn't own the farm, so I suppose it was just handed over to other people when they left. I guess that was probably the best part of twenty years ago now."

"What was the name of the farm? Do you remember?"

"I do, because it struck me as so charming at the time. It was called Apple Tree Farm, because it had a large orchard that stood just inside the wall that ran along the road at the edge of the property."

"Michael told me he was staying somewhere that had a lot of 'unintentional ventilation,'" said Sheelagh. "Can you think of anywhere like that near or around the farm where he might have headed? Perhaps a place that's fallen into a state of dilapidation or disrepair?"

"Yes, I can," said Anne thoughtfully. "He always waxed lyrical about an old caravan that stood somewhere on the farm. When he was a teenager, his grandparents let him take it over and make it into a den for himself. He even slept there overnight. He really loved it. I have no idea if it's still there, now that the farm has new owners, but if it is I can imagine he would feel safe there, even if it was falling apart."

"We'll find out about that," said Jackie, making a note on her pad.

"But how do you feel about all this?" asked Sheelagh. "How do you feel about Michael? It can't have been easy for you since he disappeared."

Anne's eyes filled with tears again. "It's been hell. Not knowing, being frightened for his life, fearing the worst. Most of all, I feel so sorry and hurt that he couldn't turn to me and let me support him. We'd always been such a strong couple, but when this all happened I guess the embarrassment and humiliation over the way he was undermined and then replaced brought him to some kind of emotional and physical breakdown. I knew how stressed he was. I mean, he'd talked to me endlessly about it in the early months because he was so determined to bring the whole project together and make it the success it should have been. But then so much went wrong – some of it coincidental – but a lot of it was quite vitriolic and hurtful.

"Michael has always been a sensitive man, especially where the welfare and needs of other people is concerned. I know he was upset at how bad workmanship and lack of professional behaviour in others had caused delays he had no control over, and he was genuinely upset about the implications for the workforce, because he could see it had made their jobs so much harder. But the man at the top always gets the blame, doesn't he? And Michael took that blame squarely on his own shoulders. He just worked around the clock. He rarely came home before midnight and then was off again soon after seven the next morning. He looked dreadful. His skin was grey, there were huge black bags under his eyes and he lost a couple of stone in weight. I suppose that only gave ammunition to his attackers, who judged him by his physical appearance rather than by his work achievements."

"And he hasn't been in touch with you at all since the day he disappeared?"

"There's been nothing. But I need you to understand that Michael was a wonderful husband. Ours had always been a really loving family. This behaviour is so out of character for him. That's why I'm convinced he had some sort of mental breakdown that made him believe flight was the only answer. I wonder if his dismissal made him feel like such an utter failure that he thought everyone would be better off without him, even the family who loved him unconditionally and he adored without question. I think he decided to run away – away from the problems, away from the embarrassment, away from a world that had become unbearably hostile towards him, and sadly away from those of us who simply love him."

Her voice had become shaky and Anne's despair was palpable as she bowed her head, her shoulders heaving with quiet sobs. Sheelagh moved along the settee to put an arm around her, saying nothing, simply offering compassion and support. By the time Anne had recovered a little, Jackie had returned from the kitchen where she'd made another round of tea.

"I need to see him. When can I see him?"

Sheelagh smiled at her. "We were hoping you'd say that. The answer is, we'd like you to come as soon as possible."

"We need to work out the best way to plan that meeting," said Jackie. "I'm hoping Michael will feel reassured in the face of your obvious love for him. Let's pray, Anne, that you can lead him home."

That conversation replayed in Sheelagh's mind the following Monday afternoon as she hovered anxiously around the main door of Hope Hall, hoping for a glimpse of Michael in his usual place behind the large oak tree at the far end of the old school playground wall. She glanced down at her watch once again, dreading that something may have happened to prevent him from coming. As she busied herself serving food parcels and then got caught up chatting to a group of mothers who were hoping to persuade their children to try on some clothes that might fit them, she was on the verge of deciding he wasn't going to come that day at all.

And then she saw him. He had been brave enough to come out from behind the tree and was sitting on the wall looking at the door, as if he was waiting for her to come. She immediately excused herself from the group she was with, quickly poured out two cups of tea, and picked up the food package she'd prepared before walking out to sit down beside him.

"It's good to see you, Michael. How have you been?"

He shrugged, then reached into the bag of food to see what was there.

"Have you found a bed at all this week?"

"I'm okay where I am."

"And where is that?"

He sank his teeth into a sandwich without giving a reply.

"Could it possibly be at Apple Tree Farm?"

He looked up with a start.

"What a lovely place that is," Sheelagh continued, "especially in the summer months."

He didn't answer for more than a minute. He just kept eating, although his eyes were clouded with suspicion.

"I've got a place there. I'm okay."

"Don't you find it lonely?"

"I find my own company better than the presence of most other people."

"Isn't there anyone you're fond of? Anyone you miss who's been dear to you in the past?"

"That's not relevant. I have nothing. I *am* nothing."

"That's really not true, Michael. And if you don't believe me, just take a look over there at the seat around the corner from the main door. There is someone there who has never, for one minute, stopped loving you. Someone who's longing to put her arms around you and show you how much you *are* loved."

Michael raised his eyes to search the playground for the bench on which his wife was sitting. Aware of his gaze, Anne got to her feet, looking anxiously at him as if uncertain she'd be welcome if she moved nearer. Then he too slowly got to his feet, not giving the impression that he would turn and run, but more as if he were drawn to move towards her. Encouraged by his expression and body language, Anne slowly walked towards him as Sheelagh quietly rose from her seat on the wall and moved back towards the main door of the hall.

From there she kept a watchful eye on the couple as they sat together on the wall for more than quarter of an hour, before she finally saw Michael get to his feet once again. What was happening? Was he leaving? But then Anne got up too and put her arms lovingly around his neck. His head lowered on to her shoulder, and Sheelagh could see that his whole body was shaking with emotion. Together they stood as Anne quietly whispered to him, stroking his face and hair, reaching for his hands.

By this time the Food Bank had closed, their clients had come and gone, and just a few members of the team were left clearing up and stacking away whatever remained. Where there had been activity and chatter, a new silence fell on Hope Hall. At this point, Sheelagh ventured to approach the couple, hoping her presence wouldn't be seen as an intrusion.

Anne turned to her immediately. "Michael's coming home."

"That's good to hear."

"It's not going to be easy. He doesn't want to go back to

Basingstoke and I agree with him on that. Our children are both away at university now, so he and I must find a new place where the two of us can make a home. And together we'll work to bring my beloved husband back to health again. He needs good food, the right medical care, and he needs love. Most of all he needs love, and I think he knows now that he has that in me. My darling Michael, I love you more now than at any other time in our marriage, and we have many years of married life ahead of us, during which I'll make sure you never doubt my love and devotion for you."

"And we'll help you both in any way we can as you plan your future," said Sheelagh.

"Thank you." Michael's voice was gruff as he spoke, his eyes on Sheelagh. "You're an interfering busybody, and one of those awful do-gooders I hate. But what you did for me was..." He stopped, plainly overwhelmed by what he was feeling. It was a while before he could speak again. "It was good. Thank you."

And once again his eyes filled with tears, but he was smiling. And for the rest of her life, Sheelagh would never forget that smile.

Chapter 12

By the first week in August, the town had a completely different air to it. Schools had broken up and suddenly there was high-pitched chatter everywhere from pupils young and older, in the parks, on their bikes, hanging around the High Street, and in the gardens on either side of Maggie's apartment in Linden Avenue. She loved it. It reminded her of her own children growing up, with their squeals of laughter and their occasional outbursts of "he said, she said".

But then, rather than the town changing, perhaps it was Maggie herself who was feeling, after a long time of darkness, the rays of sunshine not just on her face but in her heart too. She threw back the bedclothes every morning, keen to discover what the day would bring her way. And the first discovery she wanted to make within minutes of getting up, or coming back to the apartment later in the day, was to see what was waiting in her inbox.

Would there be another message from Phil? There nearly always was. As soon as Maggie had replied to his email explaining that he was now divorced from his wife Sandra, their conversation had continued at first daily, then gradually within a couple of weeks twice or more each day. She had started by giving a very brief description of her break-up with Dave and their subsequent divorce, which had led to her having to move out of their family home and into the apartment that had come to mean so much to her. It was Phil who had probed with gentle questions; not just about the logistics of that whole process but, more importantly, how she felt about it along the way. Maggie had been surprised at how healing it had been to share her reactions and thoughts with someone who was able to take a caring yet detached point of view. In the past, as each revelation and stage in that awful period of upheaval had unfolded, she had really only spoken without reserve to Steph or Darren, not wanting to air the family's dirty washing in public, or the depth of her hurt to others who really didn't need to know.

She found herself thinking about why it seemed so much easier to share the whole painful business with a man who really was a stranger to her. They may have had a passing acquaintance all those years ago when they were both still young enough to be at school, but she was forty-seven years old now, and Phil forty-nine, so there was a stretch of more than three decades since they'd last seen each other.

She soon realized, though, that what gave her the freedom simply to be herself in her responses was the fact that they were physically miles apart and never actually in each other's company. They weren't speaking face to face. They had not exchanged photos. He had suggested they should, but she had come up with excuses not to. He must have noticed and been curious, but he hadn't brought the matter up again, for which she was deeply grateful. So he was probably under a rosy illusion of what she looked like based on how he remembered her all those years ago. The moment he realized she was almost as broad as she was high, and that she had completely lost control of her eating habits throughout the divorce, he would be off like a shot. Of course he would! What man wouldn't? He'd run for the hills, and she wouldn't blame him one bit.

However, until that awful and probably inevitable time when he would want more and become disappointed and disillusioned with the barriers she had built up around herself, she was enjoying every moment of their absorbing, supportive, entertaining and often hilarious email conversations. They made her day. They put a spring in her step. Life had become not just bearable but joyful again.

So with a plate of toast and marmalade in one hand and a cup of tea in the other, Maggie sat down at the computer with a smile on her face, anticipating the pleasure of another email exchange to set her up for the day ahead.

When Michael Sayward and his Historical Society friend Beryl rang Mrs Jessop's bell, it was her son Derek who opened the front door.

"Hi Michael. It's great to see you without your handlebar moustache! It was a good rehearsal the other night, wasn't it?"

After exchanging some brief chat about the barbershop choir to which they both belonged, Michael introduced Derek to Beryl.

"Mum's waiting for you in the lounge," said Derek. "She's very excited to hear about all this. Go in and say hello, and I'll put the kettle on. Tea okay for you both?"

Joyce Jessop was sitting in a comfy, well-worn armchair beside the window, from where she had a view up and down this street of terraced houses in which net curtains had probably been twitched by neighbours keeping an eye on each other since the estate was first built back in Victorian times. She was a slightly built woman with a shock of white hair that had been permed into neat regulation curls. Her striking blue eyes looked enormous behind the lenses of her tortoiseshell spectacles, which sparkled with shiny studs and jewels along each of the arms that hung over her ears. Her feet were enclosed in pink fluffy slippers that were resting on a leather pouffe, and she wore a flowery apron over her blue skirt, which was topped by what looked like a hand-knitted pink jumper.

Once the introductions had been made and everyone was

settled and organized with a cup of tea and biscuits, Michael delved into his briefcase to draw out the letters that had been found behind the Hope Hall foundation stone. Pushing her glasses safely up her nose, Joyce began to read, her huge blue eyes filling with tears as she got to the end. It took her a minute or two to recover before she felt able to speak.

"How I wish my granny Edith were here to see this. She spoke of these letters, of course. She knew they'd been placed in the wall, and she had very mixed feelings about it. In those days, you couldn't copy any letters you had. There was just this one sheet that Gerry had written to her from the trenches, and of course she treasured it. It broke her heart to part with it in this way, but she knew it meant so much to Leonard and Rose. It felt like a public recognition of what their son and their family had sacrificed in that dreadful war."

"Like so many others," agreed Beryl. "That's what's especially moving about these letters. They represent the dreadful pain that was shared by countless mothers, fathers, wives and children in families just like yours."

"That's why Leonard did it. He built Hope Hall because he agreed that a memorial hall was a good and fitting tribute, but he just didn't feel that a sparkling new building alone reflected the depth of the pain and suffering they and all their neighbours had gone through. The words of those letters are able to convey that in a way bricks and mortar never could."

"I suppose he hoped they would be rediscovered one day in the future," commented Michael. "And a hundred years on, here they are. Leonard could never have imagined how much the world would change in that time, or all the other wars we've seen around the world since Gerry died."

"But these letters still speak out loud and clear, don't they?" stated Joyce. "The pain in them is as moving today as it must have been back then. I'm glad for him. Glad for my granny Edith too, who never ever recovered from the death of her husband. She had a sadness about her for as long as I can remember."

"When did you lose her?"

"She was ninety-five when she died, so she reached a grand old age in spite of everything. That was in 2003. It was no dramatic illness; she just died because she was very old. She was a wonderful lady, really."

"Did she ever think about remarrying?"

Joyce smiled. "I remember asking her about that once, and she just said that she'd married the man she loved and that she could never love that way again."

"How tragic," mused Beryl, glancing down at her notes. "When did she and Gerry marry? Oh, here it is. They married in April 1916, and that was within weeks of national conscription being brought in for all men over the age of eighteen. Gerry was twenty-two by then, and Edith was only nineteen years old. They must have decided to tie the knot as quickly as possible so they could have some time together before he was called up. In the end, they had just three weeks before he was shipped off to Europe along with thousands of other young men. He never made it home again and never saw his baby son Walter. Just over a year later he died in the Battle of Passchendaele."

"And Granny Edith never recovered from the shock of it." Joyce's voice was flat as she spoke. "She devoted her life to her little boy, my father, because he was the only living reminder she had of her beloved husband. And when Dad grew up and married Mum, Granny devoted her life to us and then to our children. She was always there with a lap to cuddle up on and a pocket full of fruit sweets to make everything better."

"Well, Joyce, we're very much hoping you might come and share some of that with all of us during our Centenary Celebration

Day. We're having a service in the church, but then we'll be moving across to Hope Hall to lay our own centenary plaque with modern-day thoughts and items stored behind it, just as your great-grandad Leonard did with the original foundation stone all those years ago. Would you consider coming along as our guest of honour on that day, and perhaps saying a few words about your grandparents, and about Leonard too, who was thoughtful enough to enclose these letters?"

Joyce's face lit up as a slow smile crossed her face. "I would really love to."

"And are you happy to decide for yourself what you'd like to say?" asked Michael. "Do let us know if we can help you with any details you might need."

"I know exactly what to say. I'm going to borrow Granny Edith's words, because she put a great deal of thought into what the ceremony should include, even though she knew she wouldn't be there herself. I'm going to make sure she's there in spirit."

Michael smiled as he realized that during their ceremony, as they all marked the history of a hundred years ago in the presence of Joyce, with her links to the past, along with a new young generation of schoolchildren making their contribution for the future, they would all be creating a moment in history that would speak to everyone who visited Hope Hall in the years to come.

Much to the disappointment of the Grown-ups' Lunch Club members that week, Maggie and her team held back on providing too many cakes and puddings for their lunch, in honour of their guest speaker that day. The local Health Service dietician was going to give them all a talk on eating healthily, with advice on what foods to avoid and what should be encouraged.

"I bet she'll say we shouldn't be eating bread," wailed Betty. "I *love* bread. I love bread almost as much as I love potatoes, especially when they're made into nice hot crispy chips. But I don't love bread *or* chips as much as I love Maggie's cakes, and we're going to be starved of those today. This talk is really going to upset me."

"I never eat fried food," stated Ida.

"My mum used to say that bread is like the sun," said Doris, joining in with the conversation. "It rises in the yeast and sets in the waist!"

"Well, if this dietician has a thing for lettuce leaves," grumbled Percy, "I'm going off down the chip shop for my lunch. Apart from mushy peas, I don't get on with eating anything green. I haven't eaten salad for eighty years and I don't plan to start now."

"I've been trying to diet," moaned Flora, "and I must be doing okay. I just dug out something I used to wear five years ago and it actually still fitted! I felt so proud."

"Really?" gasped Betty. "That's impressive."

"Actually, it was only a scarf, but I've got to start somewhere!"

And the group around her all joined in as Betty threw back her head and laughed.

"Well," said Robert, "when it comes to my body, I am losing something, but it's not my weight. I filled up with petrol the other day and saw someone had dropped their glasses on the ground by the pump. So I did the right thing and took them in to the cashier, because I thought a driver would probably come back looking for them. But when I got back in the car, I couldn't find my driving glasses. It was really embarrassing having to go and ask the same lady if I could have my own glasses back!"

Robert's story went down as well as Betty's had done with the delighted group members.

"So you're losing your marbles then, Robert!" hooted Percy. "Join the club, mate. Join the club."

"Right, pin your ears back because I'm only going to say this once!"

Everyone jumped with a start as Shirley's voice bellowed across the foyer.

"We've got some lovely photos from our summer outing to Southsea. We've put them up on the display board over in the corner. If you want a copy of any of them, there will be no charge because we can print them off here. Just let me know the numbers on the photos you'd like, and we'll make sure you get your order as soon as possible."

Eyes strained to see where exactly the photos were, with stiff necks turning and fingers pointing in the right direction to indicate the location of the board for all who weren't sure.

"*And...*" continued Shirley, her voice louder than ever, "on the twenty-eighth of this month – that's about two weeks away – you're all invited to be guests of honour at the Hope Hall centenary celebrations."

A buzz of excited chatter broke out around the room.

"There's a church service over at St Mark's in the morning where, if you put your name down on the list, there will be a reserved seat for you in the front few rows. Afterwards, we'll all be making our way back here to Hope Hall for the laying of our new centenary plaque."

The level of chatter grew even louder, but so did Shirley's voice as she carried on speaking.

"Once the ceremony to lay the new stone is over, you're all invited inside the hall for a celebration buffet. There'll be some entertainment laid on too, so it should be fun. If you need transport to get here that day, put your name and address on the transport request list. Is that clear? Any questions?"

"I've never been a VIP guest before," gasped Betty. "Do I have to wear a hat?"

"I like hats," agreed Flora. "Would my wedding hat do? I've only got one!"

Shirley shook her head with exasperation. "Ladies, you don't need to wear hats."

"I could wear my trilby at a jaunty angle," quipped Percy. "I'd look like Frank Sinatra then."

"No hats," explained Shirley with exaggerated patience. "Not for you, Percy. Not for anyone. Any more questions?"

"Is there likely to be a minute's silence during the ceremony in honour of the men who died during the First World War?" asked Ida. "After all, this hall *is* dedicated to their memory."

Shirley's expression softened. "The ceremony is being very carefully planned for just that reason, Ida. This is all about those young men who died, and the other young men and women who have lost their lives or health in subsequent conflicts. Thank you for asking."

Ida nodded gravely.

"Right, our guest speaker is ready to start now and she suggests you all move into the main hall, because she has quite a lot of demonstration items set up in there. Take your time, but could you start moving into the hall now, please?"

There was general bustle as chairs were pushed back, creaking knees straightened and walking sticks grabbed as the Grownups' Lunch Club members started their exodus from the foyer into the main hall.

Ida remained seated to allow slower members to move on ahead of her. She suddenly became aware that someone had stopped as they walked past her. She looked up to see Percy at her side.

"Thank you for asking that question," he said. "I was glad to hear the answer."

She smiled for just a second before reaching into her bag as if she were searching for something important. "Run along, Percy. I'll be right behind you."

He smiled too, then turned and headed for the main hall door.

When Terezka and Mili reached the old school classroom where their English lessons took place the following morning, they were surprised to see their Spanish friend Mariana already sitting at her desk.

"Mariana!" squealed Terezka. "Where have you been? You weren't at the dance night on Friday when everything happened with Carlos. You weren't there!"

"I had headache," replied Mariana. "I stay home."

"You stay home?" challenged Terezka. "Wherever Carlos is going, you always want to go too!"

Mariana sniffed. "Not any more."

"Why not? He broke with you?"

Clearly offended, Mariana's eyes flashed with anger. "I broke with him!"

Mili and Terezka looked at her in fascinated amazement.

"Well," said Terezka, "good. But a shock. I never think you will do that."

"I did nothing... Carlos did. I find him kissing the girl who works in kitchen at the pub."

"No!"

"Yes!"

"What did you do?"

"I made that pig man less pretty. His eye have big bruises."

"Oh dear. I hope not too serious," sighed Terezka, trying unsuccessfully not to giggle.

"And I told kitchen girl she can have him. Welcome!"

"What did Carlos say?"

"He says he go to London, where people love him."

"Bon voyage, then!" grinned Terezka.

"But you're okay, Mariana?" enquired Mili. "You had a big love for Carlos."

"*Carlos* had a big love for Carlos!" snapped Mariana, before her expression changed to one of mischievous fun. "And did you see the new student from Estonia?" She gestured over to the corner of the classroom, where a good-looking young man was flicking through the pages of his exercise book. "His name is Nelu. His hair is yellow. Yellow hair and blue eyes. He's pretty, no?"

Along the corridor, in her office, Kath noticed the email from Celia Ainsworth straight away, and allowed herself one big calming breath before clicking the button to read it. The email came from Celia's Apex Finance account, with her full office details and credentials as Director of Apex PLC Pension Fund displayed at the bottom:

Dear Ms Sutton

I write to inform you that the Good Neighbours minibus is now ready for delivery. Richard told me how very helpful you were in selecting the modifications that would best suit the elderly and disabled people who will benefit most from this minibus. Thank you for your valuable input. We very much hope this will be an asset to all your future work.

As previously requested, we would like to feature some of the local people whose lives will be improved by this magnificent vehicle in a range of publicity material about the event that raised the funds for its purchase.

Could you suggest a time next week when our photographer can come along to capture the moment

of delivery? And would you mind inviting some of your
most enthusiastic members to welcome the new arrival?
Yours
CELIA AINSWORTH

Kath sat back for a minute or two to think about her reply, initially struggling with how she should address Celia. Should she use her Christian name, which was how Celia had been introduced to her in the first place? Or should she echo the formality of the email and address her as Ms Ainsworth? She finally started typing:

Dear Celia

Thank you so much for letting us know that our wonderful new minibus is ready for delivery. We're still coming to terms with the generosity of this gift, knowing the wide-ranging benefits it will bring to this community, especially our most vulnerable and needy members. I know I speak on behalf of everyone at Hope Hall when I thank you most sincerely for your thoughtfulness in helping our work in this way. In addition, I would like to thank you again for opening up your home and garden for that unforgettable summer party. Your guests were incredibly benevolent, and we hope you'll pass on our grateful thanks to them all.

Having been fortunate enough to play a small part in the choice of modifications to the new vehicle, I know there will be no shortage of enthusiastic members to welcome its arrival. May I suggest that any time after eleven o'clock next Tuesday morning would be a good opportunity for your photographer to come? About fifty elderly people from the area will be here for their regular Grown-ups' Lunch Club at that time. Many of them have mobility problems and will be greatly helped by the new bus. I have no doubt they would all be absolutely thrilled at the prospect of being photographed on this wonderful occasion, and I hope that among the pictures your photographer takes, there might be at least one showing the whole group. I can guarantee that such a photograph would take pride of place on the wall here at Hope Hall for many years to come! After that, groups or individual members can be selected by your photographer as needed – for as long as our ladies and gentlemen have the energy to stand and the patience to wait for their lunch!

I hope you'll be able to join us for this happy occasion, although we understand that the demands of your very busy professional role may make that impossible. That is all the more reason for me to thank you for agreeing to come to our Hope Hall centenary celebrations taking place on 28th August. We are particularly delighted that you have offered to speak at the laying of our new centenary plaque. I believe it was your own great-grandfather, Reginald Ainsworth, who was the moving force behind the planning and completion of this much-loved building. Therefore, it seems appropriate and fitting that you'll be here to remind us of your family's long involvement with Hope Hall on our special day of celebration and thanks for all it has meant to this community over the past hundred years.

We look forward to welcoming you here very soon.

Every good wish

Kath Sutton

Kath read the email through again before pushing the Send button. She hoped it sounded formal enough, but friendly and suitably humble too. It *was* really generous of Celia to help Hope Hall in this very practical way. Kath felt nothing but gratitude towards the high-powered, efficient, professional woman.

She didn't have to *like* her though.

As Maggie turned into her road at the end of another long working day, she was surprised to see her son Darren's car parked outside the Linden Avenue flat. She peered through his side window to see that he had pushed back his driver's seat and was stretched out with his eyes closed as he waited for her. She knocked gently on the window, not wanting to alarm him. He woke immediately and wound down the window.

"This is a lovely surprise!" she exclaimed. "Have you been here long?"

"Not really," he muttered, rubbing his eyes. "I started work early this morning, so I finished quite early too."

"I'll put the kettle on and you can tell me all about it."

Ten minutes later, the two of them were perched on high stools either side of the breakfast bar in Maggie's new kitchen, cups of tea in hand and large slices of home-made ginger cake laid out on a plate between them.

"So, something more important than my ginger cake has brought you here. I'm guessing it's your dad."

"He's not doing very well, Mum."

Maggie said nothing.

"I saw him last night. He looks dreadful. His face is really thin, as if he's lost a lot of weight. His hair's gone grey."

"Steph said he'd started dying it. Copper-coloured, she said it was."

"Not any more. I don't think he's got the time, the energy or the money for anything like that now."

"And you're telling me because…"

"Because I know you. I know what a soft heart you have. I know you were hurt so badly by what Dad did to you because he's the only man you've ever truly loved. And I'm guessing you still love him enough not to want him to be ill or as desperately unhappy as he obviously is right now."

"Has he asked you to speak to me?"

"Not exactly. He said he'd written to you but that you hadn't replied."

"Trouble in paradise, is there?"

"I think things are very hard at home with Mandy and the children."

"And what do you think I should do about it, Darren?"

"Oh, it's not my choice, is it? He treated you really badly, so I have no idea how this makes you feel."

"What do you think my choices are?"

"Would you ever consider taking him back?"

"Is that what he'd like?"

"He did mention it, yeah."

"I'll think about it, Darren. I don't think it'll take me long to make a decision, but I promise to think about it."

"Okay," said Darren, getting up to give her a hug. "I hated having to come here to say this. Just don't shoot the messenger, okay?"

She smiled at him, ruffling his hair as she used to do when he was a small boy. "You look exhausted. Go home and get some rest."

And giving his mum another kiss on the cheek he headed out.

Hearing the click of her front door shutting, Maggie sat in the kitchen, her mind a mass of conflicting thoughts. Darren was right. Dave *was* the only man she'd ever truly loved. She had met him when she was sixteen years old, and they had married when she was just twenty-two. She felt as if she'd spent her whole life with him.

And now it seemed there was the prospect of turning the clock back, of welcoming this man she'd shared so much with back into her life and back with their family. But the deep and cutting pain she'd felt over the past year was only partly due to the shock that Dave had chosen another woman over her. Hardest of all was the huge void that had been carved out of the centre of her world when Dave walked away from the home they had shared for more than twenty-five years.

He had done that. *Dave* had done that. Not the comfortable, familiar Dave she'd always known and loved, but another version of that man. A person she didn't recognize at all.

Was it possible to turn the clock back? Could old feelings be rekindled in the face of such pain and rejection?

She sighed and got up from her seat in the kitchen, heading into the lounge where her laptop was waiting. When she opened her emails, Phil's name was right at the top of the list. Smiling, she started to read:

> *Hi Megs!*
>
> *How was your day? Was the café as busy as ever? Did you sell out of cupcakes and bowl 'em over with your cream buns? How lovely it must be to spend your working day doing something you love so much. I can tell from everything you say about baking that there's nothing you enjoy more. You care, so you cook!*
>
> *I'm not great at cooking. My daughter Mel's been nagging me to get with the times in the kitchen. She says I'm stuck in an old routine and ought to try out new things. So I decided to go trendy and buy some brown sugar for my coffee instead of the usual white stuff. I poured some out into the sugar bowl, made myself a coffee and added a spoonful with great flourish – then*

spat it out again. That'll teach me not to forget my glasses when I'm out shopping. I took a proper look at the packet and found I'd bought couscous instead of demerara!

Anyway, I have a suggestion to make – one I hope you may like. I'm so enjoying our emails – they brighten my day – but what do you think about us being a bit more daring? How about swapping phone numbers and actually talking to each other once in a while? Would that terrify the life out of you?

I'll understand if you'd prefer to keep things just as they are. But on the off-chance you might enjoy chatting too, I'll put my phone number at the bottom of this email.

Over to you...

Phil X

P.S. It was hard to type that with my fingers crossed!

Maggie sat back against the settee cushions with a thump. And so it begins! Phone calls now; then what? Seeing each other, of course. And that would be the end. Without a doubt, that would be it.

An image of him shovelling couscous into his coffee brought a grin to her face. That was the thing about Phil. Without even trying, he made her laugh. They shared the ups and downs of their days. They opened up. They pooled their thoughts. They covered everything in the comfortable way old friends did – everything, that was, except the pleasure of having a proper conversation.

Suddenly, she knew she wanted to hear his voice very much indeed. Without giving herself a moment longer to change her mind, she picked up the phone and dialled his number.

Chapter 13

Once the Grown-Ups' Lunch Club members heard the news that their photos might end up in *Hello!* magazine, there was a buzz of excitement in the air. Local hairdressers reported an unprecedented increase in bookings for pensioner cuts, restyling and perms. The department store in the High Street almost ran out of "summer dresses for the young-at-heart", meaning any lady over retirement age. Gentlemen's white shirts were snapped up in the supermarkets, and shoe departments noted record sales in wide- and *very*-wide fitting shoes.

At eleven o'clock on that Tuesday, the time at which members would usually start arriving on prearranged transport or meandering in under their own steam, the foyer was already full.

"Blimey, they scrub up well!" grinned Liz, Maggie's assistant, who was putting the finishing touches to the lunch that would be served at noon.

"I've never seen so many blue rinses or red roses in gentlemen's buttonholes," agreed Maggie, as she handed a tray of hot muffins over to their work experience kitchen assistant, Kevin, so he could arrange them on a serving tray.

"The photographer's already arrived," said Kevin. "Did you see him? He's got lights, reflector boards, laptop computers and a whole range of cameras to choose from. I'd like to go and have a look. Could I do that later?"

Maggie looked at him sternly, but with a kind understanding in her eyes. "Once you've finished all your work here, you're very welcome. Believe me, Kevin, this crowd may be lining up to have their photos taken now, but they'll be much more serious about making sure of their place in the queue for lunch. When it comes to food, nothing will distract them. Not even stardom!"

Suddenly, there was a commotion outside the hall, and the members in the foyer started making a dash to squeeze through the door. The kitchen crew couldn't resist following them and arrived at the back of the crowd just in time to see a sleek, sparkling, cream-coloured minibus driving into the old school playground.

"Wow!" breathed Kevin. "She's a real beauty."

"It's got writing on the side, hasn't it?" asked Maggie, craning her neck to get a better view. "Oh, *why* am I not six inches taller? I can't see a thing!"

"It says 'GOOD NEIGHBOURS' in huge letters in the middle," read Liz, squinting a little as she tried to make out the words. "Then underneath it says 'Hope Hall' and the address. And there's something written down in the corner, with a picture of some sort. Can you see it, Kevin?"

"'A gift from the Ainsworth Family, part of this community – and from Apex Finance, caring for communities everywhere," he read. "What's Apex Finance?"

"No idea," said Liz, "but I like them already."

"Well, all this won't get that gravy made," sighed Maggie. "Come on, team. Let's get this lunch on the road!"

"Oh look!" squealed Betty as she tried her best to peer around the crowd in front of her to get a good look at the minibus. "It's got a hoist in the back. What's that for?"

"Particularly heavy ladies," whispered Percy as he stood behind her. "Are you going to put your name down for a lift?"

Flora giggled when she overheard his comment. "Betty doesn't need that. Ada over there in the corner is much heavier, and that friend of yours, Harry, is so broad in the beam he needs two seats!"

"I can't see what's going on properly from over here," grumbled Doris. "Do you think they'll be looking for models to try out the various bits and pieces on the van? Only I'd like to volunteer. Should I go and tell the driver? I definitely want to be at the front so I can see everything. Are you all coming?"

Outside, not far from where the minibus had been parked, Kath was looking anxiously at her watch. There had been no word from Celia about whether she or anyone else was planning to be with them that morning to officiate at the formal handover of the magnificent new bus. Kath couldn't help feeling that with the society photographer and several members of the press in the crowd, a formal public thank you to Celia and Apex Finance was the very least Hope Hall could offer.

"There you are! I thought I'd lost you."

Richard Carlisle's familiar voice had Kath spinning around immediately. "Is Celia with you?" she asked. "She didn't reply to my invitation, so I don't know if she's planning to be here for the handover or not."

"She's not, I'm afraid. She was hoping to get away from the office, but apparently she's having a particularly busy morning."

"Oh, I'm sorry to hear that. We'd have liked to say thank you to her properly. And all these press people are here. What are they expecting? Celia didn't let me know how she wanted the occasion to be run, but surely someone official should say a few words?"

"You're absolutely right," agreed Richard, smiling at her. "And here's your man! I'm not sure if you actually met Douglas Ainsworth at the garden party. Douglas, this is Kath Sutton, the wonderful woman who organizes everything here at Hope Hall."

Kath had seen Douglas from a distance at the party, but close up she had to admit that he made quite an impression with his well-cut suit, Rolex watch and blue eyes that were particularly striking against the suntanned skin of his face.

"Miss Sutton, I've heard a great deal about you," he drawled, shaking her hand rather limply.

"You have?"

"Indeed I have. Now, shall we get on with the ceremony? Perhaps you can introduce me by explaining the major role I've played in achieving all this. I'll say whatever needs to be said, and then, after that, the press will be able to get some good photos of me handing over the key. Agreed and understood?"

Kath nodded. She certainly agreed and understood that this was to be a one-man show.

"Don't worry," Richard whispered in her ear. "Douglas has no idea what the minibus is like at all. Do you recognize the man who's just driving through the gate now? It's Adrian Morgan, the modifications expert we met at the garage the other day. He's come along to demonstrate the facilities the minibus has to offer and to see what the Good Neighbours think of it all."

Kath breathed a sigh of relief. "Oh gosh, I'm so glad he's here. You organized that, didn't you? Thank you so much."

"Go on, then!" His eyes twinkled with encouragement as he looked at her. "Your audience awaits."

"Hello, everyone," started Kath as she stood in front of the microphone. "Well, in all of Hope Hall's hundred years, this occasion certainly rates as a Red Letter Day! This beautiful, brand-new minibus has been donated to our Good Neighbours scheme, which plays a practical and enabling role in the lives of many elderly, frail or vulnerable friends in our local community. We have always understood how challenging it can be for an elderly person to remain part of local life once mobility becomes difficult and transport is not easily available. This is the point at which they can become prisoners in their own home, isolated, unsupported and incredibly lonely.

"That's why we're so proud and fond of *our* neighbours in this town, our *Good* Neighbours in all walks of life who regularly volunteer; not just offering reliable help with transport, but all kinds of other services too – ranging from shopping to hospital visits, hairdressing appointments, social clubs, gardening and chiropody. A myriad of services is lovingly and regularly offered to those who need help in this area, making our Good Neighbours scheme one that is envied across the county. But this wonderful new minibus will catapult the service we provide to unprecedented new heights. The vehicle comes as a gift to us that we never expected in our wildest dreams. It is thanks to the generosity of the Ainsworth family, in association with Apex Finance, that this money was raised via an auction at a garden party Miss Celia Ainsworth was kind enough to host at her own home a few weeks ago. That auction raised enough to pay for this state-of-the-art minibus, which has arrived here today. We owe a huge debt of thanks to the Ainsworth family, and we are delighted to have Mr Douglas Ainsworth with us this morning."

Responding to applause from the crowd, Douglas grabbed the microphone from Kath without actually looking at her.

"Thank you. Thank you all so much," he beamed, his face an interesting mix of genuine pleasure and slightly more orchestrated humility. "Really, there's no need for your applause, because my family and I are delighted to have this chance to support our own little community in this town. Of course, we wish you to have nothing but the best, and this minibus is just that – the very best available for people like you who are getting on a bit and becoming rather unsteady on your legs. The Ainsworths have come to your rescue. We enjoyed our garden event which raised the money for it, and we hope you will enjoy riding in this bus!"

A ripple of rather bemused applause came from the crowd.

"I think it must be time for photos now!" Douglas announced, running his fingers through his hair just to make sure it was tidy.

At that moment, smiling sweetly at him, Kath stepped up to wrestle the microphone away from his grasp. "Thank you so much, Douglas, and that's exactly what we'll do in a few minutes, but first I'd like to introduce Mr Adrian Morgan, an expert on the special modifications that have been made to this minibus to make it ideal for the needs of our local users. Adrian, would you be kind enough to describe some of these very special features to us now?"

Douglas's face darkened with impatience, but his reaction was diffused by Richard, who appeared at his side to congratulate him on the speech he'd made. The audience, however, didn't notice a thing, because Adrian's explanation of all the special modifications had them applauding and ooh-aahing with approval. They loved the van and couldn't wait to give it a try. The photographer caught delighted expressions on several groups of elderly faces before finally inviting a few of the pensioners standing in the front row to take a seat in the minibus and try out some of its luxury features.

And that was how Betty, Flora and Doris, Percy and Robert, all of whom had been determined to have a front row view of the proceedings, found themselves starring in a series of photos that appeared not just in the local paper, but in the society columns of at least two national publications and a couple of glossy magazines. Betty and Flora had their picture taken along with Douglas Ainsworth, who was leaning against the front of the bus with his arms around the two ladies at his side. Doris was singled out for a shot of her being hoisted into the minibus at the back, and Robert demonstrated how the seats could twist to ease the process of getting in and out of the seating area.

But it was Percy who captured the spirit of the occasion more than anyone else. He was photographed leaning out of the driver's seat window, waving merrily with a cheeky expression of sheer delight on his face. That photo, along with several others, was displayed with pride on the foyer wall of Hope Hall for many years to come after that day, alongside a big wide shot of all the Hope Hall family gathered around the new arrival, smiling broadly for the whole world to see.

Maggie's mobile rang. It was Phil. She knew it would be. For nearly two weeks since Phil had first asked for her phone number they had slipped into a routine of having a quick chat in the morning before she headed off to work, knowing they would catch up again in the evening when there was time for more leisurely conversation. They never seemed to run out of things to say. They talked through their day, commented on the news headlines, sympathized about aches and pains, grumbled about or recommended television programmes they'd seen, giggled, reminisced and even sang songs from the old days to each other from time to time! It was easy, it was companionable and it added such anticipation to every day that Maggie glowed with the pleasure of it.

"Hello, you! How was your day?"

Maggie loved his voice; warm and deep, with the suggestion of a smile in every word.

She told him about her day – about the excitement of the new minibus being delivered, and how glamorous it had been with members of the press and photographers there, capturing every wonderful moment.

"I bet your cakes went down well!"

"Let's just say there were none left."

Phil hesitated for just a moment. An immediate shiver of cold foreboding slid down Maggie's backbone. "Any chance that I might be able to try one of your cakes before too long?"

She couldn't gather her thoughts quickly enough to answer.

"Maggie, you and I get on like a house on fire. I can't ever remember a friendship that has become so comfortable, so natural, so utterly wonderful as the one we're already sharing. You feel it too. I know you do."

Maggie cleared her throat, uncertain that her voice would work. "It's just all happening so fast..."

"Yes," he agreed, "but we are old friends. We share our roots and so much more than that. Every time we talk we discover more and more that we have in common. Megs, this just feels *right*."

She felt breathless, unable to speak.

"I can tell you're nervous. I am too. I don't want to risk losing your friendship by pushing too hard too soon. But I'd love to see you, Megs. I *long* to see you."

"Er..." Maggie stopped. She had no idea what to say.

"Promise me you'll think about it."

"Okay."

"Oh, Megs, have I done this all wrong? I'm so sorry if I have. Please don't push me away, please don't!"

She couldn't answer.

"Can I ring you in the morning?"

"Okay. Bye."

She ended the call without waiting for his reply, then slumped back into the cushions of the settee, her face pale with shock at how quickly everything had changed.

She couldn't meet him. Phil would take one look at how she'd let herself go, how plain and dowdy she was, and would know he'd made a dreadful mistake. And the thought of seeing that reaction in his eyes created a gnawing agony deep at the very heart of her. She'd been through that once already. The husband she'd loved for years had been so disappointed with the way she looked he had traded her in for a younger model. She'd learned a hard lesson from that. Looks mattered. They mattered to Dave, and without a doubt they would matter to Phil. Whatever other qualities she may or may not have, they came in a dowdy package. What man would want that?

She looked down at the phone in her hand but couldn't make out the words on the screen for the tears that were misting her eyes. Pushing the OFF button firmly, she pulled herself off the settee and headed for the kitchen in search of a comforting cup of hot chocolate.

Among all the usual bills and notices that arrived in the post that morning, Kath instantly spotted a smart-looking cream envelope addressed to her personally. Sliding her finger along the top to open it, she pulled out a single sheet of thick silky paper that had the address of Ainsworth Cottage beautifully embossed in the top right-hand corner. Glancing down the page, she saw that it had been signed, very simply, "Celia".

> *Dear Kath*
>
> *Both Richard and Douglas have spoken in superlatives about your contribution to the proceedings on the day the minibus was handed over to your Good Neighbours scheme at Hope Hall. The proof is in the delightful photographs, which captured the spirit of the day so graphically. We have been thrilled with the response to those photographs, many of which were used alongside editorial pieces in significant national and local publications.*

I wish to thank you most sincerely, not just on behalf of my own family, but also on behalf of Apex Finance, which received some very welcome and positive feedback as a result of their involvement in this charitable activity. I have no doubt that you and the Hope Hall team will put the minibus to excellent use, and wish you all many happy times as a result of it.

On a personal level, I feel that perhaps you and I didn't get off to the best of starts. Richard has told me very firmly that it was my fault, and that I was off-hand and impolite on those first occasions when we met. If that was the case, I apologize without reserve. I know there was a lot on my mind around then, but that is no excuse for rudeness. It won't happen again.

In fact, Richard and I were wondering whether you would consider joining us for dinner later this week so we can get to know each other a little better. Would Friday suit? Trevor will be with us too. Unfortunately, Mary is otherwise engaged that evening, but Trevor is happy to combine our late afternoon business meeting that day with a dinner for us all later on. I've arranged a table at the Swan Hotel at 7 pm. I hope that will be convenient for you.

I await your response.

Regards

Celia

Kath had to read the letter twice to come to terms with Celia's abrupt about-turn in attitude. She'd said that Richard had told her in no uncertain terms that she'd been rude and off-hand towards Kath, and that an apology was required. She could never have imagined Celia taking orders from anyone, but

Richard's opinion obviously mattered to her and she valued his advice.

Kath found herself wondering about the dynamics of Celia and Richard's relationship. He was able to combine efficiency and achievement with concern and kindness. Kath had been at the receiving end of both, and had sometimes found it a heady mix to be in the company of that charming, dynamic man. But when it came to dynamism, Celia won hands down. She was driven by business and the need to excel at everything she did. Richard couldn't fail to find that exciting and attractive. But it was also clear that he brought a calming, steady influence to Celia's busy life. No wonder she responded positively when her partner was such a rooted, down-to-earth, lovely man.

Perhaps the dinner on Friday evening would give Kath a bit more insight into the two of them. Having a chance to get to know such influential and altruistic entrepreneurs could only be of benefit to Hope Hall. On a personal level, however, Kath didn't particularly relish the idea of seeing just how close Celia and Richard were. That was for them to know and of no earthly relevance to her. At least Trevor would be there, so she wouldn't end up feeling like a gooseberry about to be eyed up by two hungry lovebirds.

Phil sent several emails. He texted, rang and left voice messages. Maggie was tempted to reply, but she found a new determination in herself which surprised her. She was going to stick to her decision. He would get the message. If he didn't quite understand why she had closed down on him, that was a shame. She couldn't tell him, so he didn't need to know. He'd get over it and move on.

That new-found determination helped her to decide how to respond to another appeal she had chosen to ignore. She sat down at the laptop and steeled herself to start typing.

Dear Dave

I apologize for not replying earlier to your email. In fact, I didn't know what to say, so I ended up saying nothing. But then Darren came to see me the other evening. He told me about meeting up with you and what you had said. He is plainly very worried about you and thinks that I might be able to help you in your present situation.

I've given this a lot of thought over the past few days. I can't deny that it saddens me to think of you unhappy, not coping practically or emotionally with the situation in which you now find yourself. You and I have spent most of our lives together, so I remember very clearly how you react when you're unhappy or under extreme pressure. But I also know that you can be clear-headed and determined when you decide to follow a certain path. You felt that certainty when you met Mandy. You were absolutely sure of your feelings when you set up home with her. The two of you decided to create a new life together. Pregnancy never needs to be an accident these days. Aurora is the result of that positive decision you and Mandy took together.

A new partner, a new family, a new home, a new baby – each one of these might cause stress in the most settled of relationships, but having to face all of them at once must be really tough. New babies disrupt the smooth running of any household, and Aurora is only being the new little person she is. But she's growing up day by day, and before long, when you're able to get more sleep, when your future living arrangements are more settled, and when you and Mandy can relax into the family life you've chosen, I do believe you'll feel a great deal happier and more confident than you do right now.

You asked Darren to see if I would consider taking you back. The answer is no. We have both moved on. After the dreadful upheaval, fear and pain of the past year, I'm finally finding my feet. I love my new home. I enjoy my job. I'm making new friends. I will be okay. I believe you will be too.

I don't think Mandy would appreciate the two of us being in touch at the moment when she is postnatal and probably feeling exhausted and vulnerable. Concentrate your care on her, Dave. I wish you well. I always will.

Love

Mags

Liz had set up coffee and sandwiches in the far corner of the balcony lounge as all the interested parties came together to discuss the final arrangements for the Centenary Celebration Day that was coming up at the end of the month. On this occasion, they weren't discussing the church service that was due to start the day off, but were confining themselves to what was planned to take place at Hope Hall itself once the service was over. Their conversation covered items that needed attention, such as timing, police presence for traffic control with such a large number of people crossing their busy road, transport for their elderly guests and car parking. They also needed to ensure seating was erected in the old school playground with a large video screen, which would allow the audience to see the detail of the foundation stone ceremony with ease, because there was little space in front of the plaques themselves. Another video screen and extra seating were to be placed inside the foyer in case the unpredictable British weather sent guests scurrying inside. They considered who would look after their VIP guests, who would make sure photos were taken, and what modern-day and historical displays should be on show in the foyer. Then they moved on to speak about the buffet in the main hall, to which all were invited, as well as the programme for the rest of the afternoon.

"We've decided to have a tea dance, because they would have been really popular a hundred years ago," explained Kath. "We often have them here at Hope Hall and they're always well supported. Over to you, Maggie. How are the plans going on this?"

"We'll have all of our round tables out right across the bottom end of the hall, as well as others lining the side. Each table will be beautifully laid out with white tablecloths, china crockery, proper cups and saucers, and lovely antique cake stands. We'll make sure this traditional high tea is just scrumptious, and when they've finished, our guests can work off the calories by dancing to our 1920s-style jazz band. I've seen this group before. They have a great MC and a wonderful knack for getting people up to dance. I think it should round our special day off really nicely."

The meeting went on for about half an hour after that contribution, but Maggie found her mind was wandering. She missed hearing from Phil. For days after their last conversation, she had kept her phone switched off whenever she wasn't at work, and had only turned it on when she wanted to ring someone herself. Phil had tried to get in contact with her for several days, but finally, in the last message she listened to with tears sliding down her cheeks, he said that he'd got the message. He didn't understand why their friendship had changed so dramatically, but he realized that there must be something she didn't feel able to share with him, at least not at the moment. He ended by saying that he hoped with all his heart that in time she might feel able to make contact with him again.

So that was that. The lovely man with his friendly conversation, gentle care, and wide knowledge on everything from world geography to the flavour of pizza teenagers enjoyed most – that old new friend had left her life. And this time it was for good.

Kath turned into the car park of the Swan Hotel at exactly five to seven. She felt uncharacteristically nervous. This was ridiculous, she told herself. In her previous role, at various times over the years she'd had regular meetings with senior directors of the NHS, hospital board members, the leader of the local council and even groups of MPs. She hadn't flinched then when she'd had to speak to large groups of people or answer searching questions from the press. So why did she feel like a teenager on a first date as she thought about the company she would be facing over the next couple of hours?

"There you are!" Trevor stood up to greet her as she entered the hotel lobby. "I'm the first one here. Celia and Richard are running a little late, but they're on their way."

"How did your business meeting go?"

He gave a wry grin. "I'm always glad Celia is on my side of any negotiation. She's so on the ball and frighteningly intelligent."

Kath smiled as she touched his arm. "But she obviously values you and your vast accountancy experience very highly. You have no reason to feel daunted, Trevor."

"How about you?" he asked quietly. "You haven't really met her properly yet, have you? Richard's such a good influence on her, of course, but then he's always been a thoroughly nice fellow."

"Trevor, I'm so sorry we're late!" Celia swooped through the door and dropped an air kiss on each of Trevor's cheeks. "And Kath, how nice of you to come! Richard's just parking the car. Shall we go straight through?"

Celia marched off, arm in arm with Trevor, and Kath hesitated before realizing she was supposed to follow along behind.

"Wait for me!"

She turned to see Richard approaching, the warmest of smiles on his face as he joined her.

"You look really lovely. I'm so glad you were able to come tonight."

She couldn't help smiling back at him.

They were shown into a beautiful conservatory with lush green and flowering plants, which either grew up in huge ceramic pots or tumbled down the walls and windows, adding an exotic touch to the elegant room. Their table looked out over rolling fields that during the evening gradually faded to darkness as the setting sun painted the sky a rich red on its journey towards the horizon. They ate exquisite food served with charm and refinement by waiters who barely made their presence felt.

If Kath was worried that conversation would be difficult, she was pleasantly surprised. Each of them touched on their work at some point during the evening, but generally they chatted about local people, national news, wine they loved, food they avoided, occasions that had moved them to tears and stories that made them laugh. She'd worried that her opinions wouldn't be of any interest at all in such hallowed company, but in fact it was quite the opposite. Her view was often sought, and her answers were either received with great interest or considered very entertaining. Curious to get a glimpse of the relationship between Richard and Celia, Kath found it rather interesting that they often corrected each other and even bickered in a good-natured way. They were loving towards one another, but not in the obvious way lovers often were. Kath sensed that a very comfortable friendship was the strong core at the heart of what this couple shared.

As the waiter refilled her coffee cup, Kath caught sight of her wristwatch. It was gone eleven!

"You're right, Kath." Celia was removing her serviette from her lap as she spoke. "It's time to draw this lovely evening to a close as we all have a busy day ahead of us tomorrow."

That prompted everyone to push back their seats and stand up as Trevor signalled to the waiter for the bill.

"That's all taken care of," said Celia. "Apex Finance has been glad to have you as its guests this evening."

"That's extremely kind," Kath started to say, but Celia was already heading for the door. Kath followed her as Richard and Trevor exchanged farewells, then Celia unexpectedly turned to scrutinize Kath, her expression one of friendly curiosity.

"I'm beginning to see why my cousin is so smitten with you."

Kath's face clouded with confusion. "Your cousin?"

Celia stared at her for a second before bursting out laughing. "You didn't know that Richard and I were related?"

"No," Kath stuttered in reply. "I assumed you were a couple."

"We were just a couple of kids whose mothers happened to be sisters, and who grew up as if we were one big family. He's six years older than me, so I've thought of him as my big brother for as long as I can remember – you know: bossy, thinks he knows best, that sort of thing. But we've always got along really well, and any issue about the age gap between us has disappeared completely over the years. Richard cares about me, unlike Douglas who is younger, less intelligent, more irritating and generally a waste of space as far as I'm concerned."

"Oh…" said Kath, unable to think of another word to say.

Celia winked at her. "I have a feeling this snippet of news is going to make Richard's day. *À bientôt*, dear Kath!"

And in a cloud of expensive perfume, Celia smiled to herself as she made her way out of the restaurant, leaving Kath rooted to the spot, looking totally bemused.

Maggie loved having a day off in the week. She usually pottered around the flat doing a bit of cleaning, catching up on the washing and ironing, and always phoning Steph for a nice long chat.

"What's happening, Mum?" Steph asked. "A couple of weeks ago you were like a seagull with a chip. You always had a smile on your face, and I was thinking that whatever you were taking, I wanted some too. Spill the beans! What's going on?"

"Oh, nothing much."

"Is it Dad? Darren told me he'd asked if he could come home. You didn't fall for that, did you?"

Maggie sighed. "I did think about it, but too much has happened. I wrote to him in the end. I told him he had to get on with the life he's chosen."

"Quite right too!"

"It was hard, though, to hear that he's unhappy. If he's not happy after all this, what was it all about?"

"And you? I was beginning to think you were feeling really good about life lately. I don't sense that in you now."

Maggie sighed again. "I'll get there. In the meantime I've got a lot to do. I'm planning to get cracking on that garden shed of mine today."

"Oh, what a job that will be. It was filthy dirty when you got there. I don't think it's ever been properly cleaned. Watch out for the creepy-crawlies. I reckon there's a colony of them living in that hut!"

"Oh, I'm not squeamish," Maggie laughed. "But I'm planning to wear my overalls, wellie boots and old sun hat just in case."

"Ring me later to let me know you got out in one piece! Bye."

An hour later, hot, bothered and covered in cobwebs and dirt, Maggie began to wonder why she'd ever started the job. She was on her knees scrubbing the floor when she heard the click of her garden gate and became aware of a shadow blocking out the light of the shed window.

"Just a minute, I'm on my way out!" she yelled, backing out from the shed on all fours, bottom first.

"Hello, Megs."

She immediately knew who was standing there. He was here. And he shouldn't be. She had made it abundantly clear she didn't want to see him. If he'd come anyway, he deserved what he got. Let him see her in all her awful glory! He'd get the message and run away as fast as he possibly could.

He reached down to help her up.

I hope he likes rubber gloves, she thought glumly as she took him up on the offer. She finally straightened up, ready to stare defiantly at him, but then she looked at him properly. She wasn't the only one who had changed a lot since they last met. His hair was greying at the temples and so thin on top that it barely covered his head. He had always been quite stocky and strong, but now his waistline had relaxed and his silhouette was more rounded. He no longer looked like someone strong and muscular; more like comfortable and cuddly. His face was broader too, with lines across his forehead and around his eyes and mouth that spoke of a lifetime of experience and laughter. But those eyes of his, the ones she remembered so well from all those years ago, were filled with warmth as they smiled down at her with an expression she really couldn't quite fathom.

"Megs," he said, holding his arms out towards her, "I'm sorry. I know you didn't want me to come, but I honestly couldn't stay away. And look at you! You're magnificent! Every bit as wonderful and lovely as you ever were."

Her throat choked. Her heart was pounding and her resolve melted away as she looked at him. Then she walked straight into his arms and felt them tighten around her as he held her close. And her last thought as she sank into the comfort of his embrace was that she had come home.

Chapter 14

The sun shone on Centenary Day as the congregation gathered inside St Mark's Church, which was gloriously decked out with garlands of flowers. The front four rows of pews were reserved for local elderly residents, including members of the Grown-ups' Lunch Club, who were all spruced up for the occasion. Betty, Flora, Doris and Ida were in the second row, with the gentlemen sitting in the pew behind them.

At eleven o'clock sharp, Rector James Barnard led visiting clergy and the St Mark's Choir as they processed into the church, followed by local dignitaries, including the town mayor, the chairman of the council, two councillors and their wives, and the high sheriff of the county. Once they had been shown to their places in sections of extra seating positioned in front of the choir stalls, James welcomed everyone to the special service of commemoration for a hundred years of Hope Hall, then introduced the first hymn, "O God Our Help in Ages Past".

It was an occasion that touched the emotions in so many ways. Children from Broad Street Upper School filed into the church to present a short pageant explaining the devastation of the town community after so many young men were killed during the First World War. Dressed in costumes of the time (expertly prepared by members of the local Women's Institute), they acted out how plans had been drawn up to erect a memorial hall so that the sacrifices made during the Great War would never be forgotten. One serious-looking lad, complete with bowler hat and a neat black moustache, played the leading role of Sir

Reginald Ainsworth, who had donated the land on which Hope Hall was built. Sir Reginald also contributed half the cost of the project, with the local community joining together to raise the other half. After that, the children had everyone singing along as they worked their way through a selection of songs that had been popular in 1920. The older generation in the front pews needed no encouragement to join in, with Percy's voice booming above the rest as he sang in a different key from everyone else in the church.

The service continued with short reminiscences from people who had used Hope Hall down the years, two stunning anthems from the newly reformed St Mark's Choir, and prayers that were led by three of the oldest members of the local community, including Mrs Alice Mendrake, aged ninety-seven, whose voice rang with emotion as she prayed first for the people in the town a hundred years ago who had lost their sons in the Great War and ended with a heartfelt plea that war should never again be allowed to take the life of another mother's son.

After that came two minutes of silence, and as everyone bowed their heads in reflection and prayer, Ida felt the gentle touch of a hand on her shoulder. Percy was sitting behind her. She nodded her head in total understanding.

That part of the day's events finally drew to a close, and James led their VIP guests and the whole congregation across the road, where they gathered in and around Hope Hall, finding seats and standing room in the school playground and inside the foyer to watch the foundation stone ceremony.

It was Kath who welcomed everyone, quickly explaining the importance of Hope Hall as a major hub of community life in the town.

"We've just been reminded about the generous and philanthropic contribution made by Sir Reginald Ainsworth, who enabled the building of Hope Hall. So we are honoured today to have a member of the Ainsworth family with us to unveil our new centenary plaque. She is Sir Reginald's great-granddaughter. Please welcome Miss Celia Ainsworth!"

Celia strode up to the mike, immediately and confidently capturing the attention of the audience.

"Ainsworth's Mill has been processing grain in this area for a century and a half. Many people from this town were employed there before the Great War, and during those terrible years between 1914 and 1918 when the men were at the front, the wives and mothers from our local families stepped in to continue the work that was so badly needed to feed a nation at war. So many of those women became widows over the years. Others found that their husbands and sons were terribly changed by their experience in the trenches.

"But this is a community that knows about caring for each other and working together. My great-grandfather, Reginald, had always known that from the support, commitment and loyalty he had seen again and again in his workforce at the mill. Because of that, and especially because of his Christian faith, which charged him with the divine duty of doing all he could to love his neighbours and show practical care to others, he made the decision to create Hope Hall. It was to be a memorial to the dead, but more importantly it was also to be a beacon of hope for the living. He wanted Hope Hall to be a community resource that would welcome all for shelter, enterprise, instruction, learning, entertainment and good company.

"And if Reginald could be here with us today, a hundred years on, I know he would smile with great satisfaction and pride. Hope Hall is everything he built it to be. It is at the heart of this town every bit as much today as it was during those early years. This place is a treasure, and I feel very privileged to be here to represent the Ainsworth family on this special day. May Hope Hall go from strength to strength in all the years to come!"

There was a murmur of approval from the crowd before they burst into enthusiastic applause. Kath was also clapping as she took the microphone from Celia in order to hand over to historian Michael Sayward. He started with a brief but fascinating summary of how the hall had developed its role down the decades, mentioning clubs and events that echoed with fond memories for many in the gathered crowd.

Then Michael turned to look at the site of the original foundation stone, which had been laid exactly a hundred years ago that day. He explained that, in preparation for their own celebration, the old stone had been carefully removed a few weeks earlier so it could be cleaned and renovated.

"As we removed the stone, you can imagine our delight when we came across a collection of papers, letters and photographs that had been placed here in 1920 in the hope that they would one day be discovered by a future generation. Copies of those papers and letters are on display in the foyer so you can see them for yourselves. We will be replacing the originals behind the old foundation stone as we re-lay it today. In addition, though, we will be positioning our new centenary plaque on the wall, behind which we will enclose our own time capsule of documents, photographs and letters from all generations within our town today. Again, you can see copies of those items and documents in the foyer – drawings and thoughts from our schoolchildren, local town plans, newspaper articles and a memory stick containing a video that tells the story of Hope Hall and our town over the past century.

"Most moving of all the discoveries we made among those papers behind the foundation stone were two letters from the family of Leonard Carmichael, who was the senior builder on the Hope Hall project. I'm going to ask Derek Jessop, the great-great-grandson of Leonard Carmichael, to read out the first letter for us."

Derek stepped up to the microphone and cleared his throat before starting to read. Even though many in the audience had seen a copy of the letter in the centenary display at Hope Hall, the impact of Derek's reading of his great-great-grandfather's words echoed down the years with heartrending poignancy. Eyes misted over, and couples reached for each other's hands as the words of Leonard's letter rang out through the silence.

Mrs Carmichael and I would like these letters to be placed in the wall of our memorial hall. Our eldest son Gerald Carmichael was conscripted into the army in 1916. He was twenty-two years old. Three weeks before he left, he married his sweetheart, Edith. They had been engaged for a year and could wait no longer.

Edith wrote to him often and treasured every one of his replies. I enclose his last letter, written in the trenches at Passchendaele in October 1917, in what they called the Third Battle of Ypres.

Edith heard no news at all of Gerry for many months. Then just before Christmas she received this letter and a photograph of herself, which had been forwarded to her by the Soldiers' Christian Association. It read, "Dear Madam, I am sending you this letter and photo found in a wood here in the battlefield. I am very sorry to say that I could not find the owner of the photo. I cannot say if he has been wounded or killed." That photo was the one Gerry loved best of Edith, taken on their wedding day. He must have carried it with him right to the end.

I am the chief builder of this new memorial hall. This will be a labour of love because it is dedicated to the memory of our boys who didn't come back; to my boy who didn't come back. I have no idea if anyone in the future will discover the box we are burying today in the foundations of this new building. If they do, I hope they will get some measure of the pain, fear and despair we parents feel as we lose our sons. There wasn't even a body to bring home to his mother so she could bury our beloved boy.

Signed
Leonard Carmichael
Senior Builder

There was complete stillness as Derek finished reading, the crowd deeply moved by what they'd heard. Thanking Derek, Michael started to speak again.

"When Edith received that letter, she was expecting a child. She had a son named Walter, and I'd like to introduce you to Walter's daughter, Joyce Jessop. She grew up remembering her grandmother Edith very well – and she knows how much Gerry's death affected life in the family for generations to come. Here she is."

Joyce was helped up to the microphone as the crowd fell completely silent.

"Let me start by reading you the letter Granny Edith received via the Soldiers' Christian Association months after Grandpa had died." Her voice cracking with emotion, Joyce started to read.

"Dearest, if this should ever reach you it will be a sure sign that I am gone under. I will have died with your name on my lips. I love you deeply – how much, you will never know.

I am heartened that I am leaving you with a son. I have not met him, but already I love our boy with all my heart. In the future, when your grief has worn a bit, speak to him sometimes of me.

Please tell Mother and Father that I think of them often, and brother George. I pray that this war will end before he too is called up. How could Mother bear that?

So, dear heart, I will bid you farewell, hoping to meet you in a time to come if there is a hereafter. Know that my last thoughts were of you in the dugout or on the fire step. My thoughts are always for you, the only one I ever loved.

Gerry

"Imagine how she felt reading those loving words in the handwriting of the husband she adored, penned just hours before he died. They had shared only three weeks as a married couple, but that was enough for Granny Edith. She never married again. She always said she'd married the man she loved, and no one else could ever match up to him. That wonderful lady lived to the age of ninety-five before we lost her nearly thirty years ago – but she always hoped there would be a day like this when people from the town would gather to remember the sacrifices of her generation. She spoke often of what she would like to say to you all, and eventually she gave me this letter for you to hear today.

"I write as a widow, a mother and a grandmother who has lived in this town all my life. I was married to the man whose father, Leonard Carmichael, oversaw the building of Hope Hall in 1920. It was more than a job of work for him. It was a labour of devotion, dedicated to the memory of his son Gerry, who died in the trenches along with so many other fine young men from this town, and others like it all over our country.

Gerry was my husband. How can I put into words the love we shared, having grown up together as neighbours and friends all our lives? Loving Gerry was as natural as breathing to me, and losing him simply took my breath away. He was my life and my love. I still think of him and miss him every day.

His younger brother George was spared from being called up in that war, and we all thanked God that he was saved for us. But then, at the start of yet another world war in 1939, all men between the ages of eighteen and forty-one were conscripted into service. George was thirty-nine, so he too was called up, in spite of all those hopes and prayers that this country would never see war again. Thankfully Leonard never lived to see that. It would have broken his heart.

Do we ever learn? How many mothers have raised their children with love, only to see them march off to war? How many fathers have received news, as Leonard did, that their beloved son had died? Why do we never learn?

I have no way of knowing how, or even if, the people of this town will ever hear the words of this letter. I simply want you to know the plea in my heart. Life is precious. Love doesn't end. Love life and each other enough to work tirelessly together to prevent wars in the future that rob us of our sons and daughters, our peace of mind and our reason to go on.

Hope Hall is a symbol of that plea. Treasure it with pride.

Edith Carmichael"

The emotional ceremony ended with the rededication and laying of both the old and new stones, after which everyone was ready to move into the hall to look at the displays, drink tea and coffee, and find their places at the beautifully set tables.

Maggie and the team had worked for days in advance to make sure as much as possible was prepared and ready for the serving of high tea, but she'd been excused kitchen duty that morning so that she could join the management team of Hope Hall in welcoming the local dignitaries to the church service, and then remain with them to host their attendance during the ceremony in which the original foundation stone and the new plaque were put into place. Liz, Kevin and Jan had managed to slip into the foyer to watch the proceedings on screen before nipping back to the kitchen to make sure the urns were piping hot when the crowd poured in for their drinks.

When Maggie eventually made her way into the kitchen, Liz did a double take because she hardly recognized her good friend. Wearing a pale turquoise jacket and matching blouse that caught the shine of her hair and the sparkle in her eyes, Maggie looked wonderful. But before Liz could comment she realized Maggie wasn't alone. Alongside her was a smiling man who gave a friendly wave to everyone in the kitchen as the two of them came in.

Raising her voice to get their attention, Maggie called out, "Let me introduce you all to a very dear old friend of mine, Phil Coleman. He says that you're going to be seeing him around quite a bit from now on – and if so, I hope you're going to like him as much as I do. If he isn't up to scratch, I know I can rely on you to tell him the error of his ways in no uncertain terms!"

Sometime later, after everyone had had their fill of a high tea that was universally declared to be the best ever enjoyed at Hope Hall, the band began taking their places on stage to start the dancing.

"Oh good," enthused Doris, rubbing her hands together with glee. "I hope they play a quickstep. Will you dance with me, Flora?"

"I'll have a go, but I can only be the lady. You'll have to lead, so you're the gent!"

"Are you coming, Betty? Elsie over there will dance with you. She's always good for a laugh."

"Oh no," muttered Betty nervously. "These new shoes are rubbing my corns. I'll come and watch, though. I like this song."

As the three of them hurried off towards the dance floor, Percy walked casually over to the table where Ida was sitting alone.

"Care to dance?" he asked.

Ida stiffened. "No, thank you."

Percy shrugged and started to walk away.

"But I'm glad you asked," she added before he'd gone too far.

He grinned broadly, then without looking back ambled off to his own seat.

Kath walked past at just that moment, having returned from saying goodbye to the high sheriff and his wife at the main door.

"Kath, do you have a minute?"

She turned to see Richard walking towards her. Without waiting for her reply, he took her hand and drew her over to the back of the hall, where the music was a little less loud.

"Did you really think Celia was my partner?"

She smiled, looking down with embarrassment. "Yes, I did."

"She isn't."

"I'm glad."

"So am I, because I'd never even thought about having a partner until I met you. I'm so drawn to you, Kath. I love your company. I love our conversations. I love spending time with you. I'd like to do a lot more of that from now on, if you'll let me."

She drew in a breath, her heart pounding at his words. But before she could answer, a couple of elderly ladies brushed past them, deep in conversation.

"My Joe liked dancing," said the lady in front. "Mind you, he led me a merry dance! He was a rascal, that man, but I never stopped loving him in the forty-three years we had together."

Kath looked up at Richard with a cheeky smile. "Are you going to lead me a merry dance, Richard Carlisle?"

He slipped his arms around her waist, then pulled her towards him. "Oh yes, my dear Kath. You and I are in for a very merry dance indeed!"

Who's Who at Hope Hall

Hope Hall staff, friends and family members:

Kath Sutton – Administrator of Hope Hall

Dr Jack Sawyer – Kath's partner during her time as Senior Administrator at a major London hospital, from which she resigned to look after her mother

Maggie Stapleton – Catering Manager at Hope Hall. Daughter **Steph**, married to **Dale** and mother to **Bobbie**; son **Darren**, lives with partner **Sonia**

Dave Stapleton, married to Maggie for twenty-five years before leaving to live with **Mandy** and her children, **Marlin** and **Belle**. New baby **Aurora Giselle** born in June

Sylvie – Maggie's schoolfriend, married to **Bill**, brother **Joe**

Phil Coleman – used to walk to school with Maggie every morning. Works as an architect, recently divorced from **Sandra**

Shirley Wells – Management Assistant at Hope Hall. Married to **Mick** with two sons – **Brandon** in Bristol and **Tyler**, who recently returned home and discovers new prospects – plus a daughter, **Kayla**, married to army sergeant **Gavin** in Yorkshire

Barbara Lucas – Younger sister of Shirley and dance teacher for many years. Mother of **Della**, who now runs dance classes at Hope Hall

Ray Brown – Hope Hall Caretaker, whose wife **Sara** recently died of cancer

Trevor Barratt – Hope Hall Accountant, married to **Mary**

Hope Hall kitchen staff:

Liz – Assistant Manager
Jan – Catering Assistant
Kevin – work experience Catering Assistant

Centenary committee:

Kath Sutton – Hope Hall Administrator
Trevor Barratt – Hope Hall Accountant
Michael Sayward – historian
The Reverend James Barnard – vicar of St Mark's Church
Mrs Ellie Barnard – represents Broad Street Upper School
Peter Radcliffe – Public Relations Officer for the local council
Brian Mack – building contractor
Roger Beck – Rotary Chairman
Brenda Longstone – Chair of Women's Institute
Maggie Stapleton – Catering Manager at Hope Hall
Ray Brown – Caretaker at Hope Hall

Grown-ups' Lunch Club members:

Percy – noisy character with a cheeky sense of humour. Loves making fun of Ida
Ida – very proper and disapproving, especially where Percy is concerned
Betty – often nervous, but can be led to join in with anything
Doris – won a cup for dancing the quickstep with husband **Bert** many years ago
Flora – small, rotund and always on a diet. Enjoys singing and dancing, but is more enthusiastic than skilful

Sea Cadets:

Muriel Baker – Commanding Officer of the Sea Cadets, temporarily based at Hope Hall throughout the summer months
Richard Carlisle – father of Sea Cadet Petty Officer **William**. Head of Carlisle Agricultural, which specializes in agricultural machinery. Comes from a local family with a trust fund that supports community projects, especially for the elderly and disabled

Hope Hall benefactors:

Celia Ainsworth – great-granddaughter of **Reginald Ainsworth**, the land and mill owner who originally donated the land on which Hope Hall was built, as well as half the cost. Now Pension Fund Manager at Apex Finance
Douglas Ainsworth – CEO at Ainsworth Mill, often seen in society magazines. Married to **Diana** with two sons, **Matthew** and **Barnaby**
Adrian Morgan – minibus technical expert who works on a swanky new minibus for Hope Hall, funded by the Ainsworths
Leonard Carmichael – chief builder of Hope Hall back in 1920
Gerry Carmichael – Leonard's twenty-two-year-old son, killed during the Great War. Married **Edith Carmichael** three weeks before leaving for the front
Joyce Jessop – granddaughter of Leonard

English as a Foreign Language:

Jean Morgan – class teacher
Mili Novakova – au pair from the Czech Republic who moves in with fellow Czech student, **Terezka Tumova**
Mariana Lopez – Spanish student and friend to Mili and Terezka

Friction:

Carlos – lead singer and boyfriend to Mariana
Andy – keyboard
Jake – rhythm guitar
Graham – lead guitar and boyfriend to **Ali**
Nigel – drummer, married to **Jayne**

Money Advice Service and Food Bank:

William Fenton – organizer of the Money Advice Service
Brian – organizer of the Food Bank, set up by Churches Together
Sheelagh Hallam – retired social worker and counsellor. On the
Money Advice Service board and helps out at the Food Bank
Michael Ford – mystery man who comes along to Food Bank,
married to **Anne**

Salvation Army:

Captain Sam Morse – helps Sheelagh uncover Michael Ford's
identity
Officer Jackie – also assists in the Michael Ford identity quest

COMING SEPTEMBER 2022

ISBN: 9781782642893

Enjoy more fun with all your Hope Hall favourites
in the final book of the series!

OUT NOW!

ISBN: 9781782642879

If you haven't yet read the first book in the Hope Hall series,
catch up with Kath and friends in this heartwarming tale!